THE SACRED COMBE

THE
SACRED
COMBE

THOMAS
MALONEY

SCRIBE
Melbourne • London

Scribe Publications
18–20 Edward St, Brunswick, Victoria 3056, Australia
2 John St, London, WC1N 2ES, United Kingdom

Published in Australia, New Zealand and the United Kingdom by Scribe 2016

Typeset in Adobe Garamond by the publishers

Printed and bound in the UK by CPI Group (UK) Ltd, Croydon CR0 4YY

CIP records for this title are available from the British Library and
the National Library of Australia

9781925321166 (Australian edition)
9781925228298 (UK edition)
9781925307269 (e-book)

scribepublications.com.au
scribepublications.co.uk

PROLOGUE

Imagine an English garden on the first day of May. Or rather, imagine two gardens: from our vantage point in this blossoming cherry tree we can examine the ridged crest of the wall that divides them, its ancient coping dimpled by rain-hollows and home to plump veins of moss, intrepid dandelions and the wrinkled, reddish lichens on which peacock butterflies like to sun themselves.

We look up, ignoring a touch of vertigo. Crowding against the blue sky is the massed abundance of blossoms, softly diffusing the sunlight and stirred by an almond-scented breeze. We look down into the garden on the left, where a low, sun-bleached table stands before two chairs on a stone terrace. A wisteria leans grey limbs delicately over the buttress of the wall, its long budding tails biding their time. A robin materialises for a moment on the arm of a chair, then silently darts away. From the terrace a step leads down to a flagged path, beyond which a couple of clipped yews, slightly ragged on top, cast matching shadows on a strip of lawn. For a moment we catch the placid murmur of human voices carrying along the path from some unseen conversation. Then the breeze stirs, and the sound is lost.

We now turn to the garden on the right, which pays a very different homage to Flora. Tall fronds of sorrel and budding stems of ragwort and foxglove stand like colourful ships' masts above a sea of long grass, and arching brambles crowd along the wall. Twenty blue butterflies play on a holly that rears darkly against its own buttress, bristling with a robustness and vigour unknown to its delicate counterpart beyond the wall. Now, as a cloud drifts clear of the sun, an appreciative hum of insects rises from the grasses.

But amidst this riotous concourse of the hosts of nature, the works of humankind survive: two stone busts confront each other from slender plinths, like the forlorn guardians of a treasure already plundered, each waiting for the other to surrender his post. We can see only one of the faces — the nose and one cheek have fallen away. A name is inscribed, perhaps, under yellow lichen.

With a sudden, soft batter of feathers, a magnificent bird alights on the wall. A burly presence, with pinkish plumage set off by a glittering streak of blue on each wing and a long black tail: a jay. It rocks clumsily for a moment on the blunt ridge of stone, finds its balance, then struts a few steps towards us. We hear an odd chuckling, clicking sound which we only connect to the bird with some astonishment. It cocks its big head and seems to fix on us a brilliant, perfectly round, yellow eye with a black pupil. Its beak opens a crack and emits a malevolent croaking rattle. But no, it is not looking at us — it has spied a few tiny twig-tips poking out from a hollowed crook against the trunk of our tree. It advances a few more steps, chuckling.

The robin reappears on a high branch. It hops about, puffs out its feathers, gives three sharp, ticking calls like defiant jabs of a needle. The jay ducks its head a few times, as though in mocking greeting, and steps closer to the nest. For a moment the two birds pause — not looking at each other but alert as only birds can be.

But here come the human voices again, suddenly much nearer: one man speaks softly while a second laughs in protest, over a single slow beat of footfalls on stone: tick, tock, tick. With another batter of feathers the jay is gone, and the robin flits into her precious hollow.

One disadvantage of our otherwise excellent lookout is that from here, directly above the wall, we cannot see whether it possesses, or does not possess, a door.

In a treetop already distant, the jay screams.

PART 1

FLIGHT

Sometimes I hear a fragment of music, a brief sequence of notes, that produces a resonance in some dusty, neglected string stretched between two otherwise remote and disconnected wings of my soul, that catches at me, and lifts me — but that is followed by a dull return to the imperfect, the clumsy, the misunderstood. What if that perfect resonance were sustained for the length of a symphony? What if, in the music of voices and birdsong and the tantalising echoes of other people's memories, it filled a whole valley?

1

This is the story of the seventeen weeks I spent in a strange and beautiful place, after I lost my wife and resigned from my job.

Don't misunderstand me: my wife — Sarah, the decisive woman who was my wife, I mean — is in good health. I lost her that summer almost as suddenly and unexpectedly as if she had indeed met with some fatal accident, but it was all quite deliberate. Sarah deliberated, and it was I, not she, who was destined for the thunderbolt.

But this is not her story, and, if I could get away with it, that is the only paragraph I would give her. She chose to be the Woman of Action, and I choose to be the Man of Words. Did you notice those five unremarkable words in my first sentence, 'a strange and beautiful place'? Look for yourself — they are still there. Sarah, whom I loved, has not touched them; she has never seen the sacred combe.

The day after I discovered the letter on the bed, I took my tent to the Yorkshire Dales — a dependable refuge — and stayed for three days. I spoke to no one, sought answers in my own memories, and found none. The nadir was stepping onto the southbound train at Garsdale Head on a warm, smug, gnat-filled August morning. For the first time in my calm and careful life, I felt panic.

It was very different from grief, or from what I vividly imagine grief to be, since I have never been bereaved — at its centre was a mockery, rather than an ennoblement, of that supernatural entity that I had called our love. But neither was it like that commonplace thunderbolt, the discovery of infidelity — there was none. Sarah's Actions were irreproachable. Her extraordinary disregard for the tawdry conventions of estrangement — the ceasing to communicate, the petty disputes, the first lies, the doomed reconciliations — was, I admitted, nothing less than admirable. I was almost proud of her.

But what I felt instead, as I stepped onto that southbound train, was the panic of a man whose betrayer, in a final act of pity, reveals that the Great Cause is empty, rests on a fallacy, is corrupted, has already failed — and he is the only one who didn't know. I might also write (since I am new to this art of writing an account of oneself, and uncertain in my approach) that what I felt was an urgent, physical sickness for which I could see no cure or treatment. Both statements are true, or at least as true as each other.

This feeling of panic, or of sickness, returns to me sometimes, even now, and in those moments retains all its original intensity. But as the steady months overtake me, lifting and lowering me like waves while they practise their slow sculpture of erosion, I have discovered new and greater causes to serve. This is the story of my discoveries.

I returned to work, hoping for diversion, but a sterile office is an unseemly stage for a panic of the soul. I sat at the focus of my curved bank of computer screens while the prices of the world's goods flashed green and red, ceaseless ruminations of that mighty hive-mind, the market. But for all its supposed wisdom the market offered no advice on the subjects of decisive wives and ruined hopes — the bedraggled

Dales sheep, incoherent but magnificently impervious to suffering, had been more helpful.

On the wall over my desk, an air conditioning unit ticked gently at the prompting of a thermostat. An expensive jacket hanging on the back of the nearest chair stirred, swinging a few millimetres to and fro in the flow of odourless air. The time, displayed a hundred times on my screens, once next to each price, advanced another minute. Who had I been, I asked myself, that I could have been satisfied with this? For I had been satisfied — or as satisfied as anyone who tries to make the best of what his time and place seem to offer. Who had I been, and who was I now?

The idea struck me later that week, as I walked from the office to the tube station. In order to fill the horrid vacuum beaten out by the air conditioning and the flashing prices, and at the same time to divert my attention from what I was by now used to calling my panic of the soul, I would simply read a book. For me, a good book would be, not like a window in the cell wall — that was the wrong image: there was no cell, for there were no walls — but like a standard, perhaps, fluttering over a field of battle. And the more stupid and farcical the battle, I told myself, the nobler must be the standard. Finally, since I feared that turning the last page would feel something like stepping onto that southbound train at Garsdale Head, I decided that it must be a very long book.

I enjoy reading stories, or novels, as we adults are supposed to call them, and so it was to fiction, to all those stories that I should have read but had not, that I first turned. *Ulysses*? *Don Quixote*? *War and Peace*? To each of these I considered pledging my allegiance but the colours of their nobility did not suit my obscure purpose — besides, none was long enough.

Proust. The word flashed up in my mind like a cartoon light bulb. Yes, Proust's shelf-buckling novel was long enough. But — the light bulb flickered — perhaps Proust, too, was inappropriate. I had once listened to a discussion about him on Radio Four. *Le temps perdu*. Lost time. Love, loss, memory, despair. *The sweet cheat gone.* I shuddered, and the lightbulb went out. Perhaps one day I would find succour and solace in the words of Proust, or some other high priest at the altar of love, but not yet. I wanted diversion from the sickness, not treatment.

My degree had been in Physics and Philosophy, neither of which subjects I felt inclined to explore further (hence my passage, my descent, into a career in finance). As for the many other provinces of the wide realm of recorded thought, I knew so little about them that I determined to go to a bookshop and choose by appearance, just as any sensible person chooses a bottle of wine.

Accordingly, during an illicit lunchbreak on the following day, I made my way to the Charing Cross Road. In those damp and labyrinthine basements, rich with the mingling smells of ancient drains and mouldering paper, I found several promising candidates. I weighed Vasari's *Lives of the Artists* against Butler's *Lives of the Saints*, flirted with Boswell and Pepys, and almost fell for Kinglake's *Invasion of the Crimea* in nine volumes (but I counted only eight).

At last, with my return to the office long overdue, and as I was about to settle for a tattered set of Churchill's *History of the English-speaking Peoples*, I glanced upward and my gaze lighted on a long, dark mass of uniform volumes on the top shelf of the history section. They were of substantial size and thickness (*demy octavo*, as I now know), occupying at least a foot of shelf space. A timeworn gilt tracery glimmered faintly on their broad spines. I stretched to reach the first volume, which slid out smoothly from its snug abode and tipped its weight into my hand. The cover was a rich, raisin brown textured by fine, diagonal grooves that formed a lattice of tiny squares, like, perhaps, a field that has been ploughed twice by a pair of infinitesimal farmers engaged in a mad quarrel of ownership. The dusty page-ends bore a marbled pattern of dark, bluish strands of ink, which flourished into a mass of vivid colour on the endpapers. A rectangle of pale grazes showed where an *ex libris* had been removed.

I turned to the title page. '*The Decline and Fall of the Roman Empire* by Edward Gibbon. A new edition, 1825. Printed for Thos. McLean, Jas. Goodwin, W. Sharpe & sons, G. & J. Robinson, also R. Griffin & Co., Glasgow & J. Cumming, Dublin.'

Now I had heard of this Gibbon, author of the pre-eminent masterpiece of English historical writing. I knew nothing about the subject, except for a puerile idea that the Romans had spread themselves out too thinly, like not enough butter on a slice of toast, but this was my chance to learn (I will return to the subject of my own ignorance later). In the margin of every page were the author's prompts to guide his readers through the massive river of prose. One page held a large folded map of the empire. A neat pencil inscription on the flyleaf stated: *12 vols complete. £200.* Even the fat, round figure of the price, and its grand excess over what I had expected to spend, appealed to me. I placed the book on a chair and began to take down the remaining volumes — three at a time, for I have large hands.

2

A few weeks after my wife's disappearance, or flight, I received a letter in which she expressed sympathy and concern about the shock I must have suffered, and asked whether I was adjusting to life without her. She wrote that she herself was feeling 'very strange' but had no regrets. She wanted to begin divorce proceedings as soon as possible, and, admitting (irreproachable, as ever) that she had no legal grounds on which to divorce me, she asked whether I would mind if she falsely cited 'unreasonable behaviour'. This would allow us both to 'put this all behind us' as quickly as possible.

I stared at those two words, 'this all' — a clumsy appellation for three happy years of marriage preceded by another three of passion and fidelity at university; for anxiously awaited phonecalls, joyful reunions, acts of selfless devotion on both sides; for aberrations of meanness or thoughtlessness fiercely regretted; for holidays and plans and stoic smiles on Monday mornings; for lives that chose to be defined by each other. But, after all, I could hardly expect her to be the Woman of Words as well. It occurred to me that my allegiance to that supernatural love-entity could indeed be described, with hindsight, as unreasonable behaviour. But she had been just as guilty of that — a cascade of now-incomprehensible snatches of memory allowed no doubts about it: Sarah had loved me.

I replied briefly (c/o her mother, as instructed) that she might do, say, cite as she pleased. How irreproachably correct of her to choose the medium of letters, I thought: how easy it was to write mad, phoney words that I could never have said, and to resist writing those that I could never have resisted saying. The concise madness of this reply made me feel better, and I got on with my life — in other words, I got on with reading the book.

With Edward Gibbon's strong hand in mine, I steered between the vacuum and the panic. Autumn began to tighten and darken. Sarah's birthday came and went, like unexplained laughter heard from a window. I did not send a card c/o her mother. I read slowly, sometimes lingering on a chapter for several days or referring back to an earlier one, but during my leisure hours I did little else. Whenever I was forced away from the book I felt as though I were holding my breath: urgent and vulnerable.

Upon reaching the end of chapter thirty-nine, near the beginning of the seventh volume, I made the discovery that led me to the sacred combe.

The chapter tells of Theodoric the Great, that barbaric king of the Ostrogoths who is now remembered chiefly for having ordered the execution of the philosopher Boethius. Its last lines are weird, fine and memorable in themselves, so I will quote them to set the mood for my discovery:

> *His spirit, after some previous expiation, might have been*
> *permitted to mingle with the benefactors of mankind, if*
> *an Italian hermit had not been witness in a vision to the*
> *damnation of Theodoric, whose soul was plunged by the*
> *ministers of divine vengeance into the volcano of Lipari, one*
> *of the flaming mouths of the infernal world.*

This image was vivid in my mind — my interpretation had the nasty old king falling headfirst, the skirts of his armour flapping immodestly, into a pool of white magma — as I turned the page. On its reverse, which the printer had left blank in order to begin chapter forty on the right-hand page, was pasted a small type-written notice:

```
WANTED:
Diligent volunteer to carry out two months'
painstaking archival work for private library.
Board and lodging provided;
curiosity and imagination rewarded.
Please telephone Miss S. Synder on
01092 650 0000
```

I gazed at this rectangular apparition for a long time; I even threw a glance over my shoulder, as a man might who suspected a prank. The notice did not look particularly old, but neither did it look brand new. I picked at its edge with my fingernail, but the glue held firm. I did not recognise the area code (neither will you, since I have changed the number), but it looked like a current British telephone number. Was the diligent volunteer still wanted? There was one way to find out. I chuckled at the idea, closed the book with a flamboyant snap, and went to bed. A week passed.

'Hello?' A woman's voice, on a bad line.

'Ah,' I said, confused already. 'Good afternoon. My name is Samuel Browne and I'm calling about an advertisement that I found glued into a book.' I waited for a reaction, but heard only the gentle hiss of telephone silence. 'For an archivist,' I added. More silence. 'For a private library?' I shook my head, feeling foolish — what had I expected? I had nothing to lose by one last attempt, so I suggested, 'Curiosity and imagination rewarded?'

At last the woman made a low exclamation expressive of understanding. 'I do beg your pardon, sir,' she said, cordially, 'I had forgotten all about those. To be honest, we had given up hope.' A very slight ponderousness suggested hale old age, and there was a thick provincial accent — but which accent?

'So the work still needs doing?'

'Well now,' she said, hesitating. 'He's not told me otherwise. I shall have to ask, though.'

'Oh, of course,' I said, casually, reassuringly. Then with a nervous laugh, I added, 'I didn't really expect it would. I thought I might be twenty years too late, or that the notice might be some sort of joke — it seemed such a strange place to put it.'

She ignored this comment and said, slowly, 'I'll note down a few particulars.' There was a pause as she looked for pen and paper. 'Mr Browne, did you say?'

'Yes.'

Then she made a sound with a questioning tone: '*Ee?*' I wondered if it was an abbreviated question in the local dialect.

'Pardon?'

'Do you have an "E",' she asked, irritably, 'or did your forebears lose it along the way?'

I laughed. 'Yes, I have an "E".'

'Oh good.' She sounded relieved. 'Now, what about education?'

'Yes — I mean — well — I have a degree in Physics and Philosophy, from Nottingham. A two-one.'

'Phil-os-ophy,' she murmured, writing. 'Though whether

17

they actually learn anything these days —' then she added, sharply, 'Occupation?'

For a moment I was at a loss. Then I said, firmly, 'Banker.' I thought it was the sort of language she would understand. She gave a short 'hm,' that seemed to express resigned pity.

'Interests?'

Again I hesitated. 'I am interested in many things,' I began, stupidly, 'even most things.' Well, it was true.

'In books, I hope,' she snapped, then added, patiently, as if I were rather slow, 'since you are applying for this position, I mean.' I said that some books interested me, and others didn't. 'Some books,' she murmured, 'not others.'

'And walking,' I added, wondering what the reader of this lady's report would think of me. 'Hiking, I mean. And astronomy.'

She gave a faint murmur of satisfaction as she finished writing. 'Your feet will carry you around here as well as in most places,' she said, 'and we have our share of stars.' I asked where the job was located. She told me the county, and added that they were 'a bit out of the way.' I asked her if she could tell me anything else about the work, but she replied that she thought all the details were clearly stated in the notice. Then she took my telephone number and said she would call back. 'One last thing,' she added. 'Which book was it, and where did you get it from?' I told her, and she wrote it down. She said that 'he' might be interested.

Miss S. Synder called me back the following day to tell me that she had discussed my application with the gentleman who owned the library, and that, if I was sure that I wanted the position (she was insistent on this point), it was mine. I assented, and she gave me the name of a small railway station at which I was to present myself on the evening of the first Sunday in January (it was now the beginning of December). She told me the departure and arrival times of my train, and that someone would meet me. I asked her if there was anything I should bring.

'Patience, and a head for heights,' she replied, mysteriously. 'And plenty of warm clothes.'

3

I decided to resign from my job. I was very polite — I did not mention the vacuum at all, but told my employers that I wanted to do some voluntary work for a while. One said that he could understand my wanting to 'give something back'. As expected, I was not required to work out my notice — indeed, I was virtually thrown off the premises, albeit courteously. I finished the seventh volume of Gibbon with some difficulty and struggled with the opening chapter of the eighth — my allegiance to the flag was wavering, now that I saw another on the horizon.

Christmas loomed, and then swept by painlessly in the presence of my family — a few games of chess with my silent and inscrutable brother, some earnest job advice from my father, and one undignified, brandy-fuelled outburst on the subject of Sarah to my sister and her husband. I returned to my own flat to find my P45 and the decree absolute on the doormat. Happy new year, Sam.

I had bought a rickety suitcase in a junk shop — it bore the initials 'E. G.' for Gibbon, which made me smile. Into this case went half a dozen shirts, spare trousers, a couple of jumpers and a handful each of socks and underpants. On top I laid four of the remaining volumes of Gibbon, leaving the last one on the shelf: something to come back for. I added a pair of binoculars (for the stars), a couple of notebooks and a waterproof jacket.

Sunday morning was bright, cold and still, and the outer door of the flat, formerly our flat, made a sharp sound like a pistol shot as I pulled it to (a farrier's pistol, a putting out of misery, I fancied). The local railway station was a fine, Victorian structure, built where the line passed through a cutting. Every morning Sarah and I had stood together on that narrow platform awaiting the seven-twelve. On some mornings the cutting had filled with mist; on others it was bathed in low sunlight that shone on her newly-washed hair while wrens yammered in the trees above; and on yet others, rain had beaten down into it, so that most commuters crowded under the drumming iron roof, while she and I found shelter by flattening ourselves into one of the shallow brick arches that bordered the platform — for five minutes our own intimate domain. But over the past few months it was the panic that had settled here like a fog: I seemed still to hear her voice, lent a faint resonance by the walls of the cutting, and the crisp clip of her shoes on the steps. Now it was only my shoes that shifted restlessly, crunching the scattered grit.

I crossed London on the tube, mounted onto the concourse of one of its great diesel-scented termini and boarded the long outbound train. At the door I turned for a moment, and found myself speaking out loud over the roar of the engine: 'So long, you bastards,' I said.

There are many things from which we fly. Some we can escape; others, not. When we succeed in escaping, we feel surprised and a little afraid. When we fail, we feel resigned. That is my brief treatise on flight.

I read a long paragraph of chapter forty-five for the third time. '... *the lofty tree,*' it said, '*under whose shade the nations of the earth had reposed, was deprived of its leaves and branches, and the sapless trunk was left to wither on the ground.*' A passenger sneezed, and I looked around the sealed carriage at the sleepy students and those silent, sharp-eyed elderly couples who seem as alert to the world as they are oblivious of each other. Slowly, unprofitably, I read the paragraph again, then turned to the window. Long shadows of trees and pylons reached over the sparse winter barley, and here and there a ghostly trail of frost lingered along a hedgerow. Details flashed past: a scrap of blue plastic half-submerged in deeply rutted mud, an old tree with a broken bough, a flock of starlings rising.

The sun, having given his best for a few hours, was already slipping, glowing orange on faces and the backs of empty seats, as the train pulled into the last stop. After a chill half an hour on the platform, I boarded a second train which rattled me out across twilit fields and past looming copses. Then came another change, at a market town that I had heard of but never visited, and another chill half-hour wait. A two-carriage train shuffled into the tiny branch-line platform, with which it exchanged a few silent travellers.

At each stop I peered out into the darkness, shielding my eyes from the carriage lights, in search of the name of the station. One seemed to have no name, and I suffered a moment of indecision, gripping my suitcase, poised to leap into the darkness. I stayed in my seat. Another few stops, and suddenly there it was — the sign illuminated by a dim lamp. I stepped down into the raw, windy evening, and the train rumbled away.

I started on seeing a shadow at the end of the platform, which I had thought deserted, but then its motionlessness made me sure it was just a post. As I turned towards the gate, however, it moved.

It approached, and took the form of a rough-looking, denim-clad teenage boy with tangled red hair.

'Misser Browne?' he asked, casually. He led me out onto the narrow road, past a rusting, abandoned car that leaned into a ditch. How could the local council permit such an eyesore to remain there, I wondered, right outside the station? To my surprise, the boy opened the sloping boot of this wreck (it was a Ford Cortina, I think) and motioned for me to put my case into it. He then tipped himself into the driver's seat and with a clattering roar the car lurched up onto the road. The passenger door swung open.

The cold interior smelled fiercely of petrol and stale tobacco. I glanced across at the boy, trying to convince myself that he was old enough to drive legally — he smiled to himself in the gloom but said nothing as we drove fast along narrow lanes for several miles. After a while he pushed a cassette into the ancient dashboard and a muffled, metronomic dance-beat accompanied the heaving engine: he smiled again and drove slightly faster. Soon we bore down on a lamplit village green at the foot of a looming bank of hills, and as we passed the church the boy braked hard and turned onto an unsigned track that wound behind the churchyard, straight towards the black hillside. The car bumped and jolted on the grassy ruts and puddles that I could see in the beam of the single working headlight. We did not climb steeply as I had expected, and peering out of the window I realised that we had entered a narrow, steep-sided valley. Leafless hawthorn branches hung across the track from both sides and screeched against the windows as we passed.

I had been unsettled by the post that moved and the abandoned wreck that was not abandoned: I have an adventurous disposition, I think, but now I was failing to make sense of my surroundings. I wanted to speak, to protest, but gripped my seat and said nothing.

At last, about half a mile from the village, we reached a lonely stone cottage on the right, with a lamp over the door. The car stopped.

'Here yer are,' said the boy, in a friendly way. I thanked him and fumbled with my wallet. He shook his head, muttering, 'I wunna get away with it.' I retrieved my case, and held up my hand as he threw the car into a skilful five-point turn, paused to light a cigarette, and drove away, a dark shape against the bouncing beam of the headlight.

The door of the cottage was opened by a tall, broad-shouldered, smiling woman who could only have been Miss Synder. Her steel-rimmed glasses were almost identical to my own, and her hair, rather greyer on the left and darker on the right, was neatly brushed back from a strong, finely lined forehead. She wore a sort of tunic of thick, plain dark wool with a matching skirt — but the austerity of this costume was, I noticed, relieved by a pair of fluffy blue slippers.

She led me through a small, dark hallway and a low door into what I soon learned to call the parlour. Half a dozen assorted, threadbare rugs lapped and overlapped each other to cover the floor. A black oak table stood against one wall beneath a large brass wall lamp, and two armchairs faced the fireplace, whence a cosy warmth radiated though the air was cool. A cat dropped silently from a broad and well-pawed chair arm and studied me from under the table. Countless pictures covered the darkly papered walls — old photographs, watercolours, engravings, and a number of bold and incongruous charcoal sketches of figures and faces. A heavy, carved bookcase was crammed with paperbacks. Miss Synder took my coat, offered me the un-pawed chair, and brought me a glass of a hot, spicy punch or mulled wine.

She had an air of serenity that allowed her to seem welcoming whilst speaking little and matter-of-factly. My place of employment was Combe Hall, a quarter of a mile further up the lane, at the head of the little valley or combe; I was to present myself there at nine o'clock the next morning; my employer was a Doctor Arnold Comberbache; breakfast was at eight.

After a delicious supper of beef pie and another glass of punch, Miss Synder led me up a dark staircase to my bedroom, which was one of three. It was plainly furnished, dimly lit, and so cold that I could see faint wisps of vapour as I breathed.

'Usually I only light the parlour fire and the stove,' she said unapologetically, nodding towards a small unlit fireplace in the corner, beside which stood a coal scuttle and a neat pile of kindling. 'You are very welcome to sit in the parlour of an evening, but it's as you wish.'

Three books stood on a shelf beside the bed — there was something deliberate about their presence, and I stooped to read the spines: J. L. Carr's *A Month in the Country*, the Rev. E. Donald Carr's *A Night in the Snow*, and Stella Gibbons' *Cold Comfort Farm*. I unpacked my case rather hastily and undressed, shivering. The sheets were stony cold as I climbed into bed, but there were two heavy blankets and I soon warmed up. As my body settled and my breathing slowed, I became aware of the exquisite silence. I could hear the microscopic stirring of my cheek against the cool pillow as I breathed, and the slowing pulse of my blood, and nothing else.

I wondered which horrors I had successfully escaped, and which might have followed me to this mysterious retreat.

4

I awoke to see a faint, pre-dawn glimmer around the heavy curtains, and felt a little rush of excitement as I drew the sharp, cold air into my lungs and remembered where I was. To my relief, there was a spluttering shower with hot water in the downstairs bathroom; I also had a tiny basin in my bedroom. The parlour fire was already crackling merrily as Miss Synder brought scrambled eggs, toast and tea, and sat down with me for breakfast.

I asked her how long she had lived at the cottage. 'At least as long as you imagine,' she replied, cheerfully, but without elaborating. After a while she added, as though to change the subject, 'I don't get a paper here, and the radio reception is not up to much. It's best in the kitchen,' she confided in a mildly disapproving tone, 'if you ever want to catch the news.' Then she seemed to remember something, went to the hall and brought back a small electric torch. 'Always carry this in your coat pocket,' she said, handing it to me. 'You'll need it in the evenings.'

After breakfast, I drew back the curtains in my bedroom to reveal a misty morning. The window was divided by a single stout mullion into two iron-framed casements which, though fastened shut, exuded coldness. I could see a small, sloping, frosty back garden, with a couple of fine old plum trees and a little greenhouse.

Beyond, the hillside mounted steeply into the mist in a sombre wall of bare, twisted trees and dead bracken.

At ten to nine, muffled up in coat, hat and scarf, I slipped the iron door key into my coat pocket and started cautiously along the frozen track. After a few steps I stopped at the sudden, weird sound of a robin, singing from a bony elbow of hawthorn not ten feet away. He fixed his bright, black eye just over my shoulder and sang with astonishing *quietness* — a thin, intimate whisper of beauty that only he and I could hear. The vibrations stirred the tiny feathers of his throat, whose colour, a soft, cinnamon orange, made me think of the noblest tones of ancient tapestries, and so seemed to lend that tiny, fragile, short-lived creature an air of grandeur and wisdom. After a few seconds he flew to the next tree and sang again, a tiny puff of colour leading me into the white morning. I followed along the track, delighted.

I could hear the subdued gurgle of a stream to my left, and occasionally glimpsed its frost-crusted banks over the mossy wall. Blood-red haws lingered on the twigs that hung over the track, and a few dog-roses held up sprays of fat, scarlet hips on groping branches. After I had walked a few hundred yards I caught a sudden smell of wood-smoke on the air, and the robin disappeared up the hillside. I wiped the mist from my glasses and continued.

The track curved to the right and then turned sharply left towards a graceful stone bridge, about eight feet wide and with no parapets, that crossed the stream in a single low span. Above the bridge was a sort of archway of ivy-clad branches, which confused me until I drew nearer and realised that it was a clever illusion: one ash tree on the far left side of the bridge, and another on the near right, each extended a long branch which, though parallel and separate, appeared from the track to meet in a perfect gothic arch over the bridge. How such a thing could have been contrived, I could not imagine.

The smooth slabs of the bridge were slippery, and it was not until I reached the other side that I looked up into the mist before me: I drew an arrow of sharp air into my lungs as the first of my revelations of place found its mark.

The track ended at two stout columns that marked an opening in a very low, curved wall. Beyond this reared the front of a beautiful and ancient house, seen obliquely: I could faintly distinguish vast, mullioned windows of many lights, and three high gables loomed against the sky. In front of the house, to the left as I looked, there towered an enormous beech whose highest branches were lost in the mist. One mighty silver bough, a yard wide at its base, reached low towards the house for a great distance over a bare and moss-darkened expanse of gravel.

I walked through the gateway (there was no gate), gazing always up at the house as I approached. It was not as large as that first glance had painted it: two great windows to the left of the door and one even greater to the right, and these three repeated above with slightly reduced height, and again in a trio of much smaller windows in the gables.

The single oak door was fantastically wide though of modest height, shaped at the top in a low gothic arch that the branches over the bridge had neatly prefigured. Beside it grew the twisted trunk of an ancient Virginia creeper, whose tendrils spread a vast leafless web over the pale yellow stone, around the door and the window high above it. The doorstep was worn into a shallow curve, as though sagging under the weight of years.

I stopped before the step. The air carried a damp, mossy, wintry smell. The silence was broken by the long, hoarse scream of some

28

unfamiliar bird in a distant treetop. The house, the beech and Sam Browne stood together in the mist: substantial in that otherwise ethereal morning — but *they* were ancient and majestic beside my clumsy insignificance, sure of themselves beside my doubt. With the reluctance of an intruder, I lifted the heavy iron knocker and let it fall twice. The sound seemed to wake me from my bewilderment: I stepped back, straightened myself and attempted an enthusiastic smile. After a long pause I heard a heavy latch being lifted and the door swung back to reveal the welcoming but unexpected figure of Miss Synder herself, whom I thought I had left in her cottage just a few minutes before.

'Hello again,' she said, now serious and businesslike, 'and welcome to the combe.' She ushered me into a large, dim entrance hall with a chequered stone floor that rang and swished beneath our feet like the floor of a church. The cold air was filled with the rich, sweet scent of pine, and, glancing upward, I saw a huge branch of that tree hanging in space above our heads. It was suspended from the banisters, slightly tilted from the horizontal like a huge hand raised in blessing (or warning, you are thinking, but it seemed optimistic). The only light was from a rectangular lantern window in the distant ceiling, which the branch largely obscured.

Miss Synder laid my coat over her arm and stepped into a deep, shadowy alcove on the left, which, from the sound of her softly knocking on it, evidently contained a door. A man's voice said, 'Come in,' faintly, and Miss Synder stepped back into the hall, motioned me forward with a reassuring smile, and walked away across the flagstones to another door, through which she disappeared. With a flutter of apprehension in my stomach I stepped forward, felt around in the darkness for the round doorknob, turned it and entered the room beyond.

29

It was a square room, a study, with a towering ceiling and one of those spectacular front windows filling almost the whole of one wall and admitting a flood of pale light. There was a busy, newly-lit fire in the grate behind a heavy brass guard, and the wall facing me was a wall of books: several thousand, I suppose, on shelves that reached to the ceiling and to which a long, slender ladder was fixed on rails. A man rose from his chair behind a desk on which a few books and papers were neatly arranged, advanced round it and stood before me, gazing at me intently: this was Arnold Comberbache.

He was a man of about seventy, with smooth, taut skin, finely lined only around his eyes, and faintly speckled here and there with liver spots, like an autumn leaf that has turned gold but is still sound. The slightly drawn-back set of his mouth gave him a pained expression that, I was to discover, rarely left him — not physical pain, perhaps, but the pain of having made a mistake, of having to start some task over again. His white hair was combed neatly back, darkening to a steely grey at his collar. He wore a thick herringbone jacket over a pullover, shirt and tie — the fire could not hope to warm that absurdly high space.

I introduced myself and he seemed pleased, perhaps because I had a deceptively scholarly look, with my slim, angular face, steel spectacles and tightly curled hair, and the bulky green jumper knitted by my aunt.

I told him about finding his advertisement in Gibbon. 'It had probably been on quite an adventure before it reached the Charing Cross Road,' he said, chuckling, 'since I left it, along with all the others, outside a charity shop not twenty miles from here. You will better appreciate my ruse, I hope, once I have explained the precise nature of the work.'

He rubbed his hands, in anticipation, perhaps, or to warm

30

them. 'M'Synder had her doubts,' he added, wryly. 'Did you not M'Synder?' That industrious lady, who had just stumped in through the open door carrying a full coal scuttle, set it down by the fire, gave a sardonic smile without turning to her employer, and walked out, closing the door behind her.

'You have an impressive library,' I said. The doctor narrowed his eyes for a moment as if confused, then followed my gaze up to the packed shelves behind him, and smiled.

'Yes, I've developed a rather acquisitive habit with books over the years,' he said, and turned towards a second door opposite the window. 'Unfortunately for you, all my ancestors did the same. Let me show you the seat of your labours.' He pulled open the heavy door slowly and motioned me forward. So occurred the second of my revelations of place.

5

My first glance through the doorway revealed two vast windows overlooking a perfect lawn, white with frost. I advanced into a much larger room, looked around, and back, and up. What I saw was books: I was standing in a cathedral to the glory of books.

There was a fireplace at each end of the room, nearer the window side, with a narrow green carpet running from one hearth to the other, perhaps twelve yards, in front of the windows. Above each fireplace hung a large and age-darkened portrait in a heavy frame. A gallery with slender iron railings, reached by a spiral stair in the corner, ran along the long back wall and part of another wall at half height, and near the centre of the dark oak floor stood a huge folio table. Two iron chandeliers hung from the distant, ghostly expanse of coiling plasterwork, and a squat leather armchair stood at each window.

With the exception of the objects so far mentioned, it was all books — eighteen thousand of them, I later learned. I dropped my wondering gaze from the shelves to the face of my employer, who was smiling his pained smile.

'Welcome to the library of Combe Hall,' he said, in a low voice, 'which has been two hundred and thirty years in the making.' He strode out to the long carpet and turned to look back fondly at the shelves, his thumbs hooked into his belt. 'It was established by my ancestor, Hartley Comberbache, in seventeen seventy-two. This room had been the banqueting hall, but Hartley, as you might guess from the look of him, did not hold many banquets.'

He nodded towards the weird portrait, which showed a man of forty turning hastily from a mass of papers, looking over his shoulder at the viewer, as though his work did not allow him time to sit formally. His face was thin and bloodless, his dark hair swept back into an untidy tangle behind his head, and he wore a plain coat over a creased and yellowed collar.

'That is Sarah, his wife,' added the doctor, indicating the other portrait. I cringed at his words, but recovered in a moment. Sarah Comberbache was depicted in half-profile, her head tilted slightly forward and her eyes lowered in contemplation. She wore a blue velvet dress with a high collar of dark lace about her throat. Neither husband nor wife looked happy, and now the one was destined to stare across at the other in a state of eternal distraction, never again to take up his pen, while she looked away. Now that I realised his true object, the intensity of Hartley's gaze seemed strung along the room from one end to the other, high above our heads, radiating anguish.

'I'm afraid the library does not take advantage of the latest technology — there is no computer, and light and heat come and go more or less as nature commands. The collection, however, as you can see, is in excellent order, and three centuries of correspondence and other papers are neatly filed here.' He indicated two long shelves of box-files in the folio table. 'It was my mother's hobby for several years. "So," you are asking yourself, "why am I here?"'

The look of wonder had not left my face. 'Why, indeed,' I said. The doctor lowered himself slowly into the armchair near the portrait of Sarah. I stood by the table, my fingertips poised on the cool mahogany, waiting for his reply.

'You are here because one item of correspondence is missing. Or rather, it is here, in this room, but I can't read it because I don't know where the damned thing is — and I would like you to try to find it.' He leaned back in the chair and gazed at me.

'How do you know it's here?' I asked.

'A sensible first question,' he replied, flicking his hand towards me like a teacher to an attentive pupil. 'I know because the item is not missing by accident. A few years ago I discovered that it was *put in safekeeping* by my great-uncle, who, sadly, was not a very enlightened man. To put it plainly, the stuffy old fool hid it because he thought it indecent.'

'What is it?' was my next question.

The doctor smiled, knitting his veined hands. 'It is just a letter, addressed to that gentleman.' He pointed to the painting. 'I will tell you more about it in good time. For now, it is enough to say that it is an important part of my family's history, and, perhaps, something more — a valuable document in itself.'

I walked to one of the windows. Its deep sill formed a seat of grey stone which might have accommodated six or eight people, and on which lay a few flattened and faded cushions. Outside was a narrow stone terrace and the top of a short, steep slope which dropped to the sunken lawn. High walls were visible to left and right, and at the end of the lawn a number of trees loomed faintly in the mist.

'And you think your uncle hid this letter in a book?' I asked.

'I know he did. And so you begin to see the task before you.'

I sank onto the window seat and looked up at the towering shelves. 'Presumably you have some idea where to start,' I suggested, hopefully.

The doctor now laid his hands on his knees and sighed. 'Here we come to the crux of the matter. My great-uncle Hartley — he bore the same name as his great-great-grandfather, you see, which might go some way towards explaining this miserable business — my uncle was one of that incomprehensible breed who are fond of puzzles. And he boasted to his unfortunate wife — I have found her diary — that he had hidden the letter in an "indeducible" location. A riddle designed to have no solution.

'If we are to believe the old prune, we cannot deduce the hiding place — the book — from the subject of the letter; nor can we deduce it from the originator of the letter, or its recipient. Nor from Uncle Hartley himself, his opinion of the letter or any other of his characteristics. Neither from the date of the letter's writing, nor the date of its hiding — other than that the book must have existed at that time, of course. But it has no particular characteristic to connect it to the enterprise. Furthermore — and now you will realise the full extent of my uncle's obsession — neither does the book have a particular absence of connection to the enterprise. That, too, would narrow the search.'

I frowned. 'So,' I began, slowly, 'it is just a book — one among thousands.' The doctor nodded. 'And therefore,' I went on, 'since we cannot deduce it —'

'We must search them all,' he said, triumphantly. 'Yes! Or rather you must — I'm an old man. I cannot stay on my feet for very long, I'm not much good at bending, and ladders prefer the tread of youth.'

I gave a sour little chuckle — it was not quite what I had expected. 'It sounds rather —' I hesitated.

'Repetitive?' suggested the doctor, looking particularly pained. 'It will be, certainly. Tedious? Perhaps, but consider this: you will

35

become intimately acquainted with one of the finest private libraries in the country. The collection is priceless, and extends into almost every branch of civilisation.' He had leaned forward in his chair, and there was a quiet enthusiasm in his voice. 'I don't expect you to search like a robot — there will be distractions and digressions, and there may be many other intriguing finds along the way. I will be here, in my study, ready to discuss anything of interest.'

Then he gave a mischievous smile. 'You did say that you were interested in many things, did you not?' I grinned sheepishly. 'Well, here they are!' he cried, rising from the chair and raising his arms towards the shelves. 'Many, many things!' I looked at him in astonishment. He still held his arms aloft, and waited for me to respond with a wild look in his eyes that seemed half jubilant, half beseeching.

'Alright,' I said, firmly, rising also. Here, if anywhere, was a standard to flutter over my field of battle, to raise my eyes from the mire of panic. 'I'll do it.'

'Good,' he said, with a sigh, holding out his hand, which bore a heavy gold wedding ring, and shaking mine slowly. 'Good, good, good.' Then he narrowed his eyes to twinkling cracks. 'But the missing letter is your primary mission — don't forget. Be diligent!'

'How will I know it, if I find it?'

'A long letter dated seventeen seventy — you will know it. But bring me anything that looks interesting — letters, receipts, notes in the margin, anything.'

'And where shall I begin?' I asked.

'You must decide that,' he replied, quickly, as though he had already considered the matter. 'If I tell you to start at one end or the other, it might condemn you to weeks of extra work. You do not yet know how the library is arranged, so you are not tempted to

calculate, to deduce. I will not give you a tour of the collection —
not yet — though I will answer any questions you may have. You
must choose where to start the search.'

'I must condemn myself,' I muttered, looking from one wall
to another. 'Then I will start there.' I pointed to a great narrow
bookcase nestled in the corner, between the right-hand window and
Hartley's portrait. It was four feet wide and sixteen feet high. 'I will
start at the top.'

'The top left of the whole collection, one might say,' observed the
doctor, coolly. 'Yes, why not? You will have to bring the ladder from
the other side. There is also a *roving shelf* roving about somewhere,
and you will find various other contraptions to help you.'

He went to the door of his study, but turned back to me as he
grasped the handle. 'We will have many a talk, Mr Browne, I am
sure. I have questions, as you do, and look forward to getting to
know you: I receive few visitors.' He threw open the door. 'But for
now,' he cried, theatrically, 'to work!'

The door slammed shut, and I was alone in a silent, cavernous
room. So began my first day at the sacred combe.

6

I carried the slender ladder, which was surprisingly light, across to my chosen bookcase and hooked it onto the brass bar that was bolted to the top shelf for that purpose. I grasped it with both hands and gave it a shake: it seemed secure. Then I stepped away, and decided to have a look around.

The neatly aligned ranks of spines invited, rejoiced in my wandering gaze. Here and there it was drawn to a long, uniform frieze of colour — a reference work in many heavy volumes, a journal or a testament to some individual's furious and exemplary prolificacy — but mostly the books were not at all homogeneous: slim and stout, tall and short, leather and board nestled together in that purely visual jumble that characterises a particularly well-organised library.

Every shelf bore a number on a little circle of brass, but there were no subject labels, or stickers on the spines. A few oversize shelves of double or triple height held huge books that looked like they contained maps, drawings and engravings — atlases, folios of anatomy, archaeology, architecture and art. Standing back, I realised I could not see any recent books, by which I mean those with very brightly coloured or glossy spines — only the occasional yellowed dustwrapper or glimmer of gilt punctuated the subdued, almost organic collage of tan, russet, navy and faded green.

The few incursions into this vertical realm were made by the windows, the fireplaces, and three closed doors beneath the gallery. One led to the doctor's study, as we know. There was a second door at the other end of that long wall, and a third next to Hartley's fireplace. Hanging on a hook in the deep alcove of this last door I found the 'roving shelf' — a stout wooden tray, much worn, grooved, and ink-stained, which slotted snugly onto the front of any shelf and proved invaluable in my search.

Thus equipped, I made my way gingerly up the ladder, which creaked at every step. It was steeply angled and by the time I reached the top vertigo was nudging at my stomach. I gripped the rungs tightly and remembered M'Synder's advice that I bring a head for heights — perhaps I could learn one. The very first book on the top shelf was Izaak Walton's *The Compleat Angler* in a single stout volume, once green, perhaps, now brownish, with five raised bands on the spine. I laid it on the roving shelf (still gripping the ladder with one hand, of course), opened to the title page and slowly added up the roman numerals of the date: sixteen hundred and seventy-six. It was the oldest book I had ever handled. I gently leafed through the thick, rough-edged pages, but there were no loose papers. I slid it back into place. The next book was the same work, in two taller, slimmer volumes with wrinkled spines, published in eighteen eighty-eight. The next was the more modestly titled *A Book on Angling* by Francis Francis. You get the gist.

After half an hour on the ladder I climbed down for a rest in the armchair, having progressed about a third of the way along the first shelf. I rubbed my cold hands and looked out of the window. The mist had almost cleared but the garden still lay frozen in the bluish shadow of the hills. Only the wooded valley-slopes, rising steeply behind, were now bathed in pale sunshine — great pines and cedars standing out like green jewels on the wintry grey mantle of oak and beech.

I had been working for another half an hour or so, and had nearly finished the top shelf, when the doctor returned.

'What do we have tucked away up there?' he asked, leaning back against the table. Angling, boating, shooting, I told him. He grimaced. 'Many of those would have been Uncle Hartley's, I should think — not that it matters to our search, of course.'

He watched me examine the last few books, then invited me to follow him to the kitchen for coffee. 'One shelf down,' he said, cheerfully, 'two hundred to go!' He opened the deeply recessed door by the fireplace, which led into a panelled dining room of surprisingly modest size, with French doors onto the garden. The table was large enough for eight, but only four chairs were drawn up to it. We passed on through another door into a dim corridor.

'There are the *facilitates*, should nature call in one way,' said the doctor, pointing to a door, 'and here is the kitchen, should it call in another.'

I had half expected 'M'Synder' to be bustling about in an apron, but there was no sign of her. The kitchen was a cheerful patchwork of form and function — it retained some of its Jacobean grandeur in the high ceiling from which various chains and ropes still hung, the great iron stove, now cold, the huge Belfast sinks and the high-up mullioned windows, but to these were added an odd collection of modern, or at least twentieth century, conveniences. A big electric oven and refrigerator each looked like they had seen a couple of decades.

The doctor set a heavy metal coffee-maker on the hob and opened a jar. It was strange to see him perform a domestic task

— perhaps because I owed my only experience of such houses to Victorian novels where they were attended by armies of staff — but he seemed quite accustomed to it.

'It is a magnificent house,' I said, stating the obvious, as we sat at an oak deal table in one corner.

Again the pained smile. 'Far too big for me, of course,' he replied, and then related a concise history of Combe Hall. It was built in sixteen twenty, he told me, as a consolation for the non-inheriting younger son of a Richard Kempe, the nobleman who owned this corner of the county — thus explaining, apparently, the oversized grandeur of its windows and ceilings. Hartley's grandfather, a lawyer, bought it from the by-then-ruined Kempes in the early years of the next century, and it had stayed in the Comberbache family ever since, passing down a tangled chain of sons, step-sons, daughters and cousins.

'But you have Hartley's name,' I observed, 'so the line cannot have been so very tangled.'

The doctor laughed. 'The line, as you call it, has been given a helping hand by a tradition that the owners take over the name, whether they were born with it or not. My father took it, though his was Hughes — a good enough name, but somehow not as appropriate as the house name, which was my mother's.'

'So the second Hartley —'

'Our prudish adversary …'

'— was your mother's uncle?'

'Correct. Her mother's elder brother.' He rose and swept up the empty cups. 'But I have prattled long enough! Our labours are waiting.' We retraced our steps to the library, and he vanished once more into his study.

British topography dominated the second shelf. I began to refine my technique: I would lift out the next book and only then replace the previous one; I would balance the book on its spine on the roving shelf, supported by the hand of whichever arm I had hooked around the ladder; with my free hand I would carefully work through the leaves, my glasses perched on my nose, as the various and indescribable scents of mingled words and years rose to my nostrils. I found my first few loose objects — a series of ancient flattened leaf skeletons in Stephen Graham's *The Gentle Art of Tramping*, a train ticket dated nineteen thirty-three, a blank scrap of blue paper. None of these seemed worthy of the doctor's attention.

It was a visit to those 'facilitates' that uncovered the next clue, the next line in the arcane mural that was the combe. As I returned through the dining room, I glimpsed, through the door to the gloomy hall, which was ajar, a woman at the front door. Her back was turned to me, and in a couple of seconds she had opened the door part-way, stepped quickly out with a graceful sideways swing of the hips, and closed it quietly behind her. She had been wearing a close-fitting tweed skirt, a tailored jacket and a red scarf. I fancifully thought I could detect a faint remnant of perfume in the air, but it was only the hall's heavy pine-scent wafting through on the momentary draught.

I was delighted by this new promise of interest, and as I creaked back up the ladder my mind began to hum with absurd but pleasant speculations. The doctor had not mentioned any family — had in fact implied that he lived alone — but I realised that he had told me much more about his ancestors than his own circumstances. After all, I thought with a grim smile, I'm a free man now — but that tainted reflection immediately dampened my pleasure.

At one o'clock, the doctor reappeared again and, seeming pleased with my progress, led me back to the kitchen where he began to prepare a simple lunch.

'A lad from the village brings fresh bread and milk twice a week,' he said, carving into a big round loaf. 'He has one of these bicycles with springs, you see. It's a marvellous thing — he let me ride it once. Even the eggs survive unscathed, usually.'

He told me to help myself to ham, cheese and tomatoes, and we carried our sandwiches into the dining room. As we ate, he at the head of the table, facing the garden, and I on one side, I was startled by an eerie, metallic shuddering sound that seemed to come from under the floor.

'There she goes!' said the doctor, triumphantly. 'Don't panic — it's just the central heating. I fired it up as an experiment. It is a fully functional specimen of pre-war plumbing. Let me know this afternoon if you feel any warmth.'

'Where are the radiators?' I asked, looking around the room.

'Oh, there are no radiators as such, just a few big copper pipes running about the house. I don't usually bother with it.'

I looked at my knuckles, which were bluish with cold, and grimaced jovially.

When we were back in the library, the doctor led me to a window. Heavy grey clouds had covered the sky, and a breeze swirled in the treetops and chased a couple of leaves across the lawn.

'Sleet is my prediction,' he said, peering upward. 'The house stands at an altitude of five hundred and thirty feet. As you can see, it is splendidly sheltered from the north, south and west winds — and this fact has allowed the arboretum to flourish — but our winters are cold.'

'How high are the hills?' I asked, following his gaze up towards their looming brows. A solitary buzzard circled far above.

'The highest is Grey Man, to the north-west,' he replied, pointing, 'at eleven hundred feet. Fern Top, above M'Synder's cottage, is a shade under a thousand feet and Hart Top, to the south, is rather lower.' He turned from the window. 'I will lend you a map to aid your explorations.'

I worked steadily through the afternoon. When the day began to fade I switched on the chandeliers, which flooded the library with a warm yellow light, and later, as the black dusk set in, I cranked the brass handles that hauled the great heavy curtains across the windows.

On the third shelf down, the complete works of W. H. Hudson, in twenty-four volumes, marked a gradual transition from travel writing towards natural history. There followed many varied works on botany, zoology and ornithology, and the fourth shelf began with a beautiful copy of Gilbert White's *Natural History of Selborne*, dated seventeen eighty-nine. The flyleaf bore the inscription, in spidery ink faded to brown, '*O Mother, They will sing for you, why not for me? Your son, Samuel. 18th March '90.*' Two blank pages at the end of the book had been covered in exquisite drawings of birds, insects and flowers.

Given the date, I supposed that this might have been written by a son of Hartley and Sarah, and carried it carefully down the ladder to show the doctor.

'Ah, you found the White,' he said, laying down his pen. 'Yes, I have seen it — in fact I read it many years ago.' He cast a fond glance over the drawings. 'After the death of her husband, Sarah discovered that she was a talented draughtswoman. You will see more of her work, I expect.' He handed back the volume.

44

'Hartley died young, then?' I asked.

'In his forties,' replied the doctor, absently, once again absorbed in his own work. 'It was not so very young at that time.' He scribbled an annotation on the paper he was reading, his face a picture of pained concentration. I withdrew.

So it was that these long-dead souls began to reach out to me from the pages of their books. Back in the library, I looked again at Sarah's portrait, painted when she was a young woman — perhaps my own age. She looked sorrowful, yes, but comprehending. I liked looking at her. As I looked, I remembered the other woman, the living, pine-scented one I had glimpsed in the hall.

I was on the ladder, wondering when I should stop work for the day, when a flood of sound burst into the silence, making me start and almost lose my balance. It was music — the first of Bach's cello suites. Music in a library. I half-turned on the ladder and looked out across the great room as the first few winding bars curled and rolled from wall to book-lined wall. A shiver spread slowly from my neck down my spine, a reaction to this bewildering collision of beauty. 'What is this place?' I whispered to myself.

I climbed down and stood by the table, immersed in the rich shock of sound. The inhuman fineness of Bach did not seem defiant here, in Combe Hall, as it does when you hear it in your living room, or in a city church over the indifferent mewing of traffic. It belonged here: it filled the house like air. The dark polished wood and tarnished brass, the great chill windows, the distant ceiling and, most of all, the books themselves, seemed to comprehend it, as it comprehended them. The study door was thrown open and the doctor walked slowly into the room, smiling, his arms crossed. He, too, comprehended entirely.

'Rest, now,' he said, during the brief pause between the *Prélude* and the *Allemande*. 'The working day is over.' He turned and indicated a series of small music speakers tucked unobtrusively in the shadows under the gallery. 'One of my contributions to the collection,' he said. 'I hope Hartley the elder would forgive me — I know the younger would not.'

He led me through the dining room into the hall, both of which were filled with the music. A sprinkling of long pine needles lay on the black and white flagstones.

'Usually you will dine at the cottage,' he said, 'for I keep irregular hours and eat a late supper. But tonight I have asked M'Synder to cook for us here in the house, so that we can have a talk.' He lifted my coat from a hook beside the door. 'Before that ordeal begins, I expect you will want to escape this old place and breathe some fresh valley air.'

I fastened my coat obediently, and he opened the door. 'Thank you for the sterling work,' he added, shaking my hand, 'and come back at seven o'clock.' The wide door swung shut, and I stood on the dark, mossy driveway across which the notes of a cello faintly drifted from behind heavy curtains.

7

I pulled my hat down hard on my head and walked slowly towards the bridge. It was windy and very dark, and after a few steps I gratefully remembered M'Synder's torch and let its merry pool of light lead me onward. It seemed a longer walk in the dark, and the lamp over the cottage door was a welcome sight.

'Good evening, Mr Browne,' called M'Synder's voice, as I hung up my coat in the hall. 'I'm glad to see you found your way — but there is only one way, of course.' I noticed a red scarf hanging on a peg, and a pair of elegant but muddy boots standing by the door.

'I would have been done-for without the torch,' I said, entering the warm parlour, where M'Synder sat with a book folded back in one hand and the cat curled up under the other.

'That reminds me,' she muttered, looking at the clock and rising. 'I must be going up to the house myself.'

Since it was only six o'clock, as she prepared to leave I fetched *A Month in the Country* from my room, settled myself by the fire and began to read.

'See you later, Mr Browne,' she said, at the door, 'and don't be late!' The front door swung shut, and I was alone with the shifting embers, the quick padding paws of the cat, and the ticking clock. Or was I alone? I remembered the boots, and the three bedrooms, whose doors were kept shut.

I read for half an hour, then changed into my slightly smarter pullover (sorry, Auntie June) and, after a moment's indecision, put on my moleskin jacket. I splashed my face at the little basin and brushed my frothy hair. Then I set out back along the lane.

This time the doctor opened the door. Music was still playing softly through the house — again a lone cello, but something different that I did not recognise. It produced a vaguely expectant atmosphere that reminded me of my parents' rare dinner parties when I was a child, when my mother had put on perfume but the guests had not yet arrived. I felt rather flattered as I performed the now-familiar ritual of hanging up my hat and coat, and the doctor led me through a different door, on the right this time, into a splendid panelled parlour.

'Sherry?' he asked, fetching two glasses from a corner cabinet. He lifted a decanter from a row of at least a dozen standing on a long side table.

A number of fine but well-worn upholstered chairs of different designs and periods stood in a semicircle around the fire, which was flanked by two cosy-looking corner seats below narrow windows on either side of the massive chimneypiece. There, set into the ornate marble relief and dominating the room, hung an allegorical painting of two women. One, spectacularly naked, upheld in her hand the sun, which shone on her white skin and fair, windswept hair, and the open white gown flung about her shoulders. The other cowered at her feet in supplication, wrapped in a heavy mantle of dark blue, shielding her eyes.

'That was one of the many locations where the arms of the

48

Kempe family were proudly displayed until Hartley made his alterations,' said the doctor, handing me a crystal glass. I was aware of him watching me as I studied the painting. 'These were added later, of course,' he added, pointing to two huge landscapes on the opposite wall: nineteenth century depictions of the sublime. One showed sunlight breaking through sweeping clouds over a mountain pass; the other, a red sunset beyond a lake surrounded by distant, jagged peaks, with a mass of storm clouds rolling in. 'I call them *Hope* and *Despair*,' he said, as we sat down by the fire.

'It must be a valuable collection,' I suggested, sipping the dry sherry, trying to look at ease but feeling like an undergraduate at the vice-chancellor's lodgings.

'It is valuable to me,' he replied, simply. 'If you mean that it could be a target for thieves, yes it could — but it is not, because they don't know about it. Believe it or not, very few people know that we exist, here in the combe.'

'I do believe it,' I said, laughing. At that moment I heard the soft click of the door opening, and turned in my chair.

'Ah, Rose is here,' said the doctor, rising. I sprang up too, as Rose, she whom I had earlier seen in the hall, entered the room.

The second thing I noticed about her, in that instant of meeting face to face, was that she was very young — a girl and not the eligible woman I had imagined. How old? It seems we men (forgive us!) are naturally incapable of guessing a girl's age once she has become *nubilis*. I later learned, however, that she was seventeen.

Before I noticed her youth, I saw the scar. It ran down from her temple to the middle of her cheek, dark and irregular, slightly distorting the corner of her right eye. She had sharp, pretty features, and her green irises had that rare iridescent colouring that makes eyes intense and disquieting — but of course her beauty only magnified the horror of the scar. My response to it was not that uncomfortable blend of tender, useless pity for the child and indignation at the pitiless world that one feels on seeing a small child in a wheelchair — her calm, proud eyes seemed to forbid pity, and instead I felt a kind of solemn admiration, as for one who carries with dignity a burden of grief or regret. She nodded a greeting to the doctor, and then looked at me steadily, as a young child looks.

'Allow me to present Rose, my ward,' said the doctor. 'Rose, this is Mr Browne, the man from London.'

'How do you do,' I said, as though I were in a novel, which is how I felt after this introduction. Her hand was very cold.

'Welcome to the combe, Mr Browne,' she said, in a soft, relaxed voice — her accent was keenly clipped, like the doctor's. She wore a short tunic dress with a dark bluish print and tiny beads sewn into the neckline, with dark red tights and black court shoes. He handed her a glass of a darker sherry, and we resumed our seats.

'Rose has been staying with friends for the new year,' said the doctor. 'She gets rather bored here, I'm afraid.'

'I do, sometimes,' she said. 'So do you.' The doctor shrugged and smiled. 'So will poor Mr Browne,' she added, 'I am sure. How long are you staying, poor Mr Browne?'

I hesitated. 'Until the job is done, I hope,' I replied, glancing at the doctor. 'I expect it will take a month or so.' He was holding up his glass, watching the flames through the pale sherry, and said nothing. 'Maybe you could show me around the valley,' I suggested. 'So far I've only seen it in the mist and in the dark!'

Rose took an adolescent gulp from her sherry and winced. She was sitting with her scar towards me. 'That would be fun,' she answered, in a level voice that almost suggested, but did not quite suggest, sarcasm.

There were questions that I would have liked to ask, but felt I could not, and this left me with nothing to say. At last, the doctor came to the rescue.

'Mr Browne is an astronomer,' he said, 'so you must show him the star-tree. I believe the Quadrantids are upon us this week, are they not, Mr Browne?'

'Yes,' I said, enthusiastically, glad to be steered into familiar territory. 'The maximum occurs on the third or fourth — probably early tomorrow morning. To be honest, I've never had much luck with them.'

'You could be forgiven for being less patient with a winter display,' he said. 'Did I tell you that Hartley was an astronomer? Our night skies are the darkest in England.'

'And the cloudiest,' added Rose, quietly. 'Besides, there is no view to the north, south or west.'

'Not from the valley, perhaps,' I replied, impressed by her quickness, 'but your Grey Man would make a first-class observatory.' At this suggestion, Rose seemed to glance at the doctor, whose face was frozen in a particularly pained smile.

'Indeed,' he said, after a pause, and drained his glass. Then the clear, distant note of a dinner gong sounded, and he got slowly to his feet. 'I hope you are both hungry,' he said, and we followed him to the dining room.

I barely recognised it as the room where the doctor and I had taken our simple lunch. Now the table was like a golden pool, glowing softly in the darkness and laid with silver and crystal. Four narrow candle flames flickered as we entered, and then stood upright — the only other light was a dim orange glow from the fireplace. M'Synder was laying out three steaming bowls of soup.

'Thank you, M'Synder,' said the doctor, in a low voice. 'This is a rare treat.' M'Synder bowed and left the room. The doctor sat in his usual place at the head of the table, and Rose and I faced each other on the two sides.

'Rose, I believe it is your turn to say Grace,' said the doctor, gently laying his napkin across his lap. Rose nodded, lowered her eyes, paused a moment for dramatic effect, and then gave a peculiar recitation:

'J'étais sûr de moi,' she began, with a perfect, precise accent, 'sûr de tout, plus sûr que *lui* —' she paused on that word and seemed to nod almost imperceptibly towards me '— sûr de ma vie et de cette mort qui allait venir. Oui, je n'avais que cela. Mais du moins, je tenais cette vérité autant qu'elle me tenait.'

The doctor smiled quizzically, as though trying to place the words, then nodded with approval and picked up his spoon. Without further comment or explanation, we began to eat.

8

'Banks,' said the doctor suddenly, after M'Synder had cleared the bowls, and as she poured wine from a tall carafe. 'M'Synder tells me you work for one.'

'I did,' I replied, warily. 'I resigned. In fact, I resigned when I secured this position.' The doctor looked surprised.

'Should I be flattered,' he asked, 'that my humble little notice so dramatically interrupted a lucrative career, or do you merely have an impulsive nature? Or, and this seems more likely, were you on the lookout for an excuse, an avenue of escape?'

I was determined not to mention Sarah. The twin forces that had driven me to the combe, the panic and the vacuum, seemed more absurd and tawdry than ever. And yet, for the first time, I felt tempted at that moment to consider my ruined marriage as a kind of resource, an unsuspected arrow of experience in my youthful quiver. You idiot, Browne, I thought.

'That is a fair assumption,' I said. 'I don't intend to return to my old career.' You, the reader, may recall the ticking air conditioner and the curved bank of screens on which, in a hundred different places, the time advanced by one minute. I had worked fifty hours a week at the bank for three years — it had been my only so-called permanent job (a grim but misleading designation) — so you probably expect me to tell you more about it. There is no more.

'What will you do, then,' asked Rose, simply, 'after you leave the combe?'

'I don't know,' I replied. I remembered that last volume of Gibbon standing on the shelf in London: the plan for the rest of my life stopped there. 'What about you?' I asked quickly, hearing the galloping hooves of the panic approaching. 'What do you want to do?' I was getting used to her steady, defiant gaze.

'I'll either go to art college,' she said, 'or join the Navy.' I smiled and glanced at the doctor, but he was nodding earnestly. 'Which do you think I should choose?' she demanded.

'Come now,' chided the doctor, 'that's not fair — Mr Browne has only just met you.' M'Synder re-entered with a tray bearing a magnificent roast pheasant, which she placed at the foot of the table and began expertly to carve. Rich smells of game and bacon diffused through the cool air. 'Save some good cuts for yourself,' said the doctor, as she served. He and I each received a leg and some tender slivers of wing, and Rose was given two splendid, long, wafer-thin cuts of breast.

'A happy new year to you all,' said the doctor, raising his glass. M'Synder acknowledged her inclusion in this toast with a silent nod, and left us.

'I hardly feel that I've earned such a feast by searching through a few books,' I said, as we began to eat. 'I am certain that this unfortunate bird would agree.'

'Ah, she would be a generous and a foolish creature who conceded the justice of her own consumption!' countered the doctor. 'But if you find your quarry in the library, as I fully expect, and if it is what I believe it to be, you will have earned pheasant, goose, swan — albatross if you desire it!' He waved his fork expansively.

'Wouldn't that bring bad luck?' I said, lightly. There was a moment's silence, and Rose glanced at the doctor.

'Are you superstitious, then, Mr Browne?' she asked, with a hint of accusation in her voice.

'I don't think so,' I replied, with a nervous smile. The doctor returned the smile reassuringly but said nothing, and we ate for a while in silence.

'You are searching for Arnold's precious letter, I suppose,' said Rose, later, rising to refill our glasses. I nodded. 'Well, I don't believe you'll find it,' she said, standing over me with the carafe, 'if it even exists. But don't let that stop you.'

The doctor sighed wearily, as though this were an old topic. 'We won't,' he murmured.

There followed a rich pudding with cream, and port for the doctor and me. The fire had died to a mound of faint embers, and the chill of the night began to creep into the high, shadowy spaces of the room. I felt a little tipsy, and guessed that Rose, who now spoke little, did too.

'I suggest that we all retire at this point,' said the doctor, suddenly, having drained his glass, 'before the brandy bowls beckon. We men must work tomorrow.'

'I'll go and help M'Synder,' said Rose, pushing back her chair sharply.

'Leave that to me,' he said, pushing back his own. 'You can accompany Mr Browne back to the cottage, and M'Synder will follow shortly.' Rose shrugged, indifferent.

A fine, drizzling sleet glittered in the torch-beams and prickled our faces as we crossed the bridge. Rose walked with quick, easy steps on the cracked stones, and I loped to keep up.

'So you live in M'Synder's little cottage, while the doctor has that enormous house all to himself,' I said, half joking, half curious. It was the only one of my questions that seemed broachable.

'Yes,' she replied. After a while she added, 'I used to live in the house, years ago, but I didn't like it. It —' she hesitated. 'It's a sad, gloomy old place.'

'I thought you were going to say it was haunted,' I said, and then added, mischievously, 'but of course you are not superstitious.' She hurried on in silence, looking down into the bobbing torchlight. The lamp over the cottage door appeared faintly ahead.

'A house does not need ghosts to be haunted,' she said at last, without turning. 'Memory is enough, if there's someone left to remember.'

As I lay in the absolute darkness of my room, listening to the thin, whispering patter of sleet against the window and waiting calmly for my body to warm the sheets, I thought of Rose just a few yards away at the other end of the little landing, warming her own sheets with a slender young body, and felt a pleasant glimmer of sensuality that seemed wholesomely disinterested. Then I thought of her unexplained words, and of the doctor, alone in that great empty house in the softly sleeting combe, turning out the light in some high-ceilinged bedchamber, his face pained in the darkness, remembering.

9

We breakfasted together — Rose, M'Synder and I — but there was little conversation and Rose quickly disappeared into her room. The doctor was similarly taciturn when he opened the door to me at nine o'clock, and I was soon on the ladder, running my eyes along the occupants of the fifth shelf.

He did not appear for coffee, which I made myself, or for lunch, which was provided in the shape of a fresh loaf, cheese which in that house had no need of artificial refrigeration, and a bowl of apples. I began to think that he had gone out — but whither, and how? Did he drive a car? I had not seen or heard one. During a break from the search, as I strolled about the library, swinging my arms and flexing my stiff ankles, I noticed again the third door, which I had not yet seen opened. It would lead to a room in the front corner of the house, beside the doctor's study. I approached it, listened for a moment and then guiltily turned the handle: it was locked.

As the daylight was beginning to fade, the doctor at last appeared from his study, looking weary. He gave me a little wave of acknowledgment, turned on the lights, sat down in what seemed to be his favourite chair, beneath the portrait of Sarah, and watched me. I leafed through the second volume of William Porterfield's *A Treatise on the Eye*, stopping at each of the folding plates to check that it was not a letter in disguise. My assiduity was motivated by a dull dread that in a moment's carelessness I might miss the prize, and then spend many weeks of pointless labour discovering (or rather not discovering) my mistake. It was heightened now by the thought that a book about the eye would make an amusing hiding place — I could not prevent my mind making such connections, even though I knew they were, according to this idea of a riddle with no solution, mere distractions.

'I would have assigned Rose to the search,' said the doctor, suddenly, 'had I trusted her to be diligent. Diligence is everything in this task, I'm afraid.'

'Why should you trust me any more than her?' I asked, turning my head. He smiled, allowing me to guess his reply before he uttered it.

'Because you are of that pattern of persons who buy their own copies of Gibbon and reach the seventh volume.' This was, of course, an assumption on his part. I might have come across his advertisement by chance, whilst idly (or hopelessly) thumbing pages, or indeed a friend might have found it. But, as you know, I did find it just as he imagined, in the full flow of careful reading, and diligence is indeed one of my few virtues. Is there not something unjust about a reckless assumption that proves correct?

'What prompts a young banker-*cum*-astronomer to embark on a study of roman history?' he asked idly, as though to himself.

'I'm interested in many things,' I replied, sliding Porterfield back into place.

At half past five he reappeared to dismiss me for the evening, this time without musical accompaniment, and I walked back to the cottage. After just two days of work, my mind was swimming

58

from the thousands of glimpses I had had into hitherto unknown, unconsidered wells of knowledge and endeavour — just by leafing through a few hundred books. Too much uncomprehended information crowded the front of my memory: sprawling tables of genera, subgenera and species; diagrams of the foot or the inner ear; names of towns, rivers, forests that were perhaps not far away but that nevertheless I would never see; and countless half-read snatches of prose — a tale of a morning ride on a steaming horse now turned to dust, the key to some tiny skill I would never possess, the flavour of some plant I would never taste. The thin, ignorant narrative of my own life seemed diminished, or, to be more precise, *shown up*. Steady on, Browne, I thought — no man can know or see everything. But I did not feel consoled.

I was, at least, relieved to reach the cottage and the welcoming serenity of M'Synder's parlour. The table was laid for two, and after ten minutes — during which I merely sat watching the fire, for I could not think of reading — M'Synder entered with a steaming pot of stew.

'No luck yet, then,' she said, cheerily.

'No,' I replied, joining her at the table, 'and it's more tiring than I expected.' Then, as we began to eat, I said, 'Rose is out this evening, then?' M'Synder nodded, chewing slowly. Encouraged by that serenity in her that I have twice mentioned, I took the plunge:

'How did she come to be the doctor's ward?'

M'Synder looked at me carefully and neatly dabbed her thin mouth with her napkin. 'Her parents were friends of the family,' she replied, at last. What family? I wondered. I thought she would say no more, but she added, softly, 'They were both killed in an accident when Rose was ten. She lived with her mother's parents for a year or so, but then she came to the combe for a visit and refused to leave. To cut a long story short, she has remained here ever since.'

Is that how she got the scar, I asked myself, in the accident that killed her parents? 'What a dreadful age to suffer such a tragedy,' I said. 'Old enough to truly suffer it.'

'The poor child was much changed by it,' said M'Synder, gravely. 'Much changed. She had no brothers or sisters, and came to despise her only remaining family. Doctor Comberbache has helped to bring her back to the world.'

I thought of saying that she too must have helped, but it seemed somehow unnecessary, and the conversation ended there. That night, as I crossed the threshold of sleep, I felt my hands slip away from the rungs of the ladder and my body slowly begin to tip backward, *just the way it would*, and I awoke with a furious, instinctive convulsion of fear.

The next day was crisp and cloudless, with a heavy frost and just a few thin ghosts of mist hanging over the stream. The robin joined me on my walk but again turned back before the bridge, perhaps to regain the dazzling sunshine, for the house was still submerged in shadow. At the leftmost window, that of the locked room, I noticed the ghostly grey baffle of daylight on closed curtains.

Shortly after lunch, my search progressed to the tenth shelf down, which was the first that I could reach without the help of the ladder. I had removed this instrument of torture, and was standing on tiptoes on the oaken terra firma, reading the spines, when Rose strode into the library.

'Good afternoon, Mr Browne,' she said, walking to a window. At breakfast I had asked her to call me Samuel, or Sam, but she had frowned oddly, as though my first name were distasteful to her, and declined the offer. 'Here at last is a day that will do the garden justice,' she said. 'Would you like to see it?'

'Yes, indeed,' I replied. I had been admiring her clothes — I had never seen anyone dress as Rose dressed. Today she was wearing a short, closely tailored jacket of deep red velvet over a white shirt, with tight greenish cords and her splendid brown boots. She was anything but immaculate: the jacket's threadbare elbows were almost worn through, the trousers bore a patch, and a long smear of mud ran up the inside of one boot. What struck me was the unaffected timelessness that she carried as lightly as the doctor and M'Synder. To all these and to the combe itself, as to the sun whose light now slanted pitilessly, gloriously, onto Rose's scarred face, the era seemed to be of less consequence than the season or the time of day.

'Come on, then,' she said, turning into the shadow. 'We'll be back before Arnold notices you're skiving.' She led me into the dining room and opened the tall, glazed door onto the garden.

10

We stepped out onto the stone-flagged terrace from which a broad flight of steps descended to the lawn. There was no need for coats in the windless sunshine, which felt warmer than the house, and we stood blinking for a moment, enjoying the sensation.

'The lawn is exactly one hundred feet square,' said Rose, starting along the terrace in front of the towering library windows. 'This garden is nothing if not precise.'

A suitably precise stripe of frost survived along the south edge of the lawn, in the shadow of the massive, ivy-clad wall. Rose ignored a narrow flight of steps that led down into this chilly domain, and turned left around the corner of the house. A sun-bleached bench stood on a dais against the chimneybreast, just high enough to clear the wall's winter shadow.

'We call that the sunniest seat,' said Rose, pointing, 'because it is.' She turned to a gate a little further along the wall — a gate that had beckoned me from the library's smaller side window. It swung open smoothly, and closed behind us with a soft, resonant clang. We were now standing on a long, straight walk that followed the wall. It was flanked on one side by a broad planted border against the wall, and on the other by a row of evenly spaced but slightly ragged conical yews, behind which could be glimpsed a lower wall of weathered brick. Rose held out her arms towards the two opposite points of converging perspective.

'This is the runway,' she said. 'Two hundred and twenty-two feet and two inches. I run it in nine-point-three seconds — Arnold could only manage nine-point-six.' I raised my eyebrows at this. 'In nineteen fifty-seven, I think,' she added, with a quick, rare smile.

We followed the runway for about twenty yards, past flowering camellias and hellebores, then turned off between the yews to another gate.

'This is my garden,' she said, imperiously, as we entered. Narrow, curving rose beds were arranged in perfect, intersecting ellipses like the orbits of comets. 'Or rather,' she added, more softly, 'I've adopted it. There are eighty-one varieties. Last week I could have shown you a flower — a *Zephirine* on the east wall — but it died.'

We walked around the edge of the immaculate but flowerless garden, towards a gate on the opposite side. 'See, there it lies,' she murmured quickly, as we passed a few limp petals on the ground.

'You must have a full-time gardener, to maintain all this,' I said, realising that I had not yet seen one from the house.

'Ah-ha,' she breathed mysteriously, opening the next gate.

We emerged into a sort of meadow nestling in the bottom of the valley, with scots pines and fine pollarded chestnuts standing here and there in a sea of rough grass. A low iron fence marked its far boundary, behind which rose the wooded slopes of Hart Top. To the right, beyond the end of the garden wall, the trees grew thicker and the meadow sloped gently down to the stream. Rose led me in this direction.

We were about to pass the end of the wall when I caught sight of something lying on the grass around the corner: it was an enormous pair of wellington boots. The next few paces gradually revealed the long, horizontal pair of legs to which these boots were attached, then a long body in green dungarees, and finally a raised, black-haired head wearing a flat cap, and a pair of long arms outstretched along the ground towards a flowerbed.

I looked at Rose, who had also noticed this recumbent giant and arched her eyebrows coolly. The man saw us with a jerk of his head, and then, as we stood watching, began to raise himself from the ground in a series of slow deliberate movements: it was like watching the erection of some monumental tower — the great beams of his limbs sliding into place one by one. At last he stood upright — a full seven feet upright — and touched his cap.

'Bonjour, mademoiselle,' he said, in a deep, solemn voice. 'Il fait beau, n'est ce pas?'

'Here is your gardener, Mr Browne,' said Rose. 'This is Moan. Moan, this is Mr Browne, the archivist.' I was so surprised by being so-called that I scarcely considered whether the man's name was spelt 'Moan' or 'Mown' — the latter seemed appropriate to his profession. He touched his cap again, but did not smile.

'Lying down on the job again?' asked Rose, sharply. The gardener knitted his heavy brows.

'I am pinching out the little sweet peas.' He motioned to a row of tiny seedlings along the front of the flower bed.

'Well, don't let us interrupt,' she replied, walking on. I followed, smiling up at him as I passed. He responded with a weird, mournful nod, his grey eyes intent on mine, and then began slowly to dismantle himself back down towards the ground, as though the earth itself were the only bed long enough to bear him.

'I wouldn't like to argue with him,' I whispered to Rose.

'This is the grove,' she said, pointedly ignoring my remark. The stream meandered between a dozen tall beeches, whose fallen leaves and mast crackled beneath our feet. Beyond a stone bridge — a narrower relation of the one in front of the house — a faint path led across the level grove and mounted obliquely up the wooded hillside in a flight of broad, earthy steps. But Rose turned away from the stream and led me through another gate, back towards the house.

We entered a grand but slightly dilapidated water garden, following a row of stepping stones across a long, formal lily pond, its surface now covered in fallen beech leaves. Sunlight filtered down through distant branches onto mossy statues and dry, leaf-filled fountains in alcoves along either side. Rose stood before a seat of carved stone and raised her face to the sky.

'This is the star-tree,' she whispered. Above us stretched a fine net of branches from an ancient hazel that crouched behind the seat. It was some weirdly contorted variety whose bare twigs curled and twisted like no others I had seen.

'Why do you call it that?' I asked.

She gave a little impatient smile. 'Come out here on a clear evening and see for yourself,' she said. 'But wrap up warm. Old Moan froze to death on that seat.'

Before I could ask her to clarify this remark she was walking away towards an archway. We squeezed between two towering rhododendrons that had almost become one, and emerged at the foot of the lawn.

'Here ends the tour,' she said quickly, skipping down the steps and striding out onto the grass. 'There's plenty more to see — the kitchen garden, the paths in the woods, and so on — but you might like to explore them for yourself.'

I thanked her, marvelling at this new view of the house, whose smooth, ochre-coloured stone glowed softly in the sunshine. The many lights of the windows flared and flickered as we approached.

In the dining room, Rose raised her finger to her lips and ordered me into the library with a stern flick of her hand, as though we were a couple of truants. I smiled and obeyed, and, feeling physically refreshed but puzzled by our walk, resumed my labours.

Rose joined us for dinner that evening. As usual, neither she nor M'Synder seemed to feel any obligation to make conversation. The cat threaded its way restlessly between our legs and those of the table, purring.

'Rose showed me around the gardens this afternoon,' I said.

'Oh yes,' murmured M'Synder in acknowledgment.

'What was that you said about someone — freezing?' I asked Rose, in a concerned tone. She stared blankly at the wall, while M'Synder, with her gaze lowered, slowly laid down her knife and fork. There was a brief, helpless silence, and then the old lady spoke.

'Monsieur Meaulnes, the gardener, died the winter before last, in the garden he loved.' She pronounced the name with such dignity that I instantly realised its true spelling. 'We called him the gardener, but he also managed the woodlands, the lane, the church grounds, the village green, and many other things besides.' She spoke quietly and with great precision, as though she might thereby disguise her emotion.

'The man we saw today is his son,' said Rose, and then added, sardonically, 'Le Petit Meaulnes.'

I resisted smiling. 'How did it happen?' I asked. M'Synder sighed.

'Monsieur was a very capable and worthy man,' she began, hesitantly.

'But he drank like a fish,' put in Rose, coolly.

66

'My dear, please,' scolded M'Synder, frowning. Rose shrugged.

'Well, he did. Aren't we all allowed our vices?'

'I hope you won't speak like that of mine, when I am gone.'

'I shall,' said Rose defiantly, before adding, in a slow, sincere whisper, 'if I can think of any.'

Later, when M'Synder had left the room, Rose filled in a few more details. The Meaulnes lived in the next valley, which could be reached by an old green track that continued up the combe from the meadow and crossed a low saddle of heathland. This explained why I had not encountered 'Le Petit Meaulnes' in the lane. Old Meaulnes had kept bottles of brandy in the potting shed, she said, concealed in particular pots that she had easily discovered. She spoke of him fondly, though without M'Synder's reverence, and I got the impression that he had been a rather wonderful man. She did not mention his son again.

'Arnold found him one morning,' she said, in an odd, mechanical voice, 'sitting on that seat beneath the star-tree, with a bottle beside him. His head was tipped back, and his eyes were wide open, looking at the stars. But of course there weren't any stars left by then. There was frost on his eyebrows, and his moustache, and even his teeth.'

'How do you know all that?' I whispered, doubtfully. Rose shrugged and began to gather up the plates.

'I asked Arnold about it, and he told me.'

11

By Thursday morning I had advanced so far down the enormous
bookcase that my back began to ache from stooping, so I fetched
a cushion from the window seat and continued the search on my
knees. These have never been my strongest point, and they creaked
audibly as I shifted my weight. My task, which beforehand had not
seemed to present any great mental or physical challenges, assuming
its sheer magnitude and repetitive nature did not cow the spirit, was,
I now discovered, not only scrambling my brain but also taking a
physical toll on each part of my body in turn. Moreover, the solitary
and silent nature of the work made me keenly aware of my own
body: every ache, every sensation of cold or stiffness, every creak
of my suspiciously creaky young bones, gnawed insistently at my
consciousness until I had to turn from the books with a sudden
exhalation and throw myself into a chair.

The lower shelves were dedicated to a field with which I was
more familiar: the physical sciences — first chemistry, then geology,
then astronomy and physics. It was not a large collection by academic
standards, of course — perhaps four hundred volumes across all these
subjects, with particular strength in astronomy — but all the most
important works were present, up to about the nineteen thirties. The
doctor seemed to keep most of the post-war collection in his study.

It was mid-morning when I began on the astronomy shelf. Some of the books dated from the eighteenth century and must have belonged to the elder Hartley himself. In Robert Smith's *A Compleat System of Opticks*, published in seventeen thirty-eight, I was thrilled to find, beside the text and on the diagrams, many annotations written in a crabby, indecipherable hand in faded ink. Beside one diagram of light-rays entering a narrow slit and projected on a plane beyond, Hartley (if it were he) had scrawled two exclamation marks — though whether these were meant to express excitement or derision, I could not tell.

I was about to carry the two volumes to the doctor's study in case he was interested in these notes, when in the gap on the shelf I noticed a slim volume that had been pushed back out of sight. It was entitled *The Dawn of Astronomy: A Study of the Temple Worship and Mythology of the Ancient Egyptians* by Norman Lockyer, and was published in eighteen ninety-four. My heart leapt when I encountered what could only be a folded letter tucked into the contents page. I laid down the book and carefully opened the letter.

It was headed simply '*Combe, Tuesday*', written in a graceful, sloping hand. '*Geoff darling,*' it read, '*Can you get here this weekend? Hartless is driving me witless. It will be warm, so bring bathers. On second thoughts, don't bother. I'm awfully keen to see (and the rest) you.*' It was signed '*Stel*', with a hurried postscript: '*Do make it Friday night if you can — it's a full moon and there is something I must show you at the T.*' The word 'must' was underlined.

The private immediacy of this lover's plea caught my imagination, and I thought that had I been Geoff I would have moved mountains to satisfy it. I supposed that 'Hartless' must be the doctor's great-uncle Hartley, and took the letter, along with the *Opticks*, to show him.

He was standing at his window with a cup of coffee, gazing out across the drive towards the wooded hillside. It was raining. He set the steaming cup on the mantelpiece, took the first volume of the *Opticks* and leafed through it, nodding: he had already seen it. I began to despair of finding anything that would be new to him, but when I handed him the letter, he frowned and held it for a long time, apparently lost in thought.

'Very good,' he said, rather distantly. 'It's from my mother to my father, if you hadn't guessed.' He laid it carefully on his desk, and then raised one faint eyebrow and smiled. 'You are thinking that my mother was a rather spirited young woman,' he said, and I laughed dismissively. 'It's certainly what I was thinking,' he added.

'What does the postscript mean, do you think?' I asked. 'What's "the T"?' *Temple*, I thought suddenly, even as I asked the question. Temple.

The doctor went to a side table in the corner, poured a second cup of coffee and handed it to me. Then he slowly dragged his work chair around his desk, waving away my offer of help, and positioned it by the fire, which he stirred up with a very long poker that spared him the necessity of bending. He indicated the armchair for me, and we sat down.

'Stella, my mother, was born here in nineteen hundred,' he began. 'Her father had married late in life, and died when she was a young child. She, her elder brother Samuel, and their young mother were utterly devoted to, and dependent on, each other.

'In nineteen fifteen, Samuel went up to Cambridge as an organ scholar. Two years later he was killed at Arras. A year after that, Catherine, my grandmother, still in her early forties but aged and broken by her loss, died of influenza. My mother was eighteen, and alone.' He paused, sipping his coffee and then gazing into the curling steam.

'Like Rose,' I suggested, cautiously. He nodded, perhaps, or just stirred his head a little, without lifting his eyes.

'My mother's uncle, Hartley, moved back in,' he went on, 'and the Combe became, for eleven years, a rectory. He was not a sympathetic guardian to my mother, attributing her unabated grief to a lack of faith. She spent most of her time alone, in her room or, more often, in some quiet corner of the gardens that still guarded happy memories of her childhood.

'One day she discovered in the woods a steep flight of steps leading up the hillside, half-buried by earth and leaf litter and concealed under brambles. She traced its path up to where the precarious trees give way to heathland, but was there defeated by a wall of ferocious western gorse. The next day she returned with gloves and shears, and fought her way up onto a small, steep-sided promontory that juts southward from the plateau, but that is screened from below by tall trees, and cannot be reached, or even seen, from above because of the massed gorse and bracken.'

Here he paused again, reached his empty cup up to the mantelpiece, and took a long breath with his hands on his knees.

'There,' he began, slowly, 'my mother found the Temple of Light, consecrated by the elder Hartley Comberbache in seventeen seventy-nine, which had by then stood entirely forgotten for nearly a hundred years.'

'It was — some kind of folly?' I asked, hesitantly — I had seen the temples at Stourhead and Castle Howard. The doctor looked particularly pained at this suggestion.

'No,' he replied, sternly. 'It was a temple: a place of reverence and sanctity — of worship, even.'

'The worship of what?' I asked, incredulous. 'Of light?'

The doctor shrugged. 'If you like,' he murmured patiently, and

71

then quickly continued: 'Part of the roof had collapsed, and a birch tree was growing up through the floor. Crowberries crept up the walls and sprouted along the roof, which was home to a small colony of long-eared bats. It was however sufficiently intact for my mother to realise its beauty and strangeness, and it became her secret retreat.'

'Is it still standing?' I interjected.

'Yes,' he replied, smiling, 'and now it is rather more easily reached. Even I still manage the climb sometimes, when my knees allow it. We have reclaimed the stair, and the temple itself, from the long fingers of nature — as you will see for yourself. It could be described as an observatory, too, I suppose — high above the valley, just as you suggested.'

'And did your uncle Hartley never discover it?'

The doctor sighed. 'Hartley was, as we know, a narrow-minded man, but also, fortunately for irreligious lovers of truth and beauty, a parsimonious one. The objects of his purges — the Taboni painting in the parlour was the first to go — were not destroyed but hidden away with the intention of discreetly selling them later, and after his death my mother discovered the ignominious hoard and reinstated everything. The temple, however, thanks to my mother's ingenuity, he never discovered. Had he done so, and had he comprehended its purpose, he would undoubtedly have demolished it. But no,' he added, rising from his chair with a quick smile, 'I suspect he would not have comprehended, and would have had it restored as a summer house for his wife's tea parties.'

'Or as a chapel?' I suggested, rising also. The doctor seemed to consider this possibility for a moment.

'I doubt it,' he said, returning to the window, where I had found him. 'The advantages of its position would be quite wasted.'

72

So I returned to work, wondering when I might get to see this temple, and what other secrets I might uncover. Well, not exactly secrets, I reflected, since the doctor gave straight answers to my questions when I asked them. Mysteries, I might call them — mysteries that he preferred to let me unravel for myself, enlightening me only when my enquiries gave him no alternative. We seemed to have embarked on a game whose rules I now began to understand: if I earned my questions, they would be answered.

I thought about what I had just learned. Was the doctor's adoption of Rose, if one could call it that, motivated by the story of his mother's lonely grief, and her uncle's failings? It seemed a neat parallel, but I was not so foolish as to be satisfied with it.

For the rest of that day I worked my way through the astronomy and physics collections. Some of the books took my breath away: for example, next to the collected works of Galileo in three immaculate volumes, dated seventeen eighteen, stood a third edition of Newton's *Principia Mathematica*, rather more battered, printed in seventeen twenty-six when the author was still alive. When the doctor entered, slowly climbed the staircase and began to consult a bookcase on the gallery, I asked him why such precious books were shelved along with the others.

'This library has traditionally been organised according to the books' contents,' he said, sharply, 'not their market value.' He cautiously descended the stairs with a slim volume under his arm, and added, in a softer voice, 'They are very precious — you are right. Be gentle with them, won't you?' Then he walked out without waiting for a reply, and closed the door.

12

It was almost five o' clock by the time I slid the last book back onto the bottom shelf with a satisfied stroke of the palm of my hand. I rose creakily to my feet and stepped back: over four days I had searched — diligently, painstakingly searched, as promised — sixty-four feet of books. The hunted letter was not there.

I stepped onto the long carpet and looked up at Hartley Comberbache, still half-turned from his work, frozen in a moment of indecision — never our most glorious moments — his lips parted, his dark eyes intent on mine, holding my gaze even as I moved my head so the reflected lamplight glistened softly over the varnished canvas. I wanted to take his arm and raise him gently from his desk, untwist that wrought-up body, lead him away, pour him a drink, make him smile. What was he working on — what words might not have been written if I could really have taken his arm? And would it have mattered?

Two piercing sword-thrusts of strings burst into the silence. It was Bach again: this time the violin concerto in A minor. The doctor was already standing in the doorway, holding a tumbler in each hand.

'Finished the first case?' he asked. I nodded, by now accepting his uncanny timing, and he handed me one of the whiskies. 'To be honest, Mr Browne,' he said, drawing back his mouth and cocking an eyebrow, 'I didn't think you'd find it in that one.' I gave a protesting laugh and threw back the spirit with a flourish, while he sipped at his mischievously.

'Why not?' I demanded, my throat burning.

'Reasoning can only work against us,' he reminded me. 'It was just a hunch. Now, where next?' I eyed the left-hand end of the gallery, next to Hartley's portrait and above the door to the dining room. 'I might as well explain,' he added, before I could reply, 'that if you want continuity in your journey through civilisation, I think you might leave the gallery until the end. Here —' he turned to the case to the right of the door, beneath the gallery '— you will find engineering, architecture, and archaeology. Advancing to the right will take you through foreign travel and topography, and then —' he moved to the other side of the staircase and the study door '— ancient history, European, British, American history, politics, philosophy and — a man's last resort — religion.' He turned. 'Here in the folio table resides the law collection — five hundred volumes, remember I am descended from a lawyer to Queen Anne — and along the far wall you will find biography and letters.'

'Letters?' I repeated, automatically.

'Irrelevant!' he cried. 'Stop deducing — it will get you nowhere. Diligence is everything.'

'What *is* on the gallery, then?' I asked.

'Works of the imagination,' he replied, solemnly. 'Art, music, poetry, drama, fiction — in that order.' He drained his glass and moved towards the door. 'It is your decision, of course,' he said. 'You are doing a fine job.'

That evening at M'Synder's fireside I finished reading *A Month in the Country*, a short, puzzling novel with whose narrator I seemed to have much in common (albeit my demons seemed comic, where his were tragic: but I was used to that). I had seen nothing of Rose since the night before, and I could not help noticing that each time she was absent when she might have been present I felt what I have called my wholesome disinterest falter.

'Tomorrow I'll be out when you finish at the house,' said M'Synder, who sat opposite me, changing the batteries of a torch. 'Fridays, I go to Evensong in the village — I'll be back at about seven o'clock to cook supper.' She had a little box of loose batteries on her lap, and tried different combinations in the torch, each time shining it up into her face to check the brightness.

'You're welcome to come along, of course,' she added quietly, fixing a discerning gaze down into the torch beam. She flicked the switch, satisfied, and closed the box.

'I'd love to come,' I said. 'That is, if you don't mind sitting next to a doubting Thomas.'

I will not now describe my Friday labours over the engineering and architecture collection, lest my account become as repetitive as the task itself. It is enough to state that I made further progress in the search, but did not find the letter.

M'Synder cooked another of her delicious spicy soups for lunch, which she, the doctor and I ate together in the dining room. From where I sat, I could see Meaulnes, the gardener, standing at the southern edge of the lawn with arms crossed and feet planted far apart, studying the deep border between him and the wall. He was wearing his boots, dungarees and cap as before, and seemed oblivious of the fine drizzle that had just filled the air. As I watched he flung out one great arm, like a conductor about to begin. Then he slowly raised the other and swept it from left to right, following it with his turning head, which he nodded rhythmically. Then he dropped the first arm and pointed down at the soil, while the second shot out straight with the palm outward.

'Something in the garden?' asked the doctor, noticing my attentive gaze.

'It's the gardener,' I replied. 'He seems to be doing a sort of dance by the flowerbed.' The doctor and M'Synder chuckled knowingly.

'He's probably just mapping out the spring planting,' explained the former. 'He thinks with his limbs, you see — he inherited that eccentricity from his father.'

'But mangled it up, somehow,' added M'Synder, drily.

That afternoon I heard the sound of ringing voices in the hall and, going to investigate, found the doctor and M'Synder talking to Meaulnes, who towered over them by so much that I found myself smiling at the sight. They were all looking up at the suspended pine branch, which by now appeared rather dry and bald, having dropped, during the course of the week, thousands of long needles onto the floor below.

'Ah, Mr Browne,' said the doctor, brightly. 'You are just in time to see the lowering of our yuletide bough.'

Meaulnes, who had removed his boots and wore thick woollen socks to which clung pieces of leaf and twig, padded up the carpeted stairs (I hardly noticed that he took three at a time). He crouched for a while on the landing and then stood up holding two coils of thin rope. The branch quivered and sent down a shower of needles.

'Keep clear,' he called, and the heavy base of the branch began slowly to descend. When it reached the needle-covered flagstones, Meaulnes threw down the ropes, walked round to the other side of the gallery and lowered the branch to the floor. I had been so engrossed in this spectacle that I noticed only now that the others had vanished. Meaulnes padded back down the stairs and stooped over the branch to untie the ropes.

'I've never seen a Christmas tree like this one,' I said, stepping forward to help.

'You seem very young,' began Meaulnes in a slow, deep, heavily-accented murmur, without looking at me, 'to be an ar-chiv-ist.' He dwelled on each syllable derisively. I was taken aback by the change in his manner, now that we were alone.

'More of a filing assistant, really,' I said, trying to sound breezy. He snorted, thrust his feet into his enormous boots, lifted the base of the branch and dragged it towards the front door, which I opened for him. It took him three great heaves to get it through, then he nodded at me, either in thanks or, it seemed to me at the time, as some vague threat, and staggered away across the drive. Over the steady, grinding hiss of the branch on the gravel came the sound of his whistling, and I paused at the open door to listen. It was an odd tune — a simple theme of four notes, the first pair suspending, the second pair resolving, repeated with wavering variations. It stuck in my head all afternoon.

13

The evening was cold and damp with chilly puffs of breeze that produced short, wavering hisses in the leafless trees. M'Synder wielded the torch she had serviced the night before, and walked with the heavy, metronomic gait of a woman whose joints are not what they once were, but who is used to walking everywhere nonetheless. We were soon past the single light of the cottage and following the lane through the thin woods and rough fields that covered the lower reaches of the combe. A couple of sheep bleated in the darkness, and an owl hooted loudly, theatrically, nearby.

Ten minutes past the cottage (that may seem to imply proximity, but ten minutes' brisk walk along a dark, narrow and winding lane seemed then, to a city-dweller like me, to emphasise the combe's isolation) I saw coloured lights ahead — the lighted church windows beneath the faint silhouette of its short, square tower.

'Are the doctor's forbears buried here?' I asked, as we passed the low wall of the churchyard. The torch beam flickered over a couple of weathered headstones — one era idly, irreverently fingering another.

M'Synder left a moment's silence and then replied, 'Some of them,' in that tone at once suggestive and final, that she, Rose and the doctor seemed all to have perfected to confound me.

The service was led by a plump, red-haired man in his forties, who read his part painstakingly from the lectern as though he were a novice. There was a choir of four men, two women and three boys, and a muffled-up congregation of about a dozen which half-filled the tiny nave. In the shadows of the south transept stood an ancient harmonium, played by a woman with long silver hair in a plait, whose face I did not see.

M'Synder recited the creed and the responses in her soft but certain voice, while I kept guiltily quiet until the congregation's hymn, which I began to sing half-heartedly and then rather enjoyed. My immediate impression of the service was that it was something worthwhile: an act of reflection and appreciation that seemed appropriate after a week's work. The countless invocations of a fairytale God were like a string of loose obstacles left stupidly in an otherwise sound path — I stubbed my toes against them, stumbled over them, silently derided them, but kept my feet. It was better than no path at all.

Afterwards, M'Synder said she had to pay a visit to a friend who was now too old to come to church. I took a turn around the little triangular green before returning up the lane, and one ancient stone cottage attracted my notice. It stood at the end of a short terrace of similar dwellings, from which it was set slightly back and separated by a narrow walled gap. I called it a cottage, but what I noticed was that it was really a cottage-and-a-half — a tiny, improbable annex was built against it. This annex, not more than twelve feet wide, had its own low door beside a lovely bow-window, and another tiny window above. All the curtains were closed. I peered at a sign hanging over the door, trying to make out the faded letters in the lamplight: it looked like 'The Croked Hand'.

My Dales rambles had introduced me to the pleasures of intruding into small country pubs out of season. Often it is a genuine intrusion, into a family meal, a game, a blazing row, and yet legitimised by the timeless tradition of hospitality that the hosts have chosen to uphold as their profession — the intruder is welcomed, accommodated, entertained or left in peace as he desires, as long as he pays his bill of a few pounds. Some of my fondest and loneliest memories are of such intrusions, but I will keep them to myself.

I reached down for the door handle in the shadows, and then jerked back my hand as it met with something unexpected: another hand. The handle was a large brass hand with ice-cold, contorted fingers; I grasped it and tried to turn it; I pushed and pulled it; then with a last glance at the closed curtain I hurried back to the church and along the dark and unsigned lane.

Saturday morning was my first opportunity to explore the surrounding country in daylight. I had thought of going for a walk over the hills, and threw back my curtains to reveal a windy morning with reassuring blue breaks in the scudding clouds. I met Rose on the stairs, already dressed but wet-haired and smelling of scented soap. I mentioned my plan for the day and she casually offered to join me: 'I know all the paths,' she said.

Just a few yards from the cottage, one such path led between the garden wall and a tiny rill that tumbled down the hillside and passed under the track to join the main stream. The path climbed steeply through a birch wood, where great thick brackets of fungus grinned on the slim, mossy trunks and sinister clusters of red toadstools crowded between the roots. The trees soon thinned and we began to zig and zag up the bracken-covered flank of the rill's little valley. After ten minutes I was warm, for Rose set a keen pace, and I was glad to see a sort of stone seat at the turn of the next switchback, which seemed like a good excuse for a pause.

Already the main track traced a fine, snaking line far below us, and this spot commanded a lofty view over the cottage, half-hidden by trees but betrayed by its little white streamer of smoke, and along the narrow valley towards the house. Arnold's trees — the dark masses of pines and cedars, and the bare, ghostly crowns of the great beeches — were clearly visible in the valley and on the hillside beyond but, surprisingly, Combe Hall itself was out of sight.

'I thought we'd be able to see the house from here,' I said, as I caught my breath. Rose studied me critically, showing no signs of exertion.

'It doesn't like to be seen,' she replied. It was not the first time she had spoken of the house as though it had a personality — as though it were alive. 'We'll be in the wind shortly,' she added, as I pushed up the sleeves of my jumper.

Soon the gradient eased and the wind indeed began to build as we came up onto the plateau. The bracken gave way to gorse and heather through which the path wound faintly before a final incline brought us to a junction with the broad ridge-top path. We followed it for a hundred yards to a pile of stones.

'This is the summit of Fern Top,' declared Rose over the cold north-westerly. 'Nine hundred and eighty-one feet.' I wrapped my scarf more tightly and pulled down my hat. To the east lay the lowland regions of the county, faintly and intricately lined and gently wrinkled like one of M'Synder's faded rugs, stretching twenty miles or more to another vague band of hills on the horizon. To the west and still looming over us stood the broad but slightly pointed summit of Grey Man, marked by a great cairn standing black against the sky. We started along the path towards it, right into the teeth of the wind. A couple of grouse burst into the air with their cackling cry: 'Go back, go back, go back!'

The cairn was further than it looked, set half a mile back on the bleak, reddish moor and standing at the centre of a bog of rippled peat that was now half-frozen, and squelched and crunched alternately beneath our boots. It was a true beehive cairn, tall and regular, and I noticed a few shrivelled and frozen flowers carefully jammed between two of the stones as though in remembrance — but I said nothing.

The path turned to the south, and after a few hundred yards we passed a short, sun-bleached wooden post indicating a path on the left.

'That's the way down into the arboretum,' said Rose. 'The path crosses the bridge in the beech grove, then skirts the meadow and joins the lane right in front of the house.'

'But it's a public footpath,' I said. Rose laughed.

'It is,' she replied. 'It runs right through the middle of the grounds — haven't you looked at the map?' I had not. 'We had a big family group wander down last summer during a thunderstorm — they asked me if we had a teashop. Since then — no one.'

'Does the path go past the temple?' I asked, cautiously. She looked at me without expression.

'No. You can't see the temple from any of the paths, public or private. Only the buzzards can see it.' She looked up and I noticed the wheeling predators for the first time. 'One for sorrow,' she counted, 'two for joy, three for brazen, four for coy: five. Five remembers.'

'Six forgets?' I guessed, stupidly.

'There are only five,' she muttered, turning abruptly to walk on.

Our own path now descended steeply to a low saddle in the ridge, crossed by a rough track that climbed up from the combe and then wound down out of sight into another valley to the west.

'So that's where the gardener lives,' I said, pointing down the track as we climbed a stile. Rose nodded curtly, and I told her about my odd meeting with him in the hall. Then I added, 'Not your favourite person, I gather.' She paused after the second stile, sheltered by the dry-stone wall and a twisted hawthorn.

'I used to be fond of him, when I was a child,' she said. 'We had fun in the holidays.' She said nothing for a while, as though recollecting, and then continued: 'When I was thirteen he made me a forty-foot swing in one of the beech trees in the grove, but Arnold told him to take it down. And of course he knows all the roses — when they'll flower and when they'll die.' Then she frowned and shook her head. 'I'm afraid he bores me now — he takes things too seriously.'

He loved her as a little sister, I hypothesised to myself, but his love changed, became complex and demanding, and now she scorns him for it: a classic case. Poor fool — he must be nearly twice her age.

14

We continued round to the long, flat, third summit, Hart Top, and then dropped off the plateau and down through the woods, crossing the stream by a plank bridge. Rose went straight to her room when we returned to the cottage, leaving me to help M'Synder unpack a box of groceries that had been delivered from the village. Later, as we two drank tea by the fire after dark, she thudded down the stairs, called out that she was going up to the house, and slammed the door.

At dinner, I tried to tease a little more information from my blue-slippered landlady. Had Arnold always lived in the combe? I asked.

'I believe he moved away when he qualified as a doctor,' she replied, after her customary pause, 'about nineteen sixty, and then moved back after his mother died in seventy-five. That was when I came to the combe.' I remembered his gold ring and wanted to ask, 'Did he ever marry?' but the words faltered on my lips and M'Synder led the conversation elsewhere:

'Thirty-nine years old, I was,' she murmured, wistfully. 'Rather old, you're thinking — young, I'm thinking — I'd never seen a house like the Hall. Never heard of it, though I lived but twenty miles away.' Did *she* ever marry? That was my next unaskable question. Then I had some questions for myself: Why does it matter whether she or Arnold married? Can a person not live his or her life unsupported by that crutch? Is she, decisive Sarah, directing my thoughts even now?

'There was an advertisement in the post office,' M'Synder went on, then smiled. 'A bit like yours, I s'pose. Mine offered a post for six months. I stayed on for a while — another six months sneaked by, then six years, then another six followed, then a decade or two. You canna stop 'em.' She sat back in her chair and sighed, while the old clock ticked quietly in the corner. 'And now here I am, getting old.'

She looked straight at me, and for a moment I could think of no reply. Then I just said, 'A beautiful place to live.'

'I'm glad you think so, Mr Browne,' she whispered, her narrowed eyes twinkling behind the steel frames, 'since if my example is anything to go by — and Rose's, for that matter — you might be staying here longer than you expect.'

I slept deeply that night, and daylight was already spilling from behind the curtains when I was woken by hurried footsteps, voices and the alien sound of a car door banging shut. I got up, threw on my coat, which I used as a dressing gown, and went out to the little landing. I heard the roar of an engine and caught a hint of exhaust fumes mingled with the usual smell of toast, then through the raindrops on the landing window saw the old Cortina bumping away down the lane. I tramped sleepily down the stairs as M'Synder was shutting the front door.

'Morning, Mr Browne,' she said, cheerfully. 'You just missed Rose.' The boots, the red scarf, the little felt hat — they were all gone. 'The new term starts tomorrow.'

'Oh, I didn't know,' I said, looking at the empty peg next to the one where my old woolly hat and scarf were hanging.

'Breakfast's almost ready,' said M'Synder, and I followed her into the parlour.

The rain grew heavier, and an easterly wind blustered up the valley and flung squalls like handfuls of rice against the windows. Undeterred, M'Synder donned a long raincoat, Wellington boots and a plastic rain bonnet, tucked her old pumps into her shoulder bag and ventured out to church. Before leaving she directed me to half a pie that I could warm up for my lunch, since she was paying some visits and would not be back until the evening.

I stood at the parlour window, looking across the sodden little garden to the swaying birches, then stooped and peered up the hill, which faded into a drifting oblivion of rain and cloud. Or was it just the condensation on the streaming glass? A loud pop from the fire made me start. I could go out, I thought — could spend the day in a reassuring battle against reassuring elemental foes — but I will not. I will stay here and think.

The four volumes of Gibbon had stood untouched in the bedroom since my arrival. I fetched one now and pulled a chair up close to the fire. The book lay on my lap. I gently circled my hands on its finely textured cover and thought of those infinitesimal ploughmen. For three months, I reflected, this book had stood in my little flat in south London, above the table at which previously Sarah and I had shared our busy, happy, now-incomprehensible lives. And yet before that, before its undocumented journey to a shop on the Charing Cross Road, it had watched over the library of Combe Hall, a quarter of a mile from where I now sat, for nearly two centuries. It had known the doctor's grandmother Catherine and his great-uncle Hartley when they were squabbling Victorian children — had perhaps been read by their stern, ambitious father in preference to Dickens. It had heard the doctor's uncle Samuel playing the piano before he went up to Cambridge, and Stella's weeping when the telegram arrived. It had, I suddenly realised, seen the object of my search — the precious letter itself — when the smug and wizened Hartley, perhaps tipsy with the bishop's port, slipped it into its enduring hiding place.

I lifted the book to my nostrils and breathed the faint scent of its pages, still unmistakeably Gibbon though I had since smelt a thousand other books. I almost hoped that the scent, which was, after all, quite literally, the accumulated and concentrated essence drawn by the paper from all those lost years, might carry some clue as to the letter's whereabouts, or might at least evoke whatever it was here that excited, inspired, *quickened* me. Instead, it reminded me of my divorce.

I wonder what you, the reader, make of my story so far. You are perhaps frustrated by the superficiality of my relations with the inhabitants of the combe — a few words here, a few there, separated by hours of monotonous solitude. That my first few weeks followed this pattern (yes, I'm afraid there is more to come, but I'll try to be concise) probably reflects my character: I do not easily make new friends. I made none at the bank, and, during the two years I inhabited that last flat with Sarah, though I said hundreds of friendly hellos to our neighbours, who seemed interesting, even attractive people, I never invited them in for a drink, nor was I invited. If I knew their names, it was only from sorting the post in the hall. Sarah was just as bad: we used to joke about it, as we spent yet another Friday evening at home, and it seemed just that — a harmless joke — in those distant days when we had each other to share it.

It was not funny anymore: now, those few words here and there and those hours of solitude were the basic elements of my life. My marriage, whose long threads had been woven so deeply into my memories, into my present concerns and actions, and into my foolish hopes for the future, had been withdrawn from me: had been cut out swiftly with skilful scissors. My first reactions had been panic and flight, but now, alone in a stranger's cottage in a strange county, I began to feel something else: a slow movement, an *adjustment*, of the remaining parts of my life.

I now remembered more fondly the Christmas game of chess with my reticent brother; I quite naturally counted among my few friends the robin in the lane, with his noble cinnamon breast; I shivered at the thought of the doctor, alone and remembering in his cold, majestic, terrible house. With a chunk of my life torn away, the disordered residue began to expand to fill the gap, began to acquire new significances as it touched, yes, some *wing of my soul* that had previously been engaged and unreceptive, but that now reached out tenderly.

Here in the combe I felt immersed in and saturated by novelty, as I had not felt, for example, when I fled to the Yorkshire Dales. There, if I opened a gate into an unfamiliar field, or the door of some cosy, crowded pub, or crawled into my little tent, all I found was myself — the seeds of my panic, whispering malevolently, 'What matter where, if I be still the same?' But in the combe it was different: when I first looked up at those vast, improbable windows looming out of the mist, when I first stepped into the cool, silent cathedral of books, or when I took Rose's cold hand in the doctor's parlour, my panic seemed to give way as though ceding me to a superior power. Of course, my stubborn self was still there — it was I who saw and touched — but in the combe I barely recognised him.

The rain hammered on, and I still had not opened the Gibbon. I put it back in my room and fetched a notebook instead. As I rumbled more coal onto the fire, a gust of wind sent a little wraith of smoke out into the room. I breathed the moment of acridity and the cosy, dissipating fire-smell that followed, and then began to write a rough account of my days in the combe — an account which, as I now try to tell my story in full, sits before me as my guide.

PART 2

TEMPLES

Dear Sam,

What I write in this letter will come as a shock to you, so please brace yourself. We have been happy together but it was nevertheless a mistake for us to marry. Happiness is not enough. We did not bring out the best in each other. We were happy even as we diminished.

Imagine you are drawing a picture, and you identify some irredeemable mistake in your composition. As soon as you are sure of your mistake, you must start again on a blank sheet. I am sure, and so debating it with you would only cause more pain to us both. I really do mean to start again, so it is better you don't know where I am. I will arrange the formalities of our separation.

We are still young. We have time. I wish you the best. Go and live a better life without me.

Sarah

1

I worked steadily by day in a trance of diligence, and by night I dreamed.

In one dream, of which I was slightly ashamed in the morning, I saw Rose sitting naked under the star-tree, a slender white 'T' like Reni's *Crucifixion* — arms outstretched along the back of the seat, toes pointed towards me, head tipped back so that I saw the triangular outline of her jaw against the shadows. I approached slowly, stood over her like a clumsy, bespectacled vampire in the moonlight, my gaze wandering over her body, waiting, I suppose, for her reaction — her censure or sanction. I leaned and saw her sharp, unscarred face, of course it was unscarred: it was I who bore the scar. Then I saw the flecks of frost on the eyelashes, on the glistening teeth, and lurched backward, two steps, three, then stepped back into nothing and fell.

In another dream, I turned from swimming ranks of books to see the doctor emerge silently from the fireplace, knitting his veined hands and wearing the drawn smile — that sad smile of having made a mistake; he stared past me, behind me, did not see the scar that I again felt clawing, dragging on my face. I said something but he did not hear. He moved closer, and his eyes began to change; his smile thinned and hardened; his hands were shaking, the knuckles white, the fingers twisted, deformed. Of course he was grieving for that young uncle who shared my name; I wanted to take his arm, lead him away, but lamplight glistened over the varnished canvas, over his grieving face. I was startled by a weird shock of sound — those sword-thrusts of Bach strings, perhaps, but rough and distorted so they were almost like the screams of birds.

In yet another dream, I was hurrying through my old university library, glancing into each stall, searching for Sarah. We were to be married that day, and I had spent too long walking in the rain in the meadows, and now my clothes were soaked and we were late. My search took me to every library I knew in the city, with obstructive librarians and locked doors at every turn. I was shivering in my wet clothes but had no time to change them. Finally I wondered, with the knocking dread that is, thankfully, rarely felt outside dreams, whether she might be 'at the combe' — no, I thought, surely not there. I awoke to find the blankets slipped off my shoulder and rain or sleet softly feathering the windowpanes.

So much for dreams. Winter had established itself in the combe with the same air of serene permanence that characterised M'Synder in her parlour. The bright hips of the dog-rose had surely hung over the lane, each burdened by a gleaming white pouch of water in which the whole sky was imprisoned upside down, and would go on hanging, for as long as those numberless pictures, that seemed not to mind whether they hung quite straight, would cover the dark parlour walls. Drifts of last season's leaves surely belonged in every sheltered nook just as the lapping, rucking rugs belonged under the well-pawed armchair. And surely the only transformation that the birches knew was to present a fine reddish spray of twigs to the low sun but a black stencil to the early dusk, just as the parlour might be transformed by the fleeting presence of Rose, but would always be M'Synder's domain.

The idea of spring seemed fanciful; summer, impossible. I was cold for most of my waking hours — cold on the stairs, in the lane, in the library, in the *facilitates*. The fires in the parlour and the doctor's study acquired unexpected significance as radiant cores of comfort — the only other refuge was my double-blanketed bed, but there I had to rely on trapping my own treacherous radiance, which would eagerly seize any chance to escape, just when I was most vulnerable.

During that second week my search brought me to some of the most spectacular books in Combe Hall's collection. Architecture, archaeology, anthropology — words whose ponderous length befits the huge books by which those fields were represented, and the delicate task of searching them. The largest of all was a century-old facsimile, in a single tabletop-sized volume, of the British Museum's seventy-foot *Papyrus of Ani*, one of the surviving copies of *The Book of the Dead*. Here the act of preservation was explicit — a sort of reverent plaster cast of a fragile miracle of survival — but this monster was merely a cartoonish exemplar of the numerous analogous acts pressed together on every shelf in this chill museum of the dead.

Yes, the exemplar's subject was fitting. What, after all, did these books, for all their insistence on singularity, have in common? Perhaps the simplest characteristic of all: death. Their authors were all dead. Strictly speaking, a few might yet be clinging to life — I envisaged a retired don whose brilliant first thesis had been published in the thirties and acquired by the doctor's parents, now hunched in a high-backed chair in a different kind of common room in the same city, writing arthritic letters to eminent ex-students and flirting with the nurses in precise, anatomical Latin — but a few more years would finish them. (Who would be the very last? Perhaps the doctor should write a congratulatory letter to mark the occasion.) Notwithstanding these few premature burials the library was a graveyard: a graveyard where the dead ceaselessly delivered their solemn lectures whether or not any among the living chose to attend.

The older part of the archaeology collection, presumably once owned by the elder Hartley, recipient of letters and contriver of temples, was built around Montfaucon's seminal *Antiquity Explained and Represented in Sculptures* in six volumes, and included massive first editions of Robert Adam and Piranesi over which I lingered for longer than was absolutely necessary (piously remembering the doctor's direction that I need not search like a robot).

I was in the armchair one morning, hunched over the latter volume across whose yellowed pages the sunshine was gloriously splashed, so that every etched detail was stark, when I heard a soft tread and glanced up to see the doctor standing at the table.

'Good morning, Mr Browne,' he said, in his dry, precise voice. 'Found some picture books?' I started to get up but he raised his hand. 'Stay, and allow me to peer over your shoulder. My eyes are word-weary.'

I had been examining one of the etchings of the Colosseum — the one in which its outer wall bulges towards the viewer and spreads to left and right with meticulously, mysteriously distorted perspective.

'Have you noticed,' he began, after scrutinising the image, 'that the lap of the seated hominid is the perfect support for a large and heavy book?'

'Though tending to encourage bad posture,' I replied, straightening my aching back.

'Indeed. Turn the page.'

The next three images depicted the ruins of the Villa Adriana at Tivoli. The first showed the surviving half of a domed temple, overgrown with vegetation; the second, sunlight slanting into a gloomy space; the third, a precarious vault rent by gaping, leafy holes through which light filtered to the dappled floor.

'The Temple of Light,' I murmured.

'Have you seen it yet?' whispered the doctor, sharply. I shook my head, still gazing down at the commingling of sunlight — our own and that which Piranesi had trapped in this prism of yellowed paper — two slivers of the same star, now reunited in a dazzling collision in the lap of a divorced ex-banker, aged twenty-five years, in a cold, silent room.

'I suggest you follow my ancestor's example,' he said, already walking away, 'and carry whatever inspiration you might have drawn from these books up the hillside: visit the temple today.'

2

The day was bright but not so still as that of my first tour of the gardens, and I went back for my coat and hat. Gazing up from the terrace to where the hill met the sky, I could see only a rampart of distant treetops. I turned right, instead of left, along the back of the house, past the high kitchen windows to where another flight of steps descended to the lawn. Between the north side of the house and a row of outbuildings with black wooden gates lay a broad passage, where a scattering of damp needles, sawdust and chippings was all that remained of the yuletide bough. Through the open gate of one shed could be seen a massive wood stack and coal store.

An archway in the main garden wall led me to a spacious yard behind the outbuildings, which now presented a neat row of doors and windows, like a miniature terrace of cottages. Along the side of the yard stood a row of water butts and several heaps of branches and decaying vegetation, and trolleys, barrows and ladders stood or leaned here and there. I peeped through each of the windows: one revealed a broad bench strewn with old newspaper, broken fragments of terracotta and sprinklings of compost, with teetering stacks of pots behind; another displayed a jumbled mass of ironmongery and smooth ash wood — an inquisitor's paradise of shears, forks, saws, dibbers, hoes, rakes and other tools whose names and purposes I could not guess. The last window looked into a tiny gardener's office, with a chair and table, a little fireplace heaped high with ashes, stacks of notebooks and shelves lined with jars, bottles, a kettle and a few old books.

My attention was then caught by the faint, unmistakeable sound of a spade striking stony soil, and I walked back along these outbuildings to a doorway in another high wall. The wooden door was wedged open with a small, tapered angle of rusty metal whose broad end was bent over and pierced by a circular hole — a distinctive object that held my gaze for a moment as I tried in vain to recall where I had seen one before. Then I stepped into a realm whose finely ordered productivity gave it unexpected kinship with the library itself: it was the kitchen garden.

An ordered garden seems to impose the same nagging burden of responsibility as an ordered library: those beds, having been carefully planned and raised ought to be tended, their crops harvested and made good use of, just as a case of books ought to be read. The gifts of the earth ought to be cherished even as the slow-crafted gifts of the dead, and just as the sight of a genuine reader in a library is morally comforting (a mere letter-searcher is not enough), so is the sight of a gardener tending his crop.

And here indeed, watched by an assistant, was Meaulnes, just where he ought to be — setting his boot on a long spade, turning the soil in four neat cuts between taut lines of cord, stepping back, digging and turning again. The assistant did not actively assist — it was an elaborate scarecrow, complete with rake, watering can and drooping hat. I advanced along the brick-paved path between the pairs of beds, some of which were bare and dug over, while others bore defiant ranks of winter-hardy cabbages and leeks, or frailer crops under neat rows of upturned buckets and glinting glass cloches.

Along the south-facing wall stood two iron-framed glasshouses in need of repainting and a line of old brick incubators with lids of dewy glass. The giant gardener saw me and stopped, leaning on his spade.

'Morning,' I called, brightly but not too brightly. He nodded. 'I'm exploring,' I said as I reached him, 'and there's a lot to explore — a surprise behind every door.' I suppose this comment was intended to provoke him, but he just nodded again. A small squadron of starlings swept over the wall and he watched them grimly as they saw us, aborted their mission, swerved and vanished.

'I will be glad to answer any questions you have about the gardens, Monsieur Browne,' he said quickly, looking over my head. 'It is good to have a visitor to appreciate them.'

I was wrong-footed by this civility, and smiled awkwardly. 'There don't seem to be many visitors.'

'Not any more,' he replied, stepping over his cord and driving in the spade to begin the next row.

'Were there once?' I asked, but the question was cut off by the next fall of the spade, and I did not repeat it.

'Happy exploring, Monsieur,' he said. I thanked him and moved on, towards another door at the far end of the garden. This, I noticed, had the same distinctive hinges and latch as the first, decorated by curls of iron like representations of wind or smoke.

Wondering to what golden age of visitors Meaulnes had alluded, I now entered a small, square orchard with rickety espaliers of apple or pear and other short, gnarly trees, all now bare and grey. Rows of shrivelled and nibbled apples lined the path, which led to another door opening on the beech grove that Rose had showed me. I picked my way through the dewy mast and the first tiny, peeping, deluded bulb-shoots to the bridge over the eddying stream.

I crossed over carefully (remember — no parapets) and began to climb the stepped path that slanted up the hillside. Diverse and beautiful trees reared up on both sides, and I soon passed between the two giant Wellingtonia redwoods that could be seen from far down the valley. These dwarfed a weird cypress with long weeping tresses and a low, dark, tangled conifer that sprawled fifty feet along the slope. I continued upward through a stand of pale firs and another of scaly Scots pines, catching occasional glimpses down through the silvery crowns of the beech grove to the house, the lawn and the crisscrossing garden walls.

I soon reached a junction over which a sinister eucalypt crouched, with curved, ghostly-white boughs like heaped whalebones. One path traversed left around the hill and another climbed up to the right. Keen to gain height, I began up the right-hand, northward fork, but then remembered the doctor saying that the temple faced south, turned back and took the level path (my first choice, I later learned, was the public right of way that joined the ridge-top path at the wooden post). As I stepped over the slippery roots extended by small, mossy oaks and sycamores, a flicker of movement caught my eye and I saw a squirrel scamper along a branch — not the fat London variety but a little brownish creature with tufty ears and a wispy, off-white tail — my first red squirrel.

The path now passed among a cluster of boulders around which a pool of damp, chilly air seemed to have settled. I happened to glance around the corner of the largest boulder as I passed, and froze in my tracks. Beyond a gap no more than two feet wide, which I might easily have missed, there rose a steep, narrow stair, straight up the wooded hillside, vanishing to a point in the distant trees: on the first step was a perfectly circular ring of moss growing in a carved groove.

I stared for a few seconds and then began to climb, pushing aside the vegetation that crowded up both sides — brambles and ivy and bare saplings of birch and rowan clinging to the slope. Each step was high and narrow, so that I was tempted to use my hands as though on a ladder, but I climbed steadily and tried to forget the straight drop behind.

After a hundred steps or more, I reached the security of a small square platform where the stair turned to the left. I now looked back and down but could see only a few glimpses of the valley between the tops of pine trees that grew thickly below. Gorse crowded the slope above, its spines piercing even the thick sleeve of my coat as I pushed aside encroaching branches to follow the now-curving stair.

At last, as I climbed to the level of the highest treetops and the gorse fell back on either side, I became aware of the yawning sky and of clear horizons behind me and to each side. I followed my own jagged shadow up the last few steps and looked up: the Temple of Light blazed before me in the sun.

3

At first I saw a small, symmetrical façade of deep yellow stone with a gracefully curved and pointed gable, and a narrow black double door whose pediment was curved and pointed to match the roof. It was only as I drew nearer and stepped to one side that I perceived the great jutting prow, like a tapered blade of stone projecting from the gable above my head, its outermost point bearing two vertical iron prongs — to conduct lightning, perhaps — and supported by a pillar of black stone that was so polished and so improbably slender that I at once curved my hand around its cold surface in wonder.

I turned and looked out at the view, which was all sky: beyond the tops of those cunning, concealing pines, the hazy grey horizon swept unhindered from north-east, through south, to north-west. Only to the north, behind the temple, a steep bank of gorse reared up thirty feet towards the flattening, unobserving plateau of Grey Man.

The temple was surrounded by a neat, narrow sward of green, grazed short by rabbits or birds, and peering around the long east side I saw a row of circular stone tablets set into the grass. The first two were very old and weathered, but the text had been carefully maintained and was still legible:

Hartley Stillwell Newton Comberbache 1735 – 1782

Sarah Louise Comberbache 1745 – 1821

The other six tablets looked more recent and were cut in a slightly different stone. Below are the names and dates they bore:

Samuel Thomas Comberbache 1772 – 1837
Samuel Sebastian Comberbache 1898 – 1917
Catherine Sarah Comberbache 1875 – 1918
Geoffrey Hughes Comberbache 1897 – 1966
Stella Louise Comberbache 1900 – 1975
Margaret Joy Comberbache 1935 – 1984

Seeing these half-familiar names carved in stone, these graves, if graves they were, of characters hitherto confined to paintings and brief stories and faded spidery notes, now crossed by snails and warmed by my own January sun, seemed to transmute the entire combe from vision to chill reality — to transmute the doctor himself (a snail would one day be crossing his name), and even to work the same change in my own confused identity.

I pushed back the panic and accounted for the names one by one: spirited Stella and Geoffrey Hughes were Arnold's parents, of course. Catherine was his grandmother, Samuel Sebastian his organ-scholar uncle. Samuel Thomas must be the book-inscribing son for whom the birds would not sing — but why was his stone not weathered like his parents'? *Because after his death the temple was forgotten.* Stella must have laid the stone when she rediscovered it. As for the other ancestors, they were presumably buried in the churchyard, as M'Synder had intimated.

This stream of easy inferences was arrested by the last name: Margaret Joy had died aged forty-nine, and was the doctor's sister, or his wife. Both her names were new to the family, I noticed, and this together with Arnold's ring made me suspect the latter tie. A folly, I had called this place: I winced at the thought.

The neat row of eight stones suggested an exclusive alliance beyond the mere sharing of an outlandish name — Stella had laid stones for her beloved mother and brother but not her father, and of course Hartless the rector and his wife were absent. This thought lifted my glance back to the temple itself, which invited exploration. I returned to the pedimented entrance, turned the handle — a wrought iron wheel in the shape of the rayed sun — and the narrow door swung inward.

I stood in a small, dark vestibule (this particular word arose in my mind, perhaps, because whilst diligently thumbing pages a few days earlier I had learned that it has a surprising anatomical application). Tiny circular windows on each side provided the only light, by which I discerned a few tools (shears, a lantern, a small stepladder) standing in one alcove, and in the other a deep stone shelf bearing a leatherbound book or journal and boxes of candles and matches. With my face tingling from the sudden stillness of the air, I removed my hat, turned another wheel-handle on the single door before me and advanced into the sacred interior.

The Temple of Light was in as short supply of that commodity as its antechamber, and I stood blinking in the gloom while my eyes adjusted. A long space like a nave opened into a circular sanctum, the whole encircled by a stone seat around the wall (imagine the shape of a keyhole — such was the temple's plan). The floor was of plain, smooth flagstones, with a narrow central band of inlaid darker stone that glinted oddly and corresponded to a massive dark beam overhead, supporting arching ribs of vaulting along each side. A shallow, curved step led down to the circular floor of the sanctum, whose flagstones were great segments of the circle. At the centre, in place of an altar, I caught the ghostly glimmer of a pool of water. The roof of the sanctum was a beautifully vaulted dome, bisected by the dark beam just as the floor and pool were bisected by the inlaid band — these two strong lines were connected by a buttress of black stone at the north end, which the curving seat joined on either side.

Is my description of any use? I try to be precise (the temple demands it), but words are a poor vehicle for carrying the peculiar weights and shapes of architecture. I feel like the doctor's delivery boy optimistically loading baskets of eggs onto that bicycle, whose springs, however ingenious, will not protect them on the combe's rutted track. What you, the reader, really need — if you cannot find your way to the temple yourself — is a picture. You need a Piranesi, not a Samuel Browne; but you will have to make do with whatever broken remnants my words convey.

At first I thought the sanctum had no windows (the dim light was from long horizontal slots latticed with plain glass, high on the walls of the nave behind deep sills), but as I sat for a moment on the seat I noticed two very long, very narrow, horizontal slits, one curving round each side. I leaned to peer into one, and found that it was set with dozens of black iron fins that reached the considerable thickness of the wall. As I moved my head, a tiny square of radial light flickered along these fins, while the rest of the slit was dark. Just below each slit a band of brass was fixed to the wall, set with a polished stud or boss at each end and one in the middle, and engraved with a frieze of devices representing the changing seasons.

I stood up, frowning, and immediately noticed some cords neatly stowed along the roof-beam and hooked against the buttress. I reached up and my hand closed on something cold and hard and brought down a many-faceted sphere of glass or crystal, around

110

which the two cords were carefully bound. This I lowered in its natural arc until it hung in space, right over the pool, where both the crystal and my hand were suddenly bathed in a cold light. I gently released it, stepped back up into the nave, and gave a little chuckle of wonder: a glittering point of light hovered in the gloom. It was not bright, but ghostly and utterly compelling, shedding little flickering flecks of colour like a low star. Here was Light — the thing itself, and not the mere icon of M'Synder's church. After carefully lifting the crystal back onto its hook and one last look back (in which I suppose wonder was mingled with smug satisfaction at my powers of observation), I returned to the blinding open air.

But my first visit to the temple was not quite over. On the top step of that long, steep stair back to the valley I stopped, flung out, it seemed, from meticulous sanctuary into chaos — into a blank flood of sunlight, of rushing air and unbounded space. The long sweep of the horizon circled me like the cut of a whip, and I was ambushed by memories of Sarah. I remembered the smell of the crown of her head, the way she closed her eyes and parted her lips, her words lined up neatly on a sheet of paper, her quick heels on the platform steps: it was as though I had slipped that famous forbidden ring onto my finger, had surrendered to the sweeping gaze, the groping hand — for a moment I let the panic claim me.

I turned with a start to the temple, and felt suddenly ashamed — that I had picked over it coolly like a tourist, when I should have sought refuge and guidance like the desperate pilgrim I was. I would go back in, just briefly, and bow my head.

As I opened the door I noticed vaguely that the slender shadow of the pillar, which before had striped one side of the door (the sole flaw in the temple's ruthless symmetry) now fell almost straight down the middle. I thought nothing of it, closed the doors solemnly behind me and sank onto the cold seat at the side of the nave.

Why didn't I fight for my wife? Why not pursue her, confront her, beg her to come back? Why not *act*? Perhaps those questions occurred to you as you followed my account. But now you have read the words that were lined up on the sheet of paper I held over the immaculately-made bed on that placid, unremarkable August evening: now perhaps you understand. She was lost. But how could I *start again*, if such was my task, without knowing where I had gone wrong?

That I *had* gone wrong — supported the wrong cause, followed the wrong dream — I could hardly deny; but it was this idea of starting again that summoned the galloping hooves of panic. I sometimes caught myself imagining that my life was just a casual experiment, a comic sideshow to the noble and profound centrepiece that must be *proceeding already* behind some curtain of heavy velvet. But no, this hunched ignoramus was the only Samuel Browne, and he must start again. I looked down at my bony fingers.

A bright sliver of light sliced straight down the floor of the temple, and I started, thinking that someone had opened the door — but it was shut. The sliver intensified, and then began to *multiply*: little sharp daggers of light crept over the floor and the walls. A dazzling flare erupted on the far wall and then vanished, as a reflected beam crossed my face. I relaxed my startled grip on the edge of the seat and slowly rose to my feet, the sudden fear that I was not alone subsiding before a rising certainty that I was indeed alone, alone and yet cradled within this silent, glittering sanctuary that was not, after all, a miracle but merely a triumphant exposition of thought, calculation and craft. I began to lose my sense of space, as stone surrendered its own identity to the service of light, whose silent gliding fragments constructed their own impossible space around the blinding axis of the main beam. This steadily broadened and intensified until it seemed that the temple and the earth itself were splitting in two.

4

'A keyhole, yes!' said the doctor, slowly pacing the long library carpet with a cup of green tea. 'Well observed. And the turning sun is, of course, the key.'

I had left the temple the second time feeling, I suppose, something like the euphoria of the born-again believer. I was not sure what I now believed, but I had faced the sweeping horizon joyfully this time and descended the stair with swift, precise steps. Now the curtains hung between a restless, windy dusk and the patient library, whose grandeur had astonished me anew when I returned from my expedition.

'Hartley's design is based on the principle of confinement,' he continued, setting down the cup and placing his palms almost together, with a tiny gap between them. 'A man's eye is accommodative, like his heart — bathe it in light and the pupil contracts and becomes insensitive; but wrap it in gloom and it dilates — invites sensation and responds with rapturous intensity. By confining the sun's light to the narrowest of paths and then splintering it into a dark space, he celebrates the glories of both phenomenon and witness.'

'So the worship of light is a worship of sensation?' I asked.

'Not sensation alone,' he replied. 'Every visitor to the temple wants to know how it works: it offers a spectacle and demands thought in return. This faithful alliance of sensation and reason, under which neither one deceives the other, is the alliance of Truth — and geometry is perhaps its purest manifestation.'

'I begin to see how it works,' I said, falteringly.

'Of course you do,' he snapped back, 'you're a lapsed physicist and astronomer.'

'The radial fins I understand,' I began, 'and the brass calendars on which the beams of the rising and setting sun will shine. The dark band was of some crystalline stone, perhaps set with glass to scatter the light. But the giant prow —' I paused, frowning.

'Confinement!' he cried. 'It is not enough to have a narrow slit in the roof — the confinement must have *depth*. So much depth that you didn't even notice it though you walked right beneath it.'

'But the winter sun is too low,' I pursued, dissatisfied. 'It seemed to be streaming through the door, but the door was shut.'

The doctor cocked his eyebrow critically. 'You did not, perhaps, notice the vertical slit in the buttress at the north end.'

I obeyed the unspoken command to think. 'Which conceals a narrow strip of mirror,' I suggested, quietly.

He smiled. 'Imperceptibly curved to produce the sweeping beam. My parents had to replace some of the optics, of course, but they had all the original plans and sections. Once you see them you will quickly grasp the design.'

As the doctor paced back and forth along the carpet, I noticed that on reaching the fireplace he turned his shoe on the same spot every time, and here the fibres were almost worn through by his years of sporadic restlessness. He must have followed my gaze as I watched him approach the abrasion, for he paused on that spot and said, quietly, 'Confinement again, Mr Browne — limit the damage to one place if you can. There it can be measured, at least, if not mended.'

As he turned and walked on his gaze seemed to flicker, just for a moment, towards the locked door in the corner of the room.

The following day was just as windy but grey and much colder, and by the time I walked back to the cottage in the evening the wind was swirling around the combe in long, fearsome gusts whose approach I could hear in the trees well before they washed over me, flinging sharp sleet. Later, as I tried to sleep, one of the plum trees groaned sadly at the onset of each gust and I was reminded of a grim painting in a London gallery — a couple take their wedding vows on a human skull behind which glimmers a four-word inscription: *We Behowlde Ower Ende.*

I stepped outside the next morning and nearly slipped over on a patch of ice. I began to pick my way carefully along the track but soon slipped again, and then again. The freeze had settled itself into the combe like a dragon gloating sleepily on its spoils, silencing the stream and dismaying even the bravest of the birds so that all I could hear were my own tentative footsteps and the last satisfied sighs of the storm circling the valley. Glassy traps lurked malevolently in every chink and hollow of the lane awaiting the careless heel, and my body gradually stiffened with its own nervousness (which is distinct from that of the mind) as though it were itself surrendering to the frost.

The doctor stood at his hearth, wearing a woollen cap with comical earflaps that fastened under his chin — a garb for which he apologised, saying he was fighting off a cold. The fire was stacked high with logs which cracked and spat ferociously as I told him of my difficulties in the lane.

'Excuse me for a moment,' he said, seeming to have an idea. 'Pour yourself a coffee while I'm gone.' I heard his slow, steady tread on the stairs, and after a few minutes he returned carrying a pair of leather boots.

'My father gave me these forty years ago,' he said, examining them fondly, 'but I disappointed him — didn't follow in those particular footsteps, or boot-steps. They're tricouni-nailed boots for climbing mountains — rather superseded now, I believe, but perfect for an icy lane. He bought them large to accommodate thick socks,' he added, glancing at my feet, 'so I think you'll be able to squeeze them on. I always kept them oiled — don't ask me why.' He handed me the heavy boots, whose soles were studded with gleaming knobbles of steel.

'Your father was a mountaineer, then?' I began, as we sat down to our coffee.

'Yes, and my mother too,' he replied, with a pained nod. 'My father took it up in the thirties with a couple of Scotsmen he'd met at work. They made or adapted all their own clothes and equipment — stormproof tents, sleeping mats made of tar and cardboard, waxed coats cut short to the waist, plus-fours let out at the knee, alum-treated tam o'shanters — and that's before we even begin on the ropes and ironmongery.'

'Mainly in Scotland?' I asked, suddenly remembering Meaulnes' improvised doorstop. *Piton* — that was the word: I had seen some in a local history museum in Windermere.

'Lakeland and north Wales for rock climbing weekends in the summer, and Scotland for what he called "rock and ice" in the winter. Then in nineteen forty he joined the Marines as a medic. His first and last action was the Battle of Crete: two chaotic days of fighting followed by four years in a prison camp.

'He was allowed to send one postcard each month,' he went on, going to his desk and taking from a drawer a small leatherbound folio. 'These are the thirty-nine that arrived — the rest were lost on the way.'

The postcards were held in neat slipcases and looked almost as good as new, bearing only the creases or stains they had suffered in their original transit. Each was covered in tiny, meticulous writing accompanied by intricate ink drawings of mountain crags and the routes by which they might be scaled, or the wide vistas commanded by their summits. On the reverse, contrasting starkly with the care and love suffusing these compositions, an array of brutal postmarks was stamped beside the simple, familiar address.

'It was only when he came home that my mother realised these were excerpts from a book he had been writing — but the finished manuscript did not survive the journey, and he had to start again with only these postcards to guide him.'

'Did he send no other news of himself, and ask nothing about you and your mother?' I asked, leafing through the cards, which seemed to contain detailed accounts of past climbs, ideas for future expeditions and miniature essays on more abstract subjects, such as 'the philosophy of risk' and 'ode to a mountain crow'.

'I suppose his implication was that as a captive the only news he had was this news of his roaming mind, and that he had no request that my mother was not already doing her best to satisfy. She used to read the cards to me as extra-special bedtime stories.'

'And the book?'

'*Rocks and Remembrances* — it was published in nineteen forty-eight and sold a few hundred copies, then became something of a cult hit among climbers in the sixties and seventies. It is still occasionally reprinted by a small publisher in Kendal.'

I warmed my hands around the tall bone-china mug. The fire had settled into a murmuring, vigorous mound of flame, and began at last to radiate heat.

'And you said your mother climbed too,' I prompted.

'Ah yes, there was a bold lady,' he said, fondly. 'My father took her to the Highlands for a holiday before I was born, and she demanded to see what he had climbed. A few hours later they were a thousand feet above the valley, he anxiously taking in the rope while she swarmed up behind him with her skirt hitched up, brightly pointing out handholds that he had missed. I think she just loved to see him in his element. She climbed rather less after the war: my fault, probably.'

'But your father went back to it?'

The doctor stood up slowly and held his hands out to the fire. 'Have you ever driven through Glen Coe?' he asked. I had not, but I had crossed part of it once on a long walk with some schoolfriends. 'In that case you will remember that mountain with the gloriously forbidding name, Buachaille Etive Mòr, the Great Shepherd, which stands at the mouth of the glen, glaring out across the Moor of Rannoch.' I did remember it — a stern, seemingly perpendicular triangle of rock visible for tens of miles.

'My father was not a demonstrative man,' murmured the doctor, now leaning against the mantelpiece, 'but he broke into tears and had to stop the old baby Austin when he first saw that mountain again after the war. For the whole hour-long walk across the moor to its foot he couldn't stop crying, as he reminded himself that he was free to walk any way he chose — to stop, to turn around, to go on. When at last he laid his enfeebled hands on the first cold, soaring slab of rhyolite the years rolled away and he crumpled to his knees in a puddle of water. A description of that morning formed the epilogue for which his book was later best known — and he told my mother it was the defining moment of his life.

'It was light, you see,' he added, grasping his chair and shuffling backwards towards the desk, 'splintering into a dark space.'

5

I had now passed the study door in my search of the books beneath the gallery, and commenced work on the long history section opposite the windows. It began, appropriately, with an elegant bilingual folio edition of Herodotus, published in Amsterdam in seventeen sixty-three. On each page the columns of weird, curling Greek and stately, regular Latin were like twin indictments of my ignorance.

Did this magisterial patriarch approve of the thousand volumes ranked beneath him, I asked myself — his burgeoning brood? I was often tempted thus to consider the authors represented by a row of books as personalities which might be of diverse ages but which were nevertheless contemporary, contiguous and mutually acquainted. Their reassuring coexistence on the shelf disguised the careful branches of influence that wound through time and space to hold each volume in its own unique position relative to the others. The illusion was perhaps a consequence of *compression* — if each glistening curl of ink pressed onto a page was a tiny separate act of compression, then here was their massed accumulation: a vast web of centuries and continents pressed tightly into a matrix of shelves eight feet square. With a simple stretch, lean or stoop of his creaking young body, Samuel Browne could span the orbit of civilisation.

The next book was a stout translation from the thirties which, on its own, I would have considered a rather magnificent volume, but about whose English text a sheepish air seemed to hang. At the contents page a fine black hair nestled along the spine. I had encountered many such fragments of the restless, Heraclitian world, caught inadvertently in the adamantine crystal of compression — hairs, crumbs, a plane seed carried on a late summer breeze, a flattened midge with a faint brown stain of literary blood — trapped in the wrong domain until some gallant future reader might release them back to the swept floor of their native reality.

It was to the sudden music of Bach yet again — a cantata this time: oboe and voices in a regal dance — that the doctor released me for the evening. Or did not quite release me, since he asked me to join him for a glass of wine in the parlour where he had lit a roaring blaze.

He lit no lamps and we took our seats in the flickering orange glow of burning pine, which threw our magnified, wavering shadows onto the great glistening landscapes behind us (mine onto *Hope* and his onto *Despair* — surely accidental) and softly picked out the plasterwork relief far above. Taboni's homage to truth loomed over us in deep shadow, its subject now a faint but defiant ghost of her former radiant self, a suggestion, a promise of beauty in a window on which night had fallen.

The bottle of wine, having been warmed on the hearth 'to remind it of sunburnt mirth and the warm south,' stood between us on a little table with a peculiar silver object which as I sat down I identified as the glinting, scaly likeness of a giant walnut shell. The doctor grasped the lid, lifted it with a flourish and peered inside.

'Roasted almonds!' he murmured. 'My favourite. M'Synder never disappoints. She and I exhausted the chocolate pennies last week.' He leaned back with a satisfied sigh, holding an almond between his finger and thumb.

'This morning I gave you the image of Arnold Comberbache aged seven,' he began, 'listening from his bed in this house to his father's words spoken gravely by his mother, who holds a postcard at the lamp with a steady, long-fingered hand. But I have no corresponding image of you, Mr Browne, and I am curious. Give me one now — an image of your past.'

Overcoming an instinctive flinch of defensiveness, I followed his example and plucked an image from the harmless reaches of childhood. I told him that after my first day at infant school the teacher had declaimed sternly to my mother, 'This child can read and write, but it cannot hold a pencil!' This was merely a symptom, I explained (to the doctor, I mean), of my failure to grasp the fundamental *chirality* or handedness of the written word: at best I began each line with my left hand and then switched to my right, but often I inadvertently wrote from right to left in mirror-text, or placed correct characters in reverse order, or reverse characters in correct order, or employed some combination of all these eccentricities. The first time I wrote my name, I called myself *Mazenworb* — a name by which my sister still calls me. 'The symmetry of the temple reminded me of my own unhanded infancy,' I said, 'before I was broken in to the chiral world.'

'But of course the temple is handed in one sense,' remarked the doctor, 'just as a symmetrical keyhole belies the handed lock within. Indeed I suspect celestial motion is one source of our handedness. But tell me more about yourself.'

I told him that my father was an architect, a quiet, inventive man who had suffered frequent lacunae of unemployment; that my mother was currently a technician at an independent girls' school;

that my confident elder sister and I had attended a good grammar school, and that my nervous younger brother had deliberately failed his Eleven Plus to avoid separation from a friend, but was now vice-captain of the Cambridge University chess team.

The doctor, slowly crunching almonds and nodding attentively, seemed pleased by this feeble sketch and wanted more. In my stumbling way I told him a little about my student years: how university, for all its failings, had dazzled me with possibilities of a better, richer life — intellectual, aesthetic, sensual — when I was too timid and ignorant to seize them. *Crawling before a footmark'd stair* — the words of one of my more imaginative friends at the time. Then just when I felt I had built of myself someone worthy of participation in its mysteries, the university had examined me like a sceptical GP, given me a piece of paper declaring me fit to work, and sent me back to London to earn a living. 'I feel I'm still waiting for the new term to start, but it never will.'

'It could,' said the doctor. 'But perhaps, like me, you feel no allegiance to any particular field.' I nodded. 'My solution,' he went on, 'has been to build my own university: the venerable Combe College. I am its student, tutor and examiner all at once. I am its hopeless buffoon and its most brilliant scholar; its enthusiastic novice and its half-senile veteran; I am also, unfortunately, its bursar. M'Synder makes a fine catering manager, young Meaulnes is adequate as clerk of works, and you, for now, are its archivist.

'The quality of its library compensates for the deficiencies of its teaching. The profound problem of indolence is neatly solved by placing all potential distractions on the syllabus: if the student wishes to lay aside his main task — perhaps I didn't tell you I'm writing a book, a biography of an unexceptional man named Linley — if he wishes instead to spend a morning hunting orchids in the meadow or an afternoon spreading old photographs across the dining table, or perhaps a single uninterrupted hour in Bach's paradise, he does so freely on the understanding that he will be rigorously examined on that topic.'

'But are you always such a rigorous examiner of yourself?' I asked, puzzled by the concept. Was it so easy to be one's own tutor?

'If in doubt,' he replied, lowering his voice to a reverential whisper, 'the examiner can refer a paper to the external moderators.'

'And who are they?'

'Hartley the Elder and his wife Sarah, ably assisted by my parents.' Then he added, in a murmur like embers shifting, 'and, of course, my wife.'

I said nothing, and after a moment's silence he sat up suddenly, began refilling our glasses and said, 'I had forgotten that you are such a young man. I was expecting someone much older. I suppose you are barely thirty.' I told him my age and he slapped his knees in wonder. 'Well, well,' he added, with a sigh. 'At your age, I — ' he paused, resting his head against the chair-back and gazing up towards the shadowy painting ' — I was still living the first of my three lives — I mean, the life before I met Margaret.'

'I saw her memorial stone,' I said, 'up at the temple.'

'Yes. All the moderators are there: that is their court of arbitration.' Then he turned his pained smile to me and said, apologetically, 'Perhaps by engineering your isolation here — your confinement — I just wanted to make sure of a sympathetic companion: dilated like an eye in the dark.'

'You weren't the engineer,' I replied, smiling nervously. 'I had my own godforsaken combe in London, though quite different to yours.' The doctor gazed at me thoughtfully, tipping his glass this way and that, as though weighing its contents.

'It was cancer, of course,' he said, turning back to the fire. 'Ovarian cancer: that miraculous originator of new life exacting its price. We shared twenty years together, and now I have lived twenty more without her — twenty-one, it is now. Three lives.'

'Where did you meet?' I asked.

'She was a patient, I am ashamed to say,' he replied, distractedly. 'Nineteen sixty-four.' He told me the city in which he had been practising — it was where I had changed trains on my journey from London. 'One meets a lot of people, of course, just when they are down on their luck: when their true characters are laid bare. I liked that. Margaret was only in for hayfever, though.' Even as he answered I could tell that his thoughts dwelled on the end of those twenty years, not their beginning, and now he broke off.

'We had plenty of time to say our farewells,' he said at length, quietly as though to himself. 'We were loving and wise. At the end — the very end, we thought — she reached a kind of resignation, a state of beauty. But she did not die then: death is not obedient to our wishes or considerate of justice. She died a week later, in pain, confusion and fear.

'I carry those two last memories of her like pails on a yoke — I have no power to choose between them. Sometimes the first predominates, and I can be happy even as her absence echoes through the house. At other times the second haunts me and I am miserable.'

I just nodded — as I wrote before, I have never been bereaved. But I did think of Sarah's quick heels on the station steps, and my own contradictory memories.

6

It was midmorning on Friday when a bluish note crept into the grey light that washed those thousand fat spines of the history section. I turned, walked to one of the great windows, and stood watching with my hands in my trouser pockets.

Snow. Snow was falling in big clusters dark against the heavy, luminous sky like the German parachutes Geoffrey saw over Crete, but falling faster, falling thickly and straight down for the air was still, silently falling on the Hall and its perfect acre and the combe that held them as in a half-closed hand: steadily mottling away the colour from the lawns and the drifts of leaves and the mossy tops of walls, mottling away the miniature tectonic ridges in the dark stream of ice and the beech leaves frozen into the ponds, alighting on Meaulnes' sweet peas and hardy leeks, and on feathers and shivering squirrel fur, and cluster by cluster mottling away the names and the round stones of the dead.

A cobalt dusk was deepening when the flakes at last became smaller and fewer and then ceased suddenly, their work done: the world transformed. As I closed the curtains I glimpsed the dark figure of Meaulnes invading that pristine realm, brushing snow off the more delicate shrubs with massive gloved hands which he banged together to warm them. Later M'Synder and I tramped and creaked our way by torchlight to a thinly attended evensong, along the ghostly white ribbon of the lane, and returned beneath a blaze of stars, stepping in our own crisp footprints.

I rose early, surprising the reluctant dawn, and was excited to see that more snow had fallen but dismayed by a heavy mist enveloping the bowed plum trees. It was as though the elements had determined to do away with the world altogether — first silencing it with frost, then bleaching and blanketing it with snow, and now erasing with mist the last stubborn pencil lines of the birches and the division between earth and sky.

After tucking a borrowed map and compass and a few homemade biscuits into my jacket, I laced the nailed boots tightly and clattered out onto the swept doorstep — Sarah's quick heels echoed again, and, more distant but just as sadly, my own little rugby boots on the pavilion steps. I plunged resolutely up Rose's path into the foggy fairyland of the woods, where the heavily burdened trees found consolation in dropping snow down the back of my neck if I brushed against them, neatly complementing the sensation produced by my snow-filled boots. 'The man needs gaiters!' said Geoffrey's cheery voice in my head. 'I rustled up three splendid pairs from an old canvas horse-rug.'

Above the woods the snow was knee-deep, and my eyes had nothing to focus on except a few reassuring periscopes of bracken that guided me onward. I was hot and breathless by the time the slope eased — then, just as it had when I had climbed above the pines on the last steps to the temple, the sky seemed to open over me. A golden glow kindled in the mist to my right and, as I climbed higher, coalesced into the gleaming eye of the sunrise. Now an outcrop loomed up to my left and I laboured up it in a welter of sweat and tumbling snow, planted my boots firmly on its little summit and looked out.

I hope you are grateful — I have just toiled a second time up that hill, numbed my hands and soaked my boots a second time in my imagination, just to show you this: *the combe as a porcelain bowl brimming with fire.*

That was right for the first glance, but the details require a different simile: surely the mist laps like a golden lagoon around the snowy bay of the hilltops, and to the east lies in a blazing ocean over the frozen blue seabed county hidden beneath, its curls and ripples vanishing away into a horizon as sharp as that of any sea. We stand squinting, you and I, at the prow of this lumpy, snowy Argo, and turn our gaze to the west, to the drowned combe and the white lighthouse-cairn of white Grey Man, and suddenly there is a tiny rayed pinprick of reflected light — not from the cairn but from a little spur of land below, an insignificant wrinkle in that snowy brow, just peeping above the vaporous sea.

If the freeze had gently pushed the doctor and me closer together as though we were seeking warmth in each other, had persuaded us to relax the rules of our game, to answer a few questions, at least, without their being asked, now the silent profundity of snowfall seemed to wrap M'Synder and me in a blanket of easy fellowship. She, perhaps encouraged by my repeat visit to church, began to soften her businesslike attitude and treated me more like the son of an old friend, or a rarely seen nephew visiting from overseas. That weekend I split a few dozen logs for her (dangerous work for the clumsy and short-sighted) and then lent my height to the substantial task she called 'the annual shuffle'.

With the cassette player chirping away merrily (M'Synder shared

128

my father's enthusiasm for country and western music), our two little glasses of American beer on the mantelpiece and Dolly the cat curled up on the chair arm, sleepily batting my hand with her paw if I held it out for her ('Gimme five,' I would say), the parlour defied the monochrome grandeur of the world outside. First we took down all the pictures and stacked them on the table for dusting and polishing. Then I attacked the naked walls with a feather duster, dislodging cocoons, sleepy spiders, dusty strands of webs and traces of soot, and M'Synder brought down a box of additional pictures ('the subs bench') which now had a chance to make their case to her discriminating eye. The figure drawings I had noticed on my arrival were by Rose, of course, and M'Synder gave these particular attention.

'This un's new,' she said of one large picture, standing it on the table beneath the brass lamp. 'My Christmas present. What d'you think?' It was a charcoal drawing of a man (overalls, boots — surely Meaulnes) wielding an axe, seen half from behind. Rose had caught the moment before contact — the dark smear of the axe-head inches above the balanced log, the man's body in relaxed, effortless motion. His back and shoulders were the focus of the piece — the clothes and skin stripped away to reveal a brutal *écorché* of overlapping muscles that seemed vulnerable and wretched, as though he had been flogged, even as they perpetrated a violence of their own.

'I think it's superb,' I said warmly, flexing my own aching shoulders, 'although rather brutal.'

'Brutal?' she returned, dismissively. 'Life isn't all flowers and pretty landscapes.' She held it out to me. 'It can go right over the fireplace: top spot. As for these' — she pointed to a pair of yellowed engravings that had occupied that position — 'they can go back in the box.'

Occasionally I peered out of the fogged window and imagined

the doctor studying, tutoring, examining, alone in his chill university, or patiently remembering his earlier, happier lives.

A half-hearted thaw began on the damp, gusty Monday of my third week in the combe, and by Wednesday morning a few sheltered drifts and shovelled heaps of snow were all that remained around the house and along the lane. Only the hilltops were still a brilliant white, like clouds anchored to the earth.

I let myself in and passed through the empty study to the library, as the doctor had bidden me do if the door was standing open. Something caught my eye: a book on the near corner of his desk, with a slip of paper secured by a rubber band. The note was brief and written in a bold hand, and I had read it without thinking: '*Arnie,*' it read, '*Here is the book, you forgetful old fish. Forfeit: no whisky for a fortnight. See you next week.*' It was signed only with an elegant, inky squiggle like the hoofprint of a deer or goat.

I stood frowning for a while at the library table, fingertips again on the mahogany, listening to the silence. Yes, it is possible to remember silence — I remember it vividly as I write this. (Is silence a sensation? Discuss.) As I listened, I made adjustments to my conception of the doctor as a recluse resigned to the Boethian consolations of intellect and memory: now he was somebody's 'Arnie' as well.

Politics: that was my next station stop. On the warped and stiffened flyleaf of the first English translation of Machiavelli were scrawled the words '*That ye may know*' in the hand I now recognised as Hartley's: I supposed he was not a fan. Here too were Hobbes, Paine, Bentham and the rest, applying their formidable minds to the formidable problems of our coexistence. As for the doctor, he might occasionally receive playful notes but he did not, as far as I knew, read a newspaper. That birch-fringed hillside of Hart Top that by geological chance had shouldered into the combe from the north not only condemned the house to blue shade on winter mornings, but also screened it from the village, the county, the world — and while the sun would peep over indulgently by ten o'clock, the world and its afflictions might easily be forgotten. What were his politics? Did he vote? I could not guess.

And young Browne? The hunched ignoramus — what of his views on the coexistence of man with man? Since my last years at grammar school I had reluctantly accepted the obligation to contribute to the democratic process, and the corresponding burden of near-helplessness in the face of other people's problems (as if one's own life and impending death did not provide enough of that). I had tried to discuss politics with my friends, had voted conscientiously when called to do so, and had even joined a 'caucus' at university (that was where I met Sarah). But fear not — you will find no polemic here. The *new and greater causes* I promised are of a different nature.

7

Thursday afternoon. The sun came out and I sat for a while with hands in my coat pockets and crossed ankles on the 'sunniest seat' — the bench against the south side of the house. Somewhere a crow cawed with momentary urgency and was comforted by another. A few ivy leaves nodded unconcerned in the faintly hostile breeze. Clouds drifted.

When I had sat outside our flat in south London (there too was a bench), the purposeful hum of traffic and the sight of passers-by on determined errands had imbued the passage of time with a kind of illusory productivity: a general bustling productivity to which I need not contribute personally. If time or silence had lain heavy in the flat I could flick on the radio or the television, which instantly discharged the tension of ennui by the same process — the babbling thumbs-up of other people's activity. And the long hours of my occasional insomnia had been comforted by distant sirens and the softly waxing and waning booms of car stereos.

The combe, by contrast, was an unforgiving place for the inactive. There were no casual distractions to cheapen the currency of time: even the clock in M'Synder's serene parlour seemed to me to tick with the gentle, rising inflection of a repeated question (well? well? well?), and the silent clocks in the silent house did not have to say anything to make themselves understood. I was lucky to have an explicit purpose here, I thought, and one towards which measurable progress could easily be made (more easily than, for example, in the writing of a book about a man named Linley, whoever he might be).

With a soft batter of feathers, a large gaudy bird took possession of the wall in front of me: sandy pink, complementary electric blue, streaks of unequivocal black and white. My short-sightedness makes me a hopeless birdwatcher, but this brilliant apparition scorned any suggestion of doubt. I could even make out the round yellow eye, which stared at me unblinking as the bird ducked its head low and chuckled knowingly. There was a suggestion of *judgement* in this gesture, and I was struck by a vivid flash of perspective on the circumstances of my life, a kind of aerial view such as this bird might have were it really omniscient, simultaneously taking in the then-presence and now-absence of Sarah, the manager who could understand me wanting to 'give something back', the tedious irony of the ignoramus turning the pages of thousands of books without reading them, and, letter found or letter not found, my impending release from the sacred combe into the profane world.

I shuddered in an eddy of breeze, got up, glanced with hollow defiance at the mocking jay and hurried back along the terrace.

As I stepped up into the dining room and turned to close the door I heard a clear trickle of sound from within the house — the notes of a piano, not a recording but the real thing. Did the doctor play, or had Rose perhaps returned? I tiptoed to the hall door and opened it. I suppose music unlocks the inherent mystical potential of a door — that moment of opening a door on music, of the muffled, the indistinct suddenly stripped naked to the ear, is perhaps a sharper demonstration than Paul's '*through a glass, darkly, but then face to face*', a more perfect metaphor for revelation. Now I stood listening at the foot of the stairs, my hand on the great black oak newel, as the piece, Bach's Goldberg aria (yes, always Bach), came to its cool, stately end. I held my breath during the moment's silence that followed, and then the pianist leapt headlong into the energetic first variation, filling the high, cold, resonant space with a beaded spray of sound.

Emboldened by this *allegro mezzo forte*, I advanced up the stairs until I could peer through the gallery banisters to the large, bright room into which the landing opened. There in the pool of light from a huge window (correspondent to the parlour window below) stood a walnut grand piano. Paintings in heavy, plain wood frames hung on whitewashed walls, a battered violin case lay on a side-table, and the doctor sat in a low chair with his head tipped back and his eyes closed, listening.

I too listened. It is fortunate that I was unobserved, for I think my face hung in the slack, goggle-eyed, infantile expression (well captured in a certain photograph of me aged nine months, and in a certain miniature of Keats) that always disguises my mind's finest moments. How can the piano be played like that? The two hands commanded by one will and yet expressing two distinct truths, living two lives as they resolutely trace their invisible paths over the blank, inauspicious keyboard, perhaps crossing now and then like the paths of souls. But souls are never so sure of themselves — are they?

Seated at the piano, with her back to me: a woman, not Rose. Honey-brown hair half-trapped in the collar of her cardigan, half tumbling over her shoulder. The doctor's eyes were still closed; I silently retreated down the stairs and returned to the library and the pages of John Stuart Mill, bursting with fearsome, Bachian prose but hopelessly devoid of those loose, yellowing sheets that I always imagined awaiting me, expecting me, in the next volume.

The woman's accomplishment (I could still hear it faintly) terrified me. And yet I expected nothing less from the combe, where mediocrity was apparently unknown. She played the whole work, including all the rarely performed repeats, while I continued my unskilled labour (in case you think me a Bach scholar worthy of the combe myself, remember I have had time to research such details retrospectively for this account). Later, some time after five o' clock, I heard voices and the doctor swept in from his study, followed by the *maestra* herself.

'Ah, Mr Browne,' he said, as I balanced the current object of my search, Böhm-Bawerk's *Karl Marx and the Close of His System*, eighteen ninety-eight, open in my left hand. 'Your perseverance shames me. Mr Browne,' he added, turning back to the woman, 'has volunteered to search for the missing document. And small return he gets for his efforts, I'm afraid.'

She stepped forward, extended her hand and murmured, 'Juliet.' A small, slight woman in her early forties — cool blue eyes gazing from a faint net of lines; a wide, attractive mouth; three slender vertical furrows worn into the centre of her brow. She wore grey jeans, brogues, a blue shirt and two (or was it three?) cardigans.

'Juliet will be staying for a week,' said the doctor, absent-mindedly taking the book from my hand and leafing through it, 'so we can hope for further recitals.'

Since he did not explain their relationship, I speculated. My first impression was of a nervous intimacy between them that might easily account for the note to 'Arnie', although she now displayed none of its playfulness ('you can hope all you like,' she might have replied to his last comment, but instead just smiled wearily). If she were his daughter, surely he would have mentioned her before, or would say so now. But she was much too young to be his — what do old gentlemen have these days? Partner? Companion? Or perhaps not — there was just enough suavity in his words and gestures to make it seem possible. Strange, but possible.

'I listened from the stairs,' I said. 'It was wonderful.'

'Come and join us for a drink,' said the doctor, warmly but maintaining the calm, calculated tone that meant the game had, after the unexpected confidences of the previous week, recommenced in earnest.

We were back on the sherry: I suppose its cool, sharp formality suited the doctor's mood or purpose (there was never a choice). Juliet's gaze rested fondly for a moment on the Taboni, as though she had not seen it for while.

'Are you a professional pianist?' I asked, right on cue.

'A teacher,' she replied. 'I was a music mistress at a secondary school for many years — now I am just a plain old piano teacher.' She spoke quietly but with an engaging, almost conspiratorial warmth.

'A music mistress,' murmured the doctor, replacing the decanter. 'A mistress to music, or, alternatively, music itself as a mistress. Splendid — it should be the name of a yacht or a racehorse.'

'What do you think of the combe?' she asked. 'Arnold says you've been here for a few weeks.' He gazed through his sherry into the fire, just as he had when I had first spoken to Rose.

'I'm afraid it's given me a conflict of interest,' I replied. 'The sooner I find the letter, the sooner I'll have to leave, and go back to London — and I'm rather inclined to stay as long as possible.' The doctor smiled wryly at his glass. Juliet nodded.

'I believe he thought the bloody abominable cold would motivate you to get the job done quickly — perhaps he miscalculated the hardiness of the urbanite.' She set down her glass and gently pressed and kneaded her charmed fingers to warm them. Their tips were slender and pointed and seemed to turn up slightly, as though from the years of pressing those inauspicious keys.

'Or the extent of his antipathy towards his own life,' suggested the doctor, casually. Juliet asked what I did in London, and I went through the miserable 'lapsed banker' alibi again.

'I have a brother about your age,' she said. 'He's drifting too. It's the burden of too much choice — isn't that what people say?'

'Not a very heroic burden,' I said, seeing that unblinking yellow eye in my mind.

'Of course, it's different for the likes of us,' she added, turning to the doctor. 'We made our choices years ago.' He grimaced and sighed.

'*Each man has,*' he began, slowly, as though quoting from memory, '*at each moment in his life, certain possibilities in his future, certain paths that he has not yet passed by, but could still follow. The number and variety of these paths are for a young man at his liberty great but not infinite. He must perhaps choose the noblest and best that he can imagine, and think how he might follow it, and act on those thoughts.*'

'Abe Lincoln?' guessed Juliet.

'Hartley Comberbache,' he replied, draining his glass. 'In the diary of seventeen sixty-two, when he was about Mr Browne's age. Note that he makes no less than three demands of his young man at liberty: imagination, reason and action. But is the young man equal to the task? That's the question.'

'Yes,' I answered, grimly. 'That is the question.' Not yet passed by — those words lingered in my mind. There was hope in them, I thought. What paths had I not yet passed by?

'Our paths,' added the doctor, breaking the silence, '— mine especially — are indeed shorter, fewer and less varied. But we console ourselves by advising the young. Rose, at least, seems to have plenty of ideas.'

'She always did,' said Juliet. 'The first time I met her she said she wanted to be — what was it? A poacher! "My ambition", she called it. Each time I saw her she would have a new one.'

'I should clarify for Mr Browne's benefit,' added the doctor, 'that this was when Rose was a very young child, before she was in my charge. She is not quite so capricious now.'

'Ah, so you are claiming that influence,' said Juliet. 'Well, it is a fair claim. But really,' she went on, drily, 'to think of you as a father-figure to that poor girl, at your age. She'll be tired of life before she's lived it.'

'Nonsense,' he replied, with his grimace-smile. 'Rose is more than a match for me, and you know it.'

While they were turned to each other I caught myself gazing at Juliet's face, fascinated by those three sculpted frown lines. If the doctor's natural expression was one of pained comprehension hers was of jaded perplexity, as though she had almost given up trying to comprehend. I'm afraid I felt rather attracted to her even then, before I got to know her (yet more light splintering into a dark space?), which in turn made me feel a surprising flicker of male affinity with the doctor, a man with nearly half a century on me; I even detected a shameless whisper of covetousness. Juliet did not, of course, accompany me on the bracing walk back to the cottage for supper: only the swift, hushing phantom of a barn owl marked my passage.

8

The next morning was one of those on which the doctor was unaccountably absent from his study (I could not believe he slept late), but after an hour Juliet slipped quietly into the library wrapped in a shawl and cradling a big mug of coffee. I was kneeling on a cushion, searching the last of the economics books.

'I wondered if you'd like a hand,' she said over the mug, sitting back against the folio table. 'I could work through a few shelves if you like — maybe the music section.'

I hesitated. My heart leapt at the thought of such intriguing company after my weeks of working alone, but something made me unsure. 'It's kind of you,' I said, awkwardly, 'but —'

'You don't want me stealing the prize,' she suggested, laughing.

'I suppose it is something like that — I've come so far.' I indicated the thousands of volumes I had already searched. 'And if I don't find this thing, I want to know who to blame.'

'Well, you won't know that,' she replied. 'You won't know whether you somehow missed it or Arnold sent you on a wild goose chase.'

I looked straight into her frowning blue eyes. 'I will,' I said. 'That's the whole point.' She smiled and shrugged, and then wandered over to the portrait of Sarah.

'She looks so grave and virtuous,' she said, after a while. 'It's hard to imagine her part in the story.'

'What story?'

'Hasn't he told you? What a peculiar man he is! But he'll tell it so much better than I.' She strolled slowly across in front of the windows, peering down at the planted border and clutching the mug to her breast like a hot water bottle. Then with a last 'Happy hunting!' she left the room.

Later I heard the piano again — something chaotic and fiendishly hard that apparently stretched even her abilities, for several times she stopped abruptly or pounded out an angry discord. When I crossed the dining room to fetch my lunch she was sitting with a musician's perfect posture at the head of the table, slowly turning an orange on a plate.

'What was that you were playing?' I asked, when I returned with my bread and cheese.

'Trying to play,' she corrected, brightly. She sliced into the orange and breathed in the sweet scent. 'Chopin's *Scherzo number one in B minor* — my nemesis.'

'I didn't think it was Bach this time,' I said, with a smile.

'Ah, so Arnold hasn't spared you his obsession. He prefers not to listen to Chopin, so I wait until he's out of the house.'

'He's gone to the village?' I asked, trying to hide my curiosity. Her frown lines deepened.

'You have seen the temple, I believe.' I nodded. 'He's probably there.'

Saturday dawned grey. I went for a morning walk down to the village — half a dozen guttering tails of smoke, the sounds of a dog barking,

140

a car failing to start, a wood pigeon cooing unimaginatively from the church tower where it sat immovable like a plump gargoyle — and bought a few provisions for M'Synder from the tiny shop. A heavy middle-aged woman was seated at the counter, eating an apple, reading a newspaper. A perfectly normal person in a normal village shop. Had she ever been to Combe Hall?

When I returned, M'Synder, her mouth pursed in concentration, her glasses balanced on the tip of her nose, was sitting in her armchair with the plank of an old bookshelf resting across its arms, writing a letter. The cassette player droned gently and Dolly the cat, finding her habitual perch unavailable, sat sulkily upright on the seat of the other chair, and narrowed her eyes defensively at me as I entered. I resisted the lure of the fire's warmth, reluctant to disturb this peaceful scene, and after a few pleasantries went up to my cold bedroom and set about lighting my own fire for the first time.

It went out. I tried again, and one side began merrily crackling while the other slumped apologetically, barely singed. I delicately slid a vigorously flaming jenga-stick of kindling out of one side and inserted it into the other, where the ripple of flame faded and died with a derisive curl of white smoke. I transferred a second stick with the same result, and now the good side began to waver reprovingly. I knelt there on aching knees for half an hour, patiently insinuating matches and twists of paper, remembering the Jack London story that my father had read to my sister and me, and that had haunted me for months afterwards and earned him a telling-off from my mother, who in a rare misjudgement had thought me too young for it. Of course, I was now in a cosy English cottage where even the air pressing on the casements was several degrees above freezing (whereas Jack had specified 'one hundred and seven degrees of frost'), but that modification seemed appropriate to my prevailing ineptitude. Anyway, I got it going in the end.

I leaned at the sill for a while but nothing much was happening in the garden: there were no passers-by. So I stood my plain wooden chair by the fire and sat down — no cup of tea, no whisky, no cigarette, no newspaper, no radio. Fire, of course, still occupied in the combe the place that the television has now claimed for itself in the profane world — the centre of domestic gravity towards which all chairs are turned. But a fire gives no babbling thumbs-up — if not fed it will die; it is compelling precisely because it is dying all the time, using up its resources, measuring time by turning to ashes.

If you stare time in the face for long enough, you will begin to think about something — it is your mind's way of blinking, of admitting defeat. Soon I was thinking about Juliet, and the doctor, and, with an odd sense that she completed the trinity, I was thinking about Rose.

I knew something about each of them, but only what they had chosen to reveal — they all exhibited themselves half in shadow, like moons in a Voyager photograph, leaving me to pencil in the natural curve, to speculate. But of course we are all used to that, since every relationship is based on mutual speculation, from the passing acquaintance to that long, circling sizing-up called marriage. This circling of each other — of anyone we meet — begins very early in life, as soon as we discover that each trembling confidence inspires a new misunderstanding (only the insane persist). I am not saying that we all lie to each other, as some have claimed: it is quite possible to circle honestly.

My five years of circling Sarah began, ironically, with a cognitive master stroke. As you know I first noticed her, speaking rarely but with humour and what seemed like good sense, at the political debates I attended. It was only when I saw her in a different setting, politely, efficiently selling tickets at the theatre, that she acquired a kind of three-dimensional significance in my thoughts, and I sent her a valentine's card — just a sheet of red paper folded over, with a leaf drawn in black ink on the front and the words of Handel's aria *Ombra mai fu* neatly inscribed inside (words written not by Handel, of course, but by a librettist named Minato — to each his due). A red envelope in her pigeonhole — the only one, I remember noticing with mixed feelings (*per voi risplenda il Fato* — a fine jest, in retrospect). She (and now at last I come to the point) immediately guessed it was from me. I have no idea how, since we had barely met. It seemed a good omen — but omens, like *il fato* — fate — are pure fiction.

A jackdaw's sharp call, like a foot lifted off a creaking board, roused me from this train of thought and I jammed a log angrily onto the little fire: 'Not here,' I muttered. 'Not here.' I reeled my errant thoughts back into the combe.

The doctor, Juliet and Rose: they were like moons, too, I realised, in that they each seemed wrapped in a chill, airless solitude, and yet were united by some invisible bond, some dark planet that eluded me. I have mentioned the odd presence of the doctor's ancestors — Hartley, twisted round in his chair, and the rest — but there was something else, something nearer, nearer even than the doctor's two last memories of his wife, some heavy focus bending their thoughts just as Einstein showed mass to bend space itself. 'Haunted by memory' — those had been Rose's words.

I was soon to be enlightened.

9

Law books are a strange breed. Colleges and universities abound in separate 'law libraries' as though the books, or perhaps the students, are not quite eligible for admittance to the main collections. One such journal-crammed oubliette, never locked at night, used to host our bleary-eyed conferences in the small hours before a physics hand-in. There were always a couple of law students hiding behind barricades of books from which they had perhaps resolved never to venture forth, like hibernating toads that settle and snuggle themselves inch by inch into some heap of decaying matter.

Combe Hall had pronounced this same customary sentence on its own law collection, banishing it to the shelves of the folio table which stood apart in the centre of the room like St Helena or Alcatraz. It was here that my fourth week began — sitting on a cushion with my back to the shelves, since my knees would no longer countenance kneeling.

Here were some books that predated even Hartley, books that had belonged to his grandfather Nathaniel, who bought the house in seventeen hundred and eight. These had been the inherited nucleus of the collection, beginning with Edward Coke's *Institutes of the Lawes of England* in two volumes, published in sixteen eighty-one. The tops of the spines were broken and the top edges of the boards scuffed and split after repeated careless extractions from a low shelf: proud, distinctive battle scars of which I had now seen hundreds of different varieties. Many grand private libraries are, I suspect, padded out with books of a rather lower mileage.

I could hear the wind, very strong and turbulent that day, as a blank wash of noise in the beeches and as a more immediate and expressive whistling and buffeting around the house, as each gust searched the stonework and batted harmlessly against the ancient glass. It was during one of these buffetings that I heard a sharper sound, quiet but very near — *inside* the glass, I thought. Something small falling onto a hard surface. A twig clawing at a window, perhaps, but I had seen none. A few minutes later during another gust I heard it again — a tapping sound (*gently rapping*, I thought, *rapping at my chamber door*). I stood up and searched the room with my eyes: nothing had moved. Then my gaze fell on the locked door nearby, and it came again, very faintly this time, but I was sure: it was something behind the door.

I had, I recalled, left the doctor in his study. I smiled impulsively at the idea of a door cleverly concealed in his enormous bookcase and giving access to some secret laboratory beyond (mainstay of many a gothic tale). On second thoughts, a concealed door seemed quite possible. If it was the doctor, perhaps he made himself audible now as a signal, as part of the game — perhaps I was to be admitted, to advance another square on the unseen board.

In that spirit, I knocked gently at the door. There was no answer, except for another gentle, almost inaudible metallic flutter. I turned the heavily sprung doorknob and this time, to my surprise, the door yielded.

'Hello?' I said quietly, slowly pushing it open and stepping over the threshold. The consistently closed curtains had been drawn back, but there was nobody in the room, and no connecting door. A large table stood against that wall, draped with crimson velvet and bearing a few carefully arranged objects: a coil of yellow nylon rope, a pair of gloves, some kind of harness to which small metal blocks and screws were attached by steel loops, and, crossed in the centre, two fearsome tools like miniature pickaxes with crooked shafts and long serrated picks. These were heavily scratched and knocked about, and one of the picks was slightly twisted as though it had been subjected to a violent strain. At the end of the table lay a slim leather folder, and on the floor stood a pair of heavy boots like ski-boots with long metal spikes — crampons — strapped to the soles. These boots were not decades old like the ones I had borrowed.

On the panelled wall above the table hung a huge monochrome photograph of a snow-covered mountain, in a frame perhaps six feet wide. As I peered closer I noticed that it was marked with dozens of fine red lines drawn onto the complex rampart of cliffs, each labelled above or below by a name in tiny, neat handwriting. Some were prosaic and topographical (*Left Edge, Central Gully Right-Hand, Route II Direct*), others poetic or humorous (*Pointless, Appointment with Fear, Riders on the Storm, Big Bad Ben*). Each name was followed by a roman numeral and an Arabic digit separated by a comma — these, I guessed, indicated the difficulty of the climb. One name in particular, written in proud capitals, caught my eye: *THE TEMPLE, IX,8 (FA 07.2.97)*. This denoted a line that breached the middle of a terrifying snowless precipice, rising straight between two slender pilasters of rock and then crossing the black shadow of an overhang (like a monstrous pediment, I supposed) and continuing up ice and steep snow to the summit plateau. IX was the highest numeral I could see. Below the photograph was written the name of the mountain (somewhat surprising, given its alpine grandeur: *Ben Nevis*) and in the corner were scrawled a few words in pencil: *To Sam. in medias res. From Adam '96.*

I started on hearing the tapping, fluttering noise again just behind me, and as I wheeled round my eye caught a flicker of movement over the fireplace. An ornate brass arrow pivoted back and forth on the wall like the hand of a deranged clock. N, E, S, W — it was a wind-dial, connected to the vane on the roof. I glanced at the open door, my body still charged with the silent tension of intrusion — but it seemed right that I should see all this, that I should know.

Two more pictures hung side-by-side opposite the window. The first was an enlarged photograph of a young man's face: the pale, aquamarine glitter of his eyes narrowed against a fierce mountain sun; windburnt skin, a strong, unshaven jaw, wisps of yellow hair falling over the mirror sunglasses that were pushed back on his head, and the broad smile, in whose shape I could recognise the doctor's grimace, but which was untouched by pain or regret or anything beyond the moment. He held up a gloved fist clenched in triumph.

The second picture completed a kind of memorial diptych: it was a figure painting of a man running away into the canvas, barefoot, one leg planted down on the void, the other flung out behind him, the muscular lower back revealed by a shirt billowing up, loose flapping trousers, yellow hair tossed up by motion, and a bare arm extended with its relaxed, empty hand turned into shadow. The figure was executed in quick broad, strokes, and traces of the background, a blank red, showed through here and there, as though the man were indeed fading, receding into the canvas. In the corner was the small, blocky signature I recognised as Rose's.

A few smaller frames hung in the alcoves, some holding collages of short newspaper articles — *Lost Walkers Rescued 'In Nick Of Time'*;

Climber Found Safe After Night On Ledge; *Rescued Schoolboys 'Had Given Up Hope'*; *Avalanche Man In Stable Condition*; and many more. None mentioned the names of the rescuers, but I guessed that all these stories had at least one anonymous participant in common; there were also several group photos of mountain rescue teams — *Lochaber, Edale, Ogwen Valley*.

On the mantelpiece stood a wedding photograph like the final superfluous *QED*: the laughing younger Juliet was to the older almost what the son was to the pained, mistaken father. I turned back to the haunting diptych. Here then was the planet, the focus of all those bending thoughts: son, husband and — how did Rose fit in? That I still did not know, but I felt sure that she too was bound to the others by these pale eyes smiling out from the not-so-distant past, this running man who had escaped them all.

The wind whistled on outside. The view from the window was dominated by the great beech, from the base of its monolithic trunk to the swaying net of branches that filled the sky. The jackdaws were here too, a dozen or so, grimly clinging on like sailors sent aloft. I turned back to the table and lifted the cover of the folder. On the first page was written the single word *Requiescat* in a large, plain hand, and, in much smaller letters below, *For Sam, from J.* I turned a few pages: it was a handwritten music manuscript.

Glancing again at the open door, I froze at the sight of Juliet herself, standing at the window with her back to me, gazing across the windswept lawn — waiting for me, I thought. I closed the folder and stepped quietly back into the library.

10

'He died five years ago today,' she said, softly, reassuringly, as I approached. 'On his birthday. On Ben Nevis.'

'I'm sorry,' I said, in the stupid, helpless way that is after all quite fitting.

'I'm sorry that Arnold didn't tell you,' she replied. 'He still can't talk about it — about Sam, I mean. I suppose he ended up making quite a mystery of it all.'

'It's alright — I mean, I understand.'

Juliet frowned. 'Not fully, I expect — not yet. How about you close that door,' she said, pointing at the doctor's shrine to her husband, 'and we'll go for a walk in the garden. I could do with being blown about a bit.'

Cold air billowed into the dining room as she opened the terrace door, tinkling the crystals of the chandelier. 'Here goes,' she said, adjusting her scarf. We went the way Rose had taken me, through the gate to the long, straight promenade she had called the runway.

'Arnold told me about the notices in the old books,' she said, her voice raised over the unsympathetic wind. She smiled and shook her head disapprovingly. 'I've no idea what possessed you to answer one and come here, but I'm glad you did — he seems to have taken to you. He's a lot more cheerful than usual.'

It had never before occurred to me, despite his odd remark about 'engineering' my stay, that the doctor might simply want company. Was there a letter, after all? And if so, was it really lost? 'M'Synder seems to look after him pretty well,' I said, laying those questions carefully aside.

'Well of course, Sara's wonderful,' said Juliet. 'But she's getting older now too — and she'll always remind him of the past, of Margaret and — and Sam growing up. It's Rose who forces him to think of the future.'

'M'Synder said Rose's parents were friends of the family,' I suggested. It is true that I was curious and hoped for further revelations; but, to be fair to myself, I think I really wanted to understand this strange family because I liked them and wanted to help them — at that moment I wanted to help this lonely, frowning woman who spoke to me, a stranger, as though I deserved her confidence.

'Very close friends of ours,' she said. 'Her father was Sam's climbing partner — in fact it was Adam who introduced him to it while they were students.'

Was there a note of accusation in her voice? I don't think so. I considered how to phrase a question about that other accident, *their* accident, of which I still knew nothing. Perhaps it was the same accident? Juliet spoke again: 'You must think us rather self-obsessed,' she said, with a smile. 'We're not really — Arnold is dedicated to Rose and to his book, which I honestly believe he'll finish this year, and I — well, I have my pupils, and the piano.'

We had walked past the gate to the rose garden, and now turned instead towards the next gate, which led to a part of the garden I had not yet seen. It was a walled enclosure about fifty feet square, paved in stone and filled with statues — sculptures, busts, abstract forms, standing here and there like guests at a garden party, or perhaps like graves.

'They call this the stone garden,' said Juliet, in a softer voice, since we were sheltered here. We both looked up as a crow whipped past skilfully on the wind overhead. 'There were parties here, and plays.' Sure enough, in one corner was a miniature sunken amphitheatre, big enough to seat twenty or thirty people, with a stone bust looming high over the sunken stage — Euripides, perhaps, or more likely Aeschylus (he was the bald one, I think).

'When we got married,' she went on, wandering from one statue to the next, 'Sam and I agreed that he would have to share me with my piano, and I would share him with his mountains. But the piano is a more —' she hesitated, searching for a word '— a more temperate possessor — it holds on to the soul and shakes it like a dog's toy, but the soul is resilient and generous: there is enough for everyone. It is the body that is delicate — *indivisible* — and the piano makes little claim on that.' She held up her hands as though to prove they were unharmed.

'But the mountains —' I murmured, sadly, as we passed either side of a slender obelisk which bore at its tip an iron ring, as though it might be drawn up to heaven.

'The mountains took everything in the end.'

We reached the high wall and began to walk along it, and suddenly I saw a face staring out from a tangle of bare branches — or rather, not staring, for the eyes were closed as though in contemplation. This face was not of stone but of bronze — a smooth cast with a skin-like sheen and the sharp precision of a real face in every detail. I peered closer. Wasn't it —

'Keats,' said Juliet. 'That was what I wanted to show you. It was another Samuel — Arnold's ancestor — who got it from the man

151

who made it. He was friends with all of that bunch, apparently. No one knows it's here, of course.'

A contemporary cast of the famous life-mask — the one taken by Benjamin Haydon just before the poet published his first collection (Keats was an adolescent fascination of mine, even though I can't read poetry). And what was written on this calm young face, with its fine nose and broad, fleshy lips preserved as miraculously as the hieroglyphs on that *Papyrus of Ani*? Health: *the cornerstone of all pleasure*, Keats later called it, once he felt it slipping away.

Habeas corpus, I thought, remembering the large, curling print on the pages of Edward Coke. Juliet was right: you must have the body.

'Sam was their only child, I suppose,' I asked cautiously, as we walked back along the runway. The yews rippled and swayed along their radial of the converging perspective, whose greens and greys were subdued under the wind-hurried sky.

'Yes,' she replied, holding her hair back out of her eyes. 'And my only husband.' I glanced at her, and for the first time saw her composure wavering. Her eyes had been watering in the wind and were reddened, and now her clenched jaw slightly changed the shape of her face — she looked almost middle-aged. 'We were talking about paths not yet passed by,' she added, quickly. 'A lot of paths ended at that stupid cliff.'

'I'm sorry,' I said, suddenly wanting to get away, to be back among the long-considered and reconciled-to sorrows of the library.

11

My next find, later that afternoon, was a slip of paper bearing a list of purchases neatly written in an unfamiliar hand:

Extraordinary outgoeings since Whitsun last

Subscription to St. Matthew's schoolhouse	*2.00.0*
Lackington	*3.10.0*
Hale's Historia fr Blagdon, IIvms	*1.04.0*
Montesquiou's Sp. Of Laws, IIvms	*0.10.0*
Smith's Harmonics	*0.06.0*
Diderot's L.B.I.	*0.18.0*
Fielding's Tom Jones, VIvms	*0.12.0*
Widdow Wallis' balsam fr Hartley	*2.02.0*
Road workes	*3.01.0*
Summa	*14.03.0*

Below this list had been added, in the same hand but more hastily, *Therefore I say unto you, Take no thought for your life. Which of you by taking thought can add one cubit unto his stature? Matthew 6.* I knocked on the doctor's door gently, having decided not yet to mention my earlier intrusion into the adjacent room, or my discussion with Juliet. There was a long pause.

'Enter,' he said at last. He was sitting at the great desk with his arms limp at his sides, leaning back as though in fear of the pen which lay before him on a blank sheet of paper — as though its tarnished nib were the nail of an accusing finger. A couple of books lay open on the desk, on those reverent foam supports that protect the spines.

'Mr Browne,' he said, with a sigh. 'My saviour. What have you found?' His arms still hung at his sides as though paralysed, so I placed the list before him. He frowned, and murmured the names of the authors. 'Diderot,' he repeated. 'L.B.I.' Then, to my surprise and for the first time in my presence, he gave a peel of cracked laughter. 'L.B.I.: *Les Bijoux Indiscrets*! Well, well — you seem to have the knack of uncovering the more salacious moments of my family's past. Hartley describes that book in his diaries,' he explained, 'as one of the treasures of his early adolescence. And when his horrified mother discovered it, Arnold, his father (I'm afraid we are all named after each other, just to confuse you archivists), denied all knowledge. But here is the proof — and for eighteen shillings, no less! Incidentally you will find the book in the fiction section, if you are so inclined, but to be frank the genre has better.'

He slowly stirred himself at last, rising stiffly from his chair as though he had not moved for hours. 'And two guineas for a *balsam*,' he went on, dragging the chair towards the fire as he had done in the past. 'That's almost as good! To cure disobedience, or maybe neurosis. Wise Widow Wallis, eh?' He prodded the fire half-heartedly until it yielded a single reluctant flame, then sat down, shaking his head. 'Too wise for poor Arnold.'

'I don't think you've mentioned Hartley's parents before,' I said. 'What were they like?'

'Fetch us some tea, and I'll tell you,' he said. I did so, and when I returned he inhaled the green tea's seaweed-scented steam as though it might nourish and revive him — his own *balsam*.

'Arnold was a well-intentioned man,' he began, 'and, to his younger children at least, a good father — Hartley himself says as much, even though they were not on speaking terms for years at a time. He was a lawyer, like his own father, but a less successful one — less able, less fortunate, or perhaps just less well-connected.'

'And his wife?'

'Hester — equally well-intentioned, I suppose, but rather a hard, puritanical woman: as much admired by my own uncle Hartley as she was scorned by her eldest son. Her portrait hangs in the dining room — one only has to look at it to sympathise with her husband both for his indecent purchase and his later denial of it.'

'And yet you say the book survived her fury,' I said, with a smile.

'Yes,' he replied, wryly. 'I suppose that is odd. Who knows — maybe she felt the need to study it further when her husband was in town, just to make sure it was wholly evil. What an intriguing thought,' he added, mischievously. 'That portrait will never be quite the same.'

He again scrutinised the slip of paper, examining the blank reverse and then turning back to the list. 'What makes this note particularly interesting, to me at least, is that Arnold left very few written traces of his own life — I have only seen him through the lens of his son's rebellion. The Diderot and the ironic quotation are fascinating: his own private acts of rebellion. He did not have much money, so left no great marks on the house, though he did at least manage to cling on to it, which I suppose was the important thing. *Road workes* — that was his contribution to the combe.'

'Then how did Hartley make his money?' I asked.

'Ah. He didn't have to — it just seemed to attach itself to him. He won a hundred pounds in an ingenious bet during his first term at Cambridge, while his father was still counting every shilling. But that was just the beginning. Next came a bestselling satirical pamphlet — he used the anagrammatical pseudonym *Beachcomber*, which others have since borrowed — then a speculative investment in a cotton carding invention that paid off tenfold, and always a stream of influential friends. Within a few years of leaving home, he was wealthy enough to disown his parents and go travelling across Europe.'

'A nice talent to have,' I said, ruefully. Of course, I had earned a good salary at the bank — more than either of my parents — but money had hardly attached itself to me.

'Indeed,' he replied. 'Sadly I have not inherited it. I am a clinger-on, like my namesake. But of course I'm not really a blood-descendant of any of them.'

'Oh? I didn't realise that.'

'Hartley's son Samuel — we are now in the next century, the nineteenth — had one surviving daughter, and it was her stepson who began the tradition of inheriting both house and name, and who called his own son Hartley (my great uncle) and his daughter Catherine. There are different kinds of heredity — in my own humble way I am the elder Hartley's thought-descendant, I hope.' As he said this his voice became quiet and solemn, as though his thoughts had run forward to a different subject.

'I'm afraid I — had a look in the other room,' I said, clumsily. 'And Juliet has told me a little about Sam. I'm sorry.'

He sat still for a while, breathing audibly in the silence and seeming to shrink slightly into his chair at each breath. 'Yes,' he murmured at last. 'Well, there you are. What did *that* young man

inherit, and from whom? He too left little enough behind him —
rarely wrote so much as a postcard.' A pause, a few more deflating
breaths. 'He saved a great many lives of course, as a rescue volunteer
and as a doctor, but no one will remember him for that. The temple
he erected is the red line on that photograph you saw, through the
famous overhang. Those red lines are his works, I suppose. He was
too busy living his life to record it or reflect on it. *in medias res* —
into the midst of things — that was his motto. But answer me this
— why would anyone want to climb the same mountain a hundred
times? Why?'

I had no answer. The fire's single flame flicked indecisively
between existence and its nameless opposite, while outside the spent
wind gave a last exhausted sigh in those branches from which restless
jackdaws had long departed.

When I returned to work, the doctor, recovering some of his
brightness as though waking from a recurrent bad dream, told me to
replace the note where I had found it, since he would leave a mention
of its existence and whereabouts in the archives. I had found it, in
fact, in the very *Hale's Historia* that was apparently intended for a
Mr Blagdon (a colleague, the doctor suggested) but that, like Rose,
M'Synder and the scandalous Diderot, had settled in the combe for
good.

As dusk fell and I continued the search (by now I was as
mindlessly efficient as one of Hartley's profitable carding machines),
I reflected on the doctor's words. *Too busy living his life* — that phrase
had jangled a memory of something similar: '*Lawrence spent most
of his short life living.*' I cannot be the only one to have been struck
by this odd assertion on the flyleaf of D.H.L.'s Penguin classics.
'*Nevertheless he produced an amazing quantity of work ...*' it goes on.

Is working not living? But I suppose we know what the biographer means: Living, with a capital L. And Samuel Comberbache, the doctor's son, had spent all of his short life doing it. Which begged the question: what the hell was I doing with mine? *I am spending it hunched on a cushion*, I thought, and remembered the glimpsed crow winging effortlessly down the wind.

The other idea whose dimpled impression I contemplated was the doctor's notion of thought-heredity. The stones beside the temple recorded the passage of these precious thoughts down the swift centuries, with each legatee adding his or her own unique infusions of personality to the trickle of ideas that had steadily swelled into something like a creed. And the young doctor, the yellow-haired running man, had inherited everything and dashed it high with his own fierce appetite and energy. He had joined forces with a beautiful and talented wife, had honed his will to a razor on those gleaming ramparts of ice, and then had broken his body — died without issue, *anno MM*.

Rose was the heir to Hartley Stillwell Newton's creed now. She would receive whatever the doctor could pass on with his dry voice and pained smile, turn it in her sharp, wilful young mind, and do with it what she chose.

12

You are more than halfway through my story, and I am still describing the fourth of the seventeen weeks I promised in my opening sentence. Has the combe lived up to those *five unremarkable words*? Has it lived up to the title of the book? Not yet, perhaps. That first sentence was whispering in my head for months before I typed it out and tried to follow it with a second and a third. Months more have passed (*lifting and lowering me*, et cetera) while I try to honour my promise. 'Be silent,' reads the inscription under the hand of Salvator Rosa, who glowers down at me from the wall as I write, 'unless what you have to say is better than silence.' You and he and I are all hoping that the best is yet to come.

It was Thursday morning when I heard the piano for the last time — neither Bach nor Chopin this time, but a wandering jazz lead over a minimal, discordant left hand. I listened for a while, almost as delighted by the change in mood as I had been by the black-eyed robin on that white first morning. The shuffling, sporadic rhythm might have robbed the house of its timelessness and pinned it to the post-war era, but did not — the pianist, I thought, could equally be Juliet, or the youthful organ-scholar uncle bound for Arras, or Bach himself on his day off.

I mounted the stairs confidently this time, crossed the landing towards the piano (it was Juliet playing, after all), and was stopped in my tracks by the glimpse of a second piano in an adjoining room — at which was seated a second pianist. The music stopped and both pianists looked round. I glanced from one to the other.

'Which of us plays better?' asked Juliet, with mock sincerity.

It was a mirror. But I was unsatisfied and went to investigate. It was set in a narrow alcove, stretching from waist-height to the ceiling. On the shelf in front stood a dark greyish vase holding a spray of pine — or rather, I realised, bending over it, the perfect half of a vase standing against the glass.

'The other half is behind you,' whispered Juliet, playfully. I spun round to see an identical mirrored alcove opposite, beside the window, at which stood an identical vase. Behind it, a thousand more vases and a thousand peering ignorami tunnelled into infinity. 'It's Greek,' she went on. 'Very rare. Arnold operated on it with his father's surgical saw — a risky procedure performed without consultation, but luckily Stella saw the funny side.'

I followed her glance round to two small sketch-like portraits hanging behind the piano — an earnest, square-faced man with his hair plastered back, wearing a grey suit, tie and watch chain, and an attractive woman with short, dark, boyish hair like Rose's, feline blue eyes and thin scarlet lips. These were the moderators — the doctor's mountain-climbing parents.

'I'm sorry I interrupted,' I said, sitting on the low listener's chair. 'I just came up to listen.'

'How's the quest for the unholy epistle?' she asked, beginning to play a few experimental chords. I watched her for a while.

'Am I going to find anything?' I returned at last. 'Does this letter exist? Rose once suggested it might not.' Juliet smiled down at the keyboard, reinstating a soft treble line.

'Arnold is man a whose motives are hard to guess,' she said, lowering her voice. 'He enjoys mystery. When I first came here, fifteen years ago, I felt quite uncomfortable. I thought he was mocking me, teasing me for being unworthy of Sam. But he wasn't really. It was only years later that I learned how to get on with him.'

As she spoke I observed her body in profile — the slight incurves of her lumbar spine and the back of her neck, the forward tilt of her head, the graceful angles and convexities.

'If he says there's a lost letter,' she went on, turning to me, which made me look away sheepishly, 'then there *is* a lost letter. And if you want to know something, ask him straight.'

I let her play for a while, and then asked her if she had wanted to be a professional performer.

'I was, for a while. I performed in a trio while I was at college in London and for a few years afterwards, and gave solo recitals. But I didn't quite have enough' — she performed a little virtuoso run with the lead, of the sort that wins approving moans in jazz bars — 'consistency.'

'Do you compose?' I asked, naively.

'I improvise,' she replied, laughing, 'and make up themes that I revisit for months, sometimes years.' She shifted to a different time signature — three slow beats in the bar — and lowered her voice again. 'What you saw downstairs is the only composition I've written down since leaving college. I wasn't sure what would happen to it if I left it swimming up here.' She touched her forehead and played on. 'I suppose I was afraid that — that the feelings would fade, even that my memories of Sam would fade.'

'And — have they?' I asked, hesitantly. She glanced at me and gave a short hiss of breath that might have signified dismissal or acceptance. Then she wound the piece down into a descending tangle of notes and stopped.

'Yes — no — I'm not sure. But the sonata doesn't feel like mine anymore. It belongs to Arnold, or to Sam.'

That day and the next I was searching the reference shelves, beside the oak door in the corner that was, once again, firmly locked. The volumes were heavy and the work more than usually repetitive (bordering on the insane, I thought), so Juliet's reassurance was timely.

Even reference works have their patriarch — surely the great *Encyclopédie* edited by none other than Denis Diderot. The doctor told me that Hartley, despite his adolescent reading and later travels, had a shaky grasp of French when the first crated volumes arrived in seventeen seventy-two — but within a year he was fluent. 'He was fascinated by the scope and ambition of the *Encyclopédie*,' he said, 'and its exaltation of reason above custom and superstition. He rapidly drew up his own modified classification of human knowledge and sent it to Diderot, explaining the differences. The reply was appreciative but wearily observed that a new edition was unlikely in the present century.'

There was also a Victorian edition of the *Britannica* (a publication Hartley had shunned), an Edwardian *DNB*, and a vast *OED* from nineteen twenty-eight. Suddenly I glimpsed a ray of hope, and went to the study door. 'What year did your uncle Hartley die?' I asked, eagerly.

'Nineteen thirty,' replied the doctor, without looking up, and my heart sank: that was tomorrow accounted for, anyway.

It was the sound of a mechanical lawnmower, like the one my mother used to lean into on our little suburban lawn, that woke me from

162

a happy dream on Saturday morning. My ex-wife and I had been travelling through some warm and expansive country where to her delight and amusement everyone we met was called Samuel or Sarah, except for a couple of Arnolds (my imagination drew the line at Hartley). After waking I lay still for a while reflecting on whether, if I ever did find a second love, as I slept beside her unimaginable body in my second marriage bed I might go on blissfully dreaming of Sarah, just as, in dreams, my home was always the childhood home that my waking eyes had not seen for a decade or more — its successors remaining stubbornly unrecognised by that inscrutable arbiter of significance who rules the sleeping mind. The thought sickened me.

A lawnmower? The impossible sound faded away reassuringly, and I clambered shivering out of bed to open the curtains. Beyond the second curtain of condensation the defiantly un-mowed world glistened under drizzle leaking from a low sky.

It was Saturday, which meant bacon, and M'Synder was just bringing the plates when the lawnmower came back. I opened the front door to find Juliet standing beside the Cortina in a long fitted coat and black beret, leaning casually against it just as she had leant on the folio table. The red-haired boy was at the wheel.

'I'm off,' she said, over the rasping engine. 'Just stopped to say goodbye to you both, and to deliver a message.'

Last night Arnold had cooked her one of his famous chestnut roasts, and he was so pleased with the result that he wanted to try it on me tonight at seven-thirty — that was the message.

'And he promised to tell you the story of Hartley and Sarah and the letter,' she added. 'Make sure you hold him to it.'

She and M'Synder embraced, and then we kissed with an awkward formality. (I hate kissing women like that — the male sex is divided into those for whom it presents inexplicable difficulties and those for whom it does not. Maybe it's something to do with being too tall or wearing glasses, or maybe we hate it because we like it too much: cool pinpricks of rain from her hat grazed my cheek as I straightened.)

'You are coming for Easter?' called M'Synder, as the elegant apparition climbed into her unseemly carriage and wound the window halfway down.

'If invited,' she replied, waving, and the car lurched away through the puddles.

13

'What was the ingenious bet at Cambridge?'

'Ah-ha! I hoped you would ask.'

The chestnut roast was the doctor's own recipe of sweet winter vegetables from the combe's garden and chestnuts gathered from the meadow and stored on racks in the cavernous larder. We drank wine from squat little tumblers instead of the tall, ringing glasses we had used before, and the doctor had abandoned his tweeds and tie in favour of a thick Aran jumper — he looked quite different.

'Hartley had been discussing the subject of religious doubt with the earnest young Earl of Fakenham,' he said, 'and asserted that such doubts were characteristic of every thinking man, themselves included. To the earl's vehement protests he replied, "Does not the sun have phases, just like the moon? And yet they are hard to see because of that body's greater brilliance. So it is with your doubts, perhaps." When the bemused earl summoned his friends to hear this absurd analogy, Hartley stuck to his story and said he would prove it the next morning if the noble lord would kindly meet him in the quad with a piece of smoked glass. He sealed the bet in suitably precise terms.'

'And?'

'The next morning happened to be the twenty-sixth day of

October, seventeen fifty-three, on which a total eclipse of the sun was visible over north Africa and Spain, and seen from Cambridge as a partial eclipse in the early hours of the morning, magnitude seventy-three percent.'

'A crescent sun,' I murmured. 'Lucky it wasn't cloudy.' The doctor smiled and nodded.

'There speaks a true British astronomer,' he said. 'But Hartley seems to have had plenty of that kind of luck — an imbalance that was amply corrected elsewhere.'

'What did he do after Cambridge?' I asked.

'He disliked exams but was nevertheless named Third Wrangler (or Wangler, as he wrote in his diary — a very early use of the word if it was not a mistake) in the tripos of seventeen fifty-six. Later that year he sailed for France — ignoring the recent declaration of war — to begin his own impulsive interpretation of the Grand Tour. In Rome, where he lived for a year, he met both Robert Adam and his tutor Piranesi, whose books you so enjoyed. In Greece his money ran out, but by a persuasive series of letters — and with the earnest earl as referee — he arranged a scholarship from the Society of Dilettanti, and so continued to Egypt and the Levant. From Alexandria he travelled inland as far as the pyramids at Giza with the help of a map sent to him by the Danish explorer Frederic Norden, but after nearly succumbing to starvation and dehydration he returned to the more populated coasts. He landed at both Ephesus and Halicarnassus and searched in vain for their lost wonders, and he even appears to have glimpsed the ruins of Knidos almost half a century before they were publicly documented — but was driven off first by a storm and later by hostile Ottoman patrols.'

The doctor told the story at a leisurely pace, between mouthfuls and slow-drawn sips of wine, but produced the details without any visible effort of recollection, almost as though he were telling the story of his own life.

'It was around this time,' he continued, 'that our intrepid young Hartley reflected on those *paths not yet passed by*. His correspondence with friends shows an increasing interest in politics, in particular the question of Britain's responsibilities to its rapidly expanding empire. When he finally returned to England — after six years abroad — it was to help a clandestine campaign of influence on behalf of the American colonies.

'He lived in London and wrote articles under many pseudonyms supporting various radical causes. One of his co-conspirators, the nephew of a wealthy Bostonian merchant, had a pretty but rather silent younger sister called Sarah. She and Hartley were married a few years after his return, at a church in Edinburgh with three guests attending — almost exactly two centuries before my own wedding. There was then a reconciliation between Hartley and his father (Hester had died while he was abroad), but soon afterwards the old man was beaten by pneumonia — who can blame him, in this house! So the young couple found themselves owners of one dilapidated combe, on condition that they pay off the family debts. Arnold had ignored the advice reported by St Matthew and spent virtually nothing during his last years, since he had nothing left, and now a small loan from the Bostonian uncle was sufficient to secure the estate.'

'No inheritance tax in those days,' I said, smiling. The doctor pursed his lips and fixed his eyes on his glass.

'It was in Constantinople,' he went on, changing the subject, 'that Hartley had first eaten opium. The recollection of its effects haunted him — "it is as though my body has its own inexpressible memory," he wrote, "and yearns for remembered sensation." In

London he soon discovered the early preparations of laudanum then available, but it was not until he and Sarah settled here that his use of the drug became habitual.

'Money was not a problem: Sarah brought a small income, and Hartley had secured a generous advance for an account of his travels and dashed off frequent articles on the American question. But the combe was a strange harbour at which to end his years of voyages, bustling cities and wide vistas. Perhaps you can imagine how he felt better than I, who have lived here so long now.'

Two of his *young men at liberty*, I thought: Halicarnassus and the Charing Cross Road; curved banks of sails and of computer screens. Shown up again. 'But he was coming home,' I said. 'He was born here.'

'True,' said the doctor, 'and I think that made it worse. In any case he began to experiment with small doses of laudanum with the idea that it sharpened his recollections of faraway places, and therefore helped his writing. It also gave instant relief to the headaches he had suffered periodically since his prolonged heatstroke and dehydration in Egypt. During the first few years of his marriage, the doses gradually increased and the work faltered — journal deadlines were missed, careful plans became mired in doubts and complexity, friendships and alliances suffered. The house and grounds fell further into disrepair. At his worst he became so lethargic that Sarah had to shave and dress him.'

As the doctor spoke he slowly turned the short, square decanter from which he had poured our wine. 'This unassuming vessel held the drug,' he murmured casually, and then smiled at my wide eyes. '*O just, subtle and mighty opium!* Don't worry — it's been washed out.'

'It doesn't sound like a happy time for Sarah,' I remarked.

'No, but although he was certainly neglectful of her in practical terms, his intentions were solicitous almost to the point of obsession — the opium seemed to intensify his dedication to her even as it clouded his perception of how to act on it. And so he spent the long, silent combe days in a helpless trance of remorse, while she did her best to manage their affairs, and wrote stoic letters to friends and family.

'The story might have ended there. But in the spring of seventeen seventy, something —' he frowned, then flashed the smile '— *something* changed. "By what cause," wrote the reluctant Hartley, "and from what sweet dreg of vitality does an old stump throw a shoot?" For no identifiable reason he found himself able to reduce his dose, and began at last to make plans, receive old friends and restore his fragile health. Sarah persuaded him that they should spend the summer in London, where he could meet people, share ideas and put his renewed energy to good use. Of course she herself was eager to escape the combe, which, though she had loved it at first, had become like a prison to her.'

The doctor finished his meal with slow, precise, sweeps of his fork, and then we rose and cleared away the plates. 'He used to carry it about the house with him, just like this,' he remarked, casually cradling the neck of the decanter between his fingers as we moved into the library, where we sat beneath Sarah's portrait with the lights very low and her husband's white face gazing out of the shadows.

'The trip began well,' he resumed, relaxing into his armchair with a long sigh. 'Hartley was introduced to the Royal Society and gave a short lecture on his astronomical observations. One Fellow recalled hearing the story of the bet, and asked him to explain how he had predicted the magnitude of the eclipse. He also surprised the Dilettanti, who had long given up on him, with an illustrated essay describing his search for the tomb of Mausolus.

'After these exertions his laudanum doses once more increased, and Sarah struggled to keep him active and reasonable. One June night, as they walked back from the theatre to their rooms near Lincoln's Inn, they passed a scuffle at the door of a tavern and a dishevelled young man, having been ejected forcefully by the landlord, fell against Sarah and almost knocked her down. "Sixpence will be small enough comfort," he shouted back through the door, dusting himself off, "when thou art dead and damned!" Then turning to Sarah he offered an unexpectedly eloquent apology in his quaint west-country accent.

'"What's your name?" asked Hartley, looking him up and down.

'"I have furnished this fair damoisel with the only redress I have to offer," returned the man, or boy, with gallant defiance.

'"I know," said Hartley, kindly, "but I'm curious to know your name."

'He called it out proudly as he walked away, adding, "You will hear it again, perhaps!"

'In fact Hartley saw him the next day in a coffee house, and they had the first of a series of discussions. The boy was twenty at most but apparently already a prolific journalist, and he claimed to be interested in the recent Boston troubles and the American cause, and a staunch supporter of one of Hartley's old heroes, the radical John Wilkes. Hartley was further intrigued to learn that he wrote plays and poems, some of which, when he was shown them, he thought "entertaining and not without merit".

'One poem was very different from the rest — the boy claimed he had not composed but merely *transcribed* it, having found it with many others in a loft in his native town. Hartley didn't believe him, but this only sharpened his curiosity. "This *ballade*," he wrote, "was at first quite unintelligible. But as I formed the words a music seemed to arise from it, and it was the music that carried the visions, but then there *was* no music. It was a thing as close to magick as I dare to countenance."

'He observed in the boy the creative energy that he himself had lost, and determined to help him. He offered to find him commissions in the pro-American press, and wrote to friends who might be inclined to publish the strange poetry. But now the boy's attitude changed — first reluctant to accept help and then openly hostile. "You might spare your sweat for your own works," he snapped at last, "where it seems to be most wanted." Hartley returned some harsh words and left him. That ballad, I might add, is still in print today, which is more than can be said for any of my ancestor's writings — although they found success enough in other ways.

'By early August most clubs and societies had followed Parliament's example and closed for the summer, and many of Hartley's old acquaintances had left town. He and Sarah prepared to return home. "These past few weeks a shadow has fallen between us," he wrote. "The foreshadow, it may be, of our own future existence, which holds little enough promise for man or wife."

'They had been back in the combe for two weeks when Hartley, slumped at a mass of papers in his study — now my study — noticed a familiar hand among the pile of post brought by the maid. It was a letter from the young journalist.'

The doctor drained his glass, set it down gently on the side-table, laced his fingers and smiled at me in the gloom.

'And that was the letter?' I prompted, impatiently. 'The one I'm looking for?'

'Yes.'

'And — what did it say?' I asked, laughing at his keeping me in suspense.

'Oh come now,' he said, rising slowly to his feet. 'You wouldn't want me to spoil it, would you? I'm relying on curiosity to motivate your diligence. In any case, if I knew exactly what it said, I wouldn't have written those advertisements and you would still be a banker.' With that, he led me out to the hall.

'Answer me one last question,' I said, as he held open the massive door. 'Was the letter in any way connected to Hartley's establishment of the library, or his building of the temple?'

'Or the rescue of his health and marriage, or the writing of his most influential works?' added the doctor, quickly. 'Your memory for dates is admirable, Mr Browne. Good night!' Then I witnessed another demonstration of the mystical properties of doors: he closed it and we were both instantly alone.

14

As we know, there was a telephone in the cottage — half-buried under coats and scarves in the little hallway — and I had used it once to give my parents a brief report of my experiences so far. But my voice carried through the stone-silent cottage though I lowered it almost to a whisper, and I could feel the presence of M'Synder's sharp and expectant ears — so I kept it brief. She, perhaps guessing my predicament, presented me with a writing pad whose cover was yellowed with age, and a rather fine old fountain pen that I had to refuse, being left-handed. The first three handwritten letters of my adult life (not counting that mad reply extracted by Sarah) were composed on her writing-plank in the parlour and addressed to my parents, my brother, and a friend who had consoled me the previous autumn, and contained brief, experimental sketches of the people, places and impressions with which you are now familiar. My father, at least, seemed to appreciate this effort, for he sent a cheery reply by return of post, in the looping black handwriting that I had admired as a child and assumed I would one day acquire, but never did.

Thus I deliberately acknowledged the existence of the profane world, and, I suppose, the nonsensical story-so-far of my own life. The trance of diligence was like Hartley's opium trance in that it did not hide my predicament, and that tantalising *adjustment* of the disordered residue came in fits and starts that often left me restless and doubting.

But let me try a different metaphor: a man can redirect the course of his life by a simple act of will, but it is more likely to be changed by collisions — collisions with events, with accident or illness, with the unpredictable contents of books, or, most propitiously, with the lives of others. And I had not been so bounced about for years (maybe that's what I meant by the vacuum). I suppose I felt like a pinball charged with momentum just as it had been about to fall between the paddles, and now I wanted more. As I dropped my father's attractive but unhelpful letter into the drawer, I remembered The Croked Hand.

Monday evening was clear and still, and the rising moon beamed from a shoal of tiny clouds over the village as I made my way down the lane after supper. The low light struck a gentle relief across the graveyard, highlighting the weathered profiles of the stones and lovingly drawing out their shadows in charcoal over the faintly iridescent tufts of silver grass. Around the village green, unseen lights yellowed the edges of curtains and narrow shafts of coal smoke rose straight from chimneys without troubling the chill, clean air below. I thought I heard the distant clatter of a railway, carrying across the silent miles of fields and hedgerows and deserted farmyards.

At the door I struggled again with the brass hand, but at last felt the upturned thumb give way stiffly to lift the latch. The door opened into an unlit porch (not a vestibule, I thought), half-filled by a bulging cocoon of coats hanging on the inner door, and I stepped forward into a public house rather smaller than M'Synder's parlour. The air was warm and heavy with pipe and cigarette smoke, and the pale ruins of a huge fire glimmered beneath a long mantel loaded with books and old trophies. There were four round tables — three

174

small ones and a larger one nestling in the bow window — and pictures of village sports teams and odd bits of brass crowded the walls and the sides of the low, crooked ceiling beams.

At one table sat a man with white curly hair and a plump red face — something like Dylan Thomas had he lived to sixty — and at another sat a younger man, furtive and wiry in scruffy work clothes. Each had a partially consumed pint and his smoking paraphernalia arranged solemnly before him. A woman laid her own cigarette carefully on an ashtray on the bar, slipped down from a barstool and looked me up and down. She too was at least sixty, I suppose, but wore jeans and boots to show off a good figure, half-moon reading glasses on a chain, and lipstick that she just about carried off.

'Good evening,' she said in a husky, theatrical drawl, and it was only when she turned to the bar that I saw the long iron-grey plait and recognised her as the mysterious organist who never emerged from her shadowy nest at the side of the church. 'What can I get you, young man?' she asked. 'Cup of cocoa?'

So I spent a strange couple of hours outside the combe, or rather in a kind of alternative combe, for The Croked Hand was a sanctuary too, and a cul-de-sac of sorts. Agnes, the landlady, was not only the organist but the church warden too (surely M'Synder was a more likely candidate for that role), and had inherited the pub from her parents. The older patron was introduced to me as The Borrowed Man, because, as he cheerfully explained, he was terminally ill and living on borrowed time. 'I'm six months in the red,' he added proudly, draining his glass, 'and I don't intend to pay it back.' The younger man was a tattooed Scot named Rab, who drove milk tankers but had been in the army ('Aye, Tank Regiment,' he said, drily).

'And you?' asked Agnes. 'Just passing through?'

'I'm working for Doctor Comberbache up at the Hall,' I replied.

'Oh yes,' she said quickly, her eyes twinkling. 'I remember now — the Man from London. Paperwork isn't it?' I nodded. 'Legal stuff?'

'Not exactly —'

'Well,' she went on, 'don't let him work you too hard — we're not all scribbling recluses!' Her manner recalled the note I had seen in the doctor's study, with the hoofprint signature. Agnes, Agnus: it could have been a lamb's hoof, after all.

The two men had a couple of pints' headstart on me, and took turns telling me things they had already told each other too many times. The borrowed man, whose real name was Gabriel, was friendly at first but gradually subsided into a silent slump, while Rab started surly but became talkative. Both accepted my shyness and lack of wit as qualifications, as mere paraphernalia laid on the table alongside their own failings and their tobacco. The eye of the jay could not reach me here.

'Had a wife,' said Rab in summary, studying his bitten-down thumbnails as he rolled another cigarette, 'had a kid, drove a tank, did some time. Now I sit and drink piss wi' a borrowed man.'

'Watch that,' warned Agnes, raising a finger. The ale was called Bachebrook, supposedly because it had once been watered down from the combe's stream, which bore that name and passed behind the pub. 'Nothing wrong with it these days,' she added. 'I test it regularly for strength, freshness and flavour.'

'Don't we all,' said the borrowed man, mournfully. At ten past nine a stumping tread stopped outside the door. 'Harry o'clock,' muttered Rab, looking at his watch and kicking an empty chair into the space by the fire. Agnes opened the door for an ancient man with one leg, who stood his crutches against the chimneypiece, sat down heavily without a word and gazed into the fire through huge round glasses. Agnes brought him half a pint, which he drank in small sips over the course of about five minutes, then reached for the crutches, stood up on his one wobbling leg and shuffled out.

'Tractor accident,' explained Rab.

'Nineteen eighty-eight,' added the borrowed man. 'And he was an old bastard then.'

'Hasn't missed his half-pint since — isn't that right Agnes?'

'Yes, although we did have to carry it over the green a few times when he was poorly.'

'But he doesn't talk?' I asked. They all looked at each other mysteriously.

'Och, sometimes he talks,' murmured the Scot, flicking his cigarette-end into the fire. But during my stay in the combe I never heard Harry utter a word.

15

The last case beneath the gallery, tucked into the corner and part-obscured by the curtain of the side window, was quite out of sequence in my 'journey through civilisation' — it was filled with books about climbing mountains.

'This is the only section that postdates the prudish prune in its entirety,' the doctor had said on Monday morning, 'so I think it can be safely passed over.'

'What was here before, then?' I asked.

'Exactly what I was wondering,' he replied, frowning. 'I suspect my father made some rather drastic cuts among the worst of the theology department. We must hope that Hartless had enough heart to spare those delicate volumes the keeping of the scandal — I think it is a safe assumption.'

I had been reluctant to interrupt my ruthless campaign of diligence, but had accepted the doctor's argument and transferred my search to the slender, full-height column of books between the side window and Sarah's fireplace, which contained volumes of letters, diaries and memoirs. The collection continued to fascinate me: here, after all, was another miracle of compression — hundreds of lives trying to make sense of themselves, turned in upon themselves but each thrusting out a hand and waving a pen towards the rest of humanity. But the search! The search was by now testing my last resources of patience, curiosity and pride. I had completely worn away the prints on my thumbs, which were now hard, shiny talons, and I began to feel pricking, twitching pains along my fingers as my body protested against the repeated commands of my will — or rather, I reflected mutinously, the commands of the doctor's will. For how much longer would I obey?

On the fourth shelf, on Tuesday morning, I noticed the diary of Hartley himself in three inconspicuous black volumes ('three lives,' the doctor had said), and, rushing rather roughly through the preceding books in my eagerness to see it, I lost my grip on the second volume of John Evelyn, a heavy quarto published in eighteen eighteen, which fell twelve feet onto a standing lamp, which in turn toppled with a crash upon the hearth fender. Meanwhile I had instinctively snatched for the book and almost lost my balance, and now clung to the ladder like a very cross child stuck up a tree.

'Everything alright?' asked the doctor calmly from his study door.

'I dropped one,' I snapped.

'Biblioclast! Well, I'm glad to see you're human.' He approached the site of the disaster and stooped stiffly to pick up the projectile: the spine was torn halfway down and the front cover bent. 'From fine to fair in one fell swoop — or should that be one swooping fall? This would now be described as a *reading copy*, I believe.'

Looking down at this gentle and learned old man (for so he seemed at that moment) I felt my allegiance return. My labours were rewarded, just as his advertisement had promised. 'I am sorry,' I said, creeping rather unsteadily down the ladder.

'Think nothing of it, Mr Browne,' he said, handing the book up to me. 'Reading copies are all I need in my library.' At the door he

turned and added, 'No need to search that next diary, by the way —
it has already been well thumbed!'

I had a quick look anyway, of course. There was no inscription,
only a short editor's preface: *'This private diary was my father's property
and then my mother's, but I do not see how it can rightly be mine. I
therefore half humbly and half proudly offer it to the reading nation, the
value of plain truth being universal. Samuel T. Comberbache, 1825.'*

The first volume covered his youth and travels, and the second
his London career and subsequent decline, from seventeen sixty-two
to August seventeen seventy. Presumably the opening pages of the
third would shed more light on the letter and its aftermath, but I
took the doctor's parting comment as clarification that this would
contravene the rules of the game, and passed over it.

The frosts returned and became heavier during that fifth week,
accompanied first by mists that lingered all day and night, and then
by sleet and chill breezes that slid malevolently down the hill from
the north. I worked with the library's chandeliers blazing all day while
beyond the windows the garden lay under a gloomy pall of freezing
fog, as though morning had forgotten to break. Whenever I had to
venture outside I wore the nailed boots and all my warm clothes.

M'Synder was an uncomplicated companion in the evenings,
confining her conversation to the worsening weather, the chores
she had done or that needed doing and the critical appraisal of her
own excellent cooking. Occasionally she could be drawn into other
subjects, and one evening after two glasses of punch she surprised
me with a confidence about her own past — the first since she had
told me about answering the advert in the post office. We had been
talking about Rose, whose latest letter from boarding school had
arrived that morning.

'I'll tell you a funny thing, Mr Browne,' she said, thoughtfully stroking the cat after supper. 'I'll tell you because I'm not ashamed of it: my husband left me because I couldn't have children. Of course, at first we didn't know which of us was *to blame* — the doctors couldn't find anything wrong with me, and he refused to be tested. At least, he refused to be tested by a doctor — in the end he had the bright idea of testing himself on another woman and came up trumps, so it was "goodbye Sara".' She looked steadily down at the indifferent cat. The clock ticked.

'What a — *medieval* thing to do,' I said, uncomfortably.

'Well, swapping us was the best thing he could do by then,' she went on, 'and it served me right for marrying him. He always was a hard man. Uncompromising. Dunna ask me why I fell for that sort.' Decisive, I thought, like someone I once knew. Not like me — I couldn't even decide whether at last to tell my own parallel story. I kept silent. 'I took back my own name,' she added. 'Funnily enough he was a Brown, like you.' Oh God, I thought, you must be joking.

'*Ee?*' I asked, grimly.

'Nope,' she replied, smiling. 'That's why I'm especially fond of yours.'

By Friday the combe was glazed with mingled frost and sleet, and the stream had frozen thickly for the second time. The snow came that night, this time not cluster by cluster straight down but swirling and stinging, plastering walls and windows and the windward halves of tree trunks and streaming past my torchbeam in twisting strands over the lane. By the morning it had drifted to the window ledges on one side of the cottage.

I fought my way outside and tried to repeat my previous ascent to the snowy Argo, but the sleet scoured and needled my face and I turned back soon after the tree line. I sat in the parlour and read *A Night in the Snow*, a brief and microscopically detailed story of survival that in other circumstances might have seemed comical: '*I continued my tremendous glissade head downward, lying on my back,*' writes the earnest Reverend. '*The pace I was going in this headlong descent must have been very great, yet it seemed to me to occupy a marvellous space of time ...*' I glanced out of the window at the steep hillside looming into the storm, and shuffled my chair closer to the fire.

As dusk fell and the wind whistled on, I went upstairs to fetch my notebook. From the landing I thought I could hear slow, heavy footsteps in the snow, and wiped the slush of condensation from the stingingly cold window to peer into the lane. A dark, long-legged figure was trudging past towards the house, stooping into the blizzard and carrying a huge rucksack. A hood was drawn close around his face, but as I watched he seemed to look up at the window and slowly raised a gloved hand, the fist clenched in triumph or in determination. I raised my own hand in reply. It was as though the fading running man, the doctor's son, had turned away from death-without-issue and was fighting his way back into the sacred combe.

PART 3

THE
ROUNDELAY

See three tiny figures, black against a blue-white canvas of shaded snow: their skis make them look like upside-down 'T's. Now see them close up: man, woman, child, poling gracefully, effortlessly along a vast, gently sloping shelf of snow between the rippling, yawning, sinister glacier below, and the cliffs towering behind.

Then the child falls over. Just tips harmlessly onto her side like a beginner. The woman waves a pole wildly to keep her own balance, then looks back and stops. The man has stopped too, troubled by a momentary feeling of drunkenness that has now gone.

'What was that?' asks the woman, her voice dull in the still, cold, early-morning air. The child is struggling to her feet. The man lifts his visor and looks up.

Curls of steam — not steam, of course, but snow — are rising silently into the morning sun near the summit. The precipitous upper slopes look blurred, and he squints, trying to focus. Comprehension and adrenaline strike him just before the first sound, which is the deep, sonorous crack of one massive object disengaging from another.

Which way? Onward, or back? 'Quick,' he snaps, waving

his arm. 'Move.' The others understand: they have heard it now, and propel themselves past him and along the slope. As he follows, he sees a new fracture flickering across the middle of the next gully: the whole face is giving way. 'Stop,' he shouts. 'Back. Back.'

His wife has often parodied his use of cricketing metaphors, and he murmurs one now automatically: 'Caught between the wickets.'

1

See one tiny figure, black against the speckled white and grey of a snow-filled valley, his steady progress between the roundish smoke-puffs of trees the only movement, and his faint, crunching footsteps the only sound. Now see him close up, hands and sleeves tucked into the pockets of his long coat, trousers folded neatly into his socks above the heavy boots tied with double bows, head held high and vapour playing over his lips as he talks to himself in a low voice. What is he saying? He is saying these very words — he is me, practising the telling of my own story as I go along.

I paused before the bridge and looked up at those ivy-clad, now snow-clad ash trees whose long boughs seemed to meet in an arch. 'The two appear perfectly united,' I said to myself, still practising, 'in that ancient and celebrated junction that for millennia has borne the weight of civilisation upon its shoulders. But come a little closer, look from a different angle, and — ha-ha! — it was all just an illusion: you see two bent and lonely forms, separated by a river of ice.' There is a bridge, you say — but she threw it down.

When the cordons of habit are withdrawn, the unruly forces of the mind strike out in new directions. Our own thoughts can seem almost as unfamiliar to us as our new surroundings: reason itself begins to turn in our grasp. With this in mind, I had said nothing to M'Synder about the stooping apparition in the lane but had waited for some verification of the visitor's substance. None came on Sunday, except that I thought I could just make out the dimpled remnant of his footprints in the shifting snow.

Now it was Monday, the footprints were gone, and when the doctor opened the door he made no mention of a new guest in the house. I began to suspect I really had imagined him, invoked him from the relics laid out in the locked room, and wondered whether the mental challenges of my occupation and circumstances were exacting tolls beyond my meagre budget.

I worked hard that day nevertheless, and early the following morning I finished searching the great corner bookcase by the window, opposite the one where my labours had begun five weeks before. I estimated that I had searched about nine thousand volumes on nearly five hundred feet of shelves: now only the gallery — the works of the imagination, exalted above all others — remained. I edged up the spiral stair to survey the field.

Exalted it might be, but this collection was not so much used by the present owner, and not so well organised as the rest. The doctor had told me that Stella, and before her Catherine and Samuel, had been the great readers (and writers) of poetry and fiction, while he himself, as I had observed, mounted the stairs only occasionally, perhaps to fetch a bundle of scripts or libretti, or some sheet music of Mozart, which seemed to be relevant to his book.

'I suppose I thought my mother would have found the letter if it were up there,' he had muttered apologetically the day before. 'So I approved of the scheme of your search and, alas! perhaps encouraged it, thus falling headlong into my uncle's trap. I'm afraid you have paid the price.'

Now I wandered along the narrow gallery, agonising over whether to start at the left-hand extremity or the right. I had reached the end of the shorter walkway, next to Hartley's portrait, when I heard the soft click of a latch, followed by a dull jarring impact as a door swung open and struck the alcove. After a few shuffling footsteps, the intruder, who had entered from the dining room, emerged from under the gallery directly beneath my feet. I saw a shock of curly brown hair, and then, as he padded rather haltingly to the window, the back of a slim young man in a silk dressing gown. He stood there for a while with hands on his hips, quietly humming a tune in which I thought I recognised that same four-note theme that Meaulnes had whistled in the drive.

'Good morning,' I said, and he spun round.

'Holy Jesus, we have a bogey at six o'clock!' he cried, glancing around wildly and snatching up the only available weapon — a cushion from the sill.

'I'm the archivist,' I pleaded, ducking behind the railing, 'working for Doctor Comberbache.'

'Well done,' he said, now in a muffled voice as though speaking pained him. He dropped the cushion and raised a hand gingerly to his mouth. 'You managed to say the name with a straight face. Actually my sister left a letter for me, and she mentioned you.' I frowned.

'Oh, you mean Juliet!' I said, comprehending and straightening up. 'She mentioned you too. The — erm — drifting brother.'

'I'll give her drifting. Corvin is my name.'

It was only when I climbed down to meet him that I noticed the state of his face, which was burned bright red. His lips were chapped and badly split and the skin around his eyes and nostrils was raw and dry. His hair corkscrewed out crazily as though he had been the victim of some slapstick explosion. He was my age or a little older, and narrowed his brown eyes as he shook my hand with an easy, unconscious firmness.

'Sorry for appearing in this dishevelled condition,' he said. 'I've been in Scotland — in the mountains. Bit of a storm up there. Can't shave at the moment — my whole face would come off.'

'You weren't camping in this weather?' I said.

'Bivouacking,' he replied. 'Bothies, caves, hollow trees — whatever I could find.'

'How long for?'

'A week longer than expected. Now come and have a coffee or something.' In the kitchen he poured a whole pint of milk into a beer glass and sipped at it while I made my coffee on the hob. 'I'm building myself up,' he explained. 'Lost over a stone — got in a bit of a mess up there and ran out of provisions. Whereas you've had a full month of M'Synder! You're carrying it well, though.'

We sat in the library, Corvin wheeling two chairs round to face the great window and propping his slippered feet on the sill (as if he owned the place, I thought). The square lawn was by now a vast white map on which the intersecting courses of birds and squirrels lay painstakingly charted, as though it mattered whether a blackbird turned left or right in its vain search for an edible morsel, as though the straight, purposeful line of the fox were a pioneering passage that would ever after have borne his name, if he had only had one. Around the perimeter, on the buried paths, the straight, loping gait of Meaulnes was trodden and re-trodden like a decorative border. What name would we inscribe with flourishes along the terrace as the title of the piece? *A night in the snow*? I don't think the Reverend would mind.

'I hope you find this letter,' said Corvin, gently wiping milk

192

from his damaged lips and producing a tin of Vaseline from his dressing-gown pocket. 'I want to read it myself.'

'Everyone knows about it, then,' I said.

'Of course,' he replied indistinctly, dabbing the Vaseline and contorting his face like a clown applying make-up. His slim fingers were the only thing about his appearance that reminded me of Juliet, but the knuckles were marked by scabs and grazes, as though he had been breaking rocks. 'It's the Comberbache family legend: the scandalous last letter of Thomas Furey.'

Here was the key fact that the doctor had chosen to withhold, casually tossed in my lap by his son's wife's brother. *Furey*: another outlandish name, but half-familiar. Wasn't he a poet? Perhaps the doctor had thought I'd guess the name from the date and circumstances, but I was too ignorant — and of course I can't read poetry. In any case, either Corvin was unaware of the rules of the game or he simply disregarded them.

'The doctor's given me some background,' I said, coolly. 'It sounds fascinating.'

'Oh, all the ingredients are there,' he went on. 'Sex, drugs, lies, Chaucerian poetry. Just don't tell the tabloids — Arnold really wouldn't like that.' I knew about the drugs, but nothing else: didn't Chaucer belong to a rather different era? Then I remembered that Hartley had described the boy's ballad as unintelligible. I would consult the encyclopaedia of English literature, and then perhaps I would dare to cast myself on the poetry shelves' mercy.

I was weighing my next comment when a movement drew our eyes to the end of the lawn. The doctor emerged from the rhododendron gate and walked slowly and stiffly along the icy perimeter path towards the house. He was wearing a three-quarter-length coat and Wellingtons, and carrying a walking stick of which, however, he made only light use. In the other leather-gloved hand he dangled the grey woollen cap with the earflaps. It was the first time I had seen him outside the house.

'Speak of the devil,' said Corvin. 'Or rather, the pilgrim returns.'

The doctor stopped to knock old snow off a couple of shrubs with his stick, looked back up at the hills and the leaden sky with the familiar squinting smile, then turned to the house and noticed us at the window. He slowly raised the stick in greeting.

M'Synder roasted another pheasant that evening, and the dining room once again assumed its formal guise, lit by tall candles and a well-stocked fire. Corvin had dressed in dark pressed trousers and a white shirt which lent a comic intensity to his glowing, windburnt face. He did not seem to feel the cold.

'Corvin,' said the doctor, 'perhaps you would do us the honour of saying Grace.'

'Certainly,' he replied. Like Rose, he left a moment's silence, lifting his hands solemnly from his knife and fork. 'Ready?' he said suddenly. 'Go!' With that he snatched up the cutlery and began to attack his food. The doctor shook his head indulgently and followed suit.

Corvin, I now learned, was two years my senior, had studied history at Oxford, and had then trained at Dartmouth and served in the Royal Navy for four years (a fact perhaps not entirely incidental to Rose's ambition, I thought).

'Believe it or not,' said the doctor to me, 'the clownish figure seated opposite you was the navigation officer onboard the first minesweeper to enter the port of Umm Qasr during the invasion of Iraq. The lives of dozens, perhaps hundreds of men depended on him. Now he tests his skills in the highlands.'

'And is found wanting,' added Corvin ruefully. 'I had a relapse of that incurable disease, complacency.'

'What were you doing up there?' I asked. 'Just walking?'

'Walking was a means to an end,' he replied. 'I was working on a little research project I began last summer. Boring stuff, really — nothing much to say about it.'

'Research project!' scoffed the doctor. 'You'll have to do better than that. My suspicion,' he said confidingly to me, 'is that Corvin has found some sort of cave miles from civilisation — in an *indeducible* location, one might say — and is busy converting it into a luxurious hermitage — without troubling to notify the landowner, of course. But he will tell me nothing.' The young man ate voraciously, responding with only a wry smile. 'I hope you are not intending to carry your secret to the grave,' added the doctor. 'What a waste that would be!'

'Oh, I shan't do that,' he replied, draining his glass and reaching for the carafe. 'Perhaps I'll write it down — leave a coded message that some suitable person might understand. Directions. A grid reference.'

'Something Uncle Hartley seems to have omitted to do,' I said. 'But I suppose we are not suitable people, by his measure.' The doctor studied his empty plate in silence for a moment.

'Indeed we are not,' he said quietly, without looking up. 'But we are meeting his hostility face to face across the intervening years, and we shall find the letter. We are close now.' The fire shifted and a coal dropped through the grate with a soft clang.

2

Wednesday was the first fine day for over a week, and the combe shone. The robin was waiting for me outside the cottage, looking rather thin and weathered like Corvin but rejoicing now, escorting me along the lane and singing herald-like from every glistening perch, while for the first time he was answered by the cheerful little car alarms of great tits and the shrill wheezings of finches in the woods. The house lay under its morning pall of shadow, but the sun had already brushed its hand reassuringly over the highest branches of the beech: spring itself was not in the air, but the memory of spring had awakened.

'We're going out!' cried Corvin, striding into the library as I opened a volume of Scottish folksongs. 'It's been approved: stamped, sealed, ratified, given the nod.' He lounged back against the table — another faint family resemblance — and looked up at me expectantly.

'What on earth are you wearing?' I asked. 'You look like a —' Words failed me.

'A pantisocratist!' he beamed, slapping his thigh on the first syllable. 'Or should that be pantisocrat? I didn't bring any decent clothes so I'm borrowing some.' He had chosen to borrow a pair of tweed trousers of a particularly bold weave and close cut, a frilled, high-collared shirt, a buff waistcoat and a cravat — the red face and chaotic hair he already possessed. 'Anyway, life's more fun when you dress up for it. Come on!'

The intricate white map was being steadily consumed, burning away to ashes of wet green turf as the shadow of the house retreated, and the air was full of the fresh, damp smell of thaw. A songthrush hopped about excitedly, a fellow searcher-for-treasure showing off her own long-practised method of indiscriminate Brownian motion.

'I've known Arnold since my first term at Oxford,' said Corvin, leading me slowly around the water garden where rounded panes of ice still floated in the pools and snow lingered on the stone seats and the twisted boughs of the star-tree. 'Sam and Julie had married a couple of years earlier, and Sam told me his dad was visiting the Bodleian to celebrate his retirement and would like to meet me — we had a strange encounter in the White Horse. He was dressed something like I am now and talked about the narrative of life. Afterwards, I wondered if I'd dreamt it.'

We crossed the grove, where the vanguard of flattened snowdrops were busy picking themselves up while the next battalion, the tight-budded crocus shoots, sounded the advance.

'Tell me more about Sam,' I said, as we started up the hillside. 'If you don't mind, I mean.' Corvin frowned for a moment, but he was just deciding where to begin.

'He took me climbing on Ben Nevis before the wedding, when I was sixteen. The North-East Buttress. I was terrified — of the climb and of Sam too, I suppose, and trying not to show it. He didn't speak much — just a few words of encouragement when I hesitated. I remember those pale smiling eyes and his quick, effortless handling of the rope on the steeper sections. The sense of joy was infectious — nothing else seemed to matter.

'Near the top there's a notorious little step called the Mantrap that forced many early climbers into dangerous retreats, especially in winter — Sam's grandfather famously climbed it by standing on his partner's head in nailed boots. Sam made me go up it first, of course — he didn't believe in easy introductions or making allowances.'

'*In medias res*,' I suggested.

'Exactly. Funnily enough, I used the same climbing move a few years later when we had a class-alpha fire during exercises in the Gulf, to free a hose caught on a stanchion — the CO was most impressed. But you didn't ask me about that. Sam. Julie had met Sam in London shortly after she gave up performing and started teaching — he was a junior doctor working long hours in the wards and studying mountain medicine on his days off. Blonde, beautiful, with boundless energy — already a brilliant mountaineer but with no time to escape the city.

'A few years after they were married — about the time I met Arnold in the White Horse — Julie was appointed head of music at a good school in Derbyshire so they moved north. Sam gave up formal medicine, became a freelance first aid instructor and joined the local mountain rescue team. The following year he and Adam Forester — Rose's father — climbed what had been called the 'last great problem' on Ben Nevis, and named it *The Temple*. They also pioneered tough, long routes in the Alps and elsewhere.'

Corvin now turned off the main path, and after climbing a few steep steps we found ourselves at the foot of one of the colossal redwoods. He patted its giant hairy root as one might pat a favourite horse.

'Talking of which, how are you with heights?' he asked, with a mischievous smile.

'Getting better,' I said, thinking of the accursed ladder.

'Good. Then you won't want to miss this. Look up there.' I craned my neck and gave a groan of dismay: I could see a kind of treehouse hidden in the rich foliage. It must have been sixty or eighty feet above the ground.

'How on earth —' I murmured.

'Elevators,' he said, triumphantly. 'Two of them.' He led me round the back of the tree, where a series of thick, taut ropes were secured to steel rings bolted to the roots. 'I reckon you're a bit heavier than me, so you have the twelve-stone lift, and I'll have the eight and do a bit of hauling. Sam made all this — it's quite safe if you use it sensibly.'

Eventually I was persuaded to stand on a wooden platform rather smaller than M'Synder's writing plank, attach a steel clip to my belt and hold a fixed line while Corvin did likewise and pushed two levers to release the ropes.

'Now try pulling yourself up,' he said, grinning, 'and we'll see what M'Synder's cooking has done to you.' I pulled down on the rope, and to my horror began to rise from the ground as if gravity had given me up. Corvin kept level with me by hauling himself hand over hand, while the ground dropped away and the counterweights — two small bulging sacks — drifted down past us. He assured me the pulleys had a mechanism like that on a seatbelt, which stopped them running too fast. 'Of course, sometimes the buggers get stuck halfway,' he added casually, 'and then the real fun begins.'

The treehouse encircled the mighty trunk, and was enclosed on the west side and furnished with a curving table and matching bench; from the windows one peered through foliage up the hillside towards the Temple of Light, whose pointed prow was from here outlined against the sky. On the east side an open balcony commanded a magnificent view down the combe, but a great shaggy branch obscured the garden and all but the highest windows of the house.

'This is where I like to come sometimes,' announced Corvin simply, leaning his hands confidently on the wooden parapet. 'Sam built it for Julie but she never quite had the head for it.'

'It does look like he got a bit carried away.'

'Like Hartley and his temple?' he said. 'Or Arnold and the Attic *oenochoe* — the vase? *To surprise by a fine excess* — that is expected here.' He peered down at the bristling chimneys and gables of the house, and the single thin spectre of smoke. 'You've come at rather a sad time, though — it was a magical place ten years ago. There were big, sprawling gatherings at Christmas or Easter or midsummer: guests would come and go as they pleased — Sam and Julie, my parents, the Foresters, Arnold's eccentric old friends-of-the-family. I would often crash the party with a couple of lucky college friends. We'd stay in those attic rooms' — he pointed at the little gable windows — 'which are full of amazing old junk, like the musket balls Sam used for the counterweights. Old Meaulnes the gardener — you've heard about him? — would rig up awnings and ancient bunting in the garden, get drunk and recite Baudelaire from the top of a wall, while his son dressed up little Rose as a garden fairy and sent her to spy on us from the bushes. And of course Arnold would preside: the all-seeing Magus, brimming with quiet energy.'

Now his face fell and he looked at me as though deciding whether to go on. 'Everything changed in May ninety-eight. It was the day before the start of my finals — Julie called me to save me finding out from the newspapers, but I didn't hear the full story until much later. Adam, Pippa and Rose had been cross-country skiing near Chamonix, and by chance Sam was there too, running a course on mountain rescue. The Foresters were caught in a massive freak avalanche set off by an earth tremor. Sam was on the first helicopter to arrive, only minutes later. He spotted Rose's red scarf just under the snow and managed to dig her out, unconscious but alive. During his frantic digging he had struck her face with the edge of his shovel, and by the time he finally resuscitated her they were both covered in blood. The bodies of Adam and Pippa were recovered some time later — they were buried much more deeply but only a few yards apart. In those last minutes they wouldn't have been aware of each other, which could I suppose be considered a small mercy. It's a death better not imagined.'

He stared out along the thawing combe as I kept my well-practised silence, then turned suddenly and put a slim, calloused hand on my shoulder as he showed me the way down.

3

Following our wobbly descent, Corvin offered me a choice of routes back to the house and I selected the path along the meadow and through the rose garden, reversing my first tour of the grounds. There in Rose's walled domain we found Meaulnes, holding a pair of long-handled loppers in a pose of concentrated expectation, as one might hold a partner before the dance begins. As we watched he stooped over a gnarly old bush, amputated a sizeable limb and without looking lobbed it in a high arc into his waiting barrow, which received it with a deep, booming clang. When he saw us he smiled and saluted cheerfully.

'Hello, old chap,' said Corvin, squinting up at him.

'Monsieur,' he replied grandly, sweeping off an earthy glove and shaking his hand. 'Welcome back.' He gave me a respectful nod.

'I have to say I'm very disappointed in you, old chap,' said Corvin, sternly. Meaulnes' dark brows curled upward in a look of comic horror.

'Mais pourquoi?' he demanded.

'Look at this place,' complained the pantisocratist, waving his arms and then planting them on his hips. 'Everything's dead. Not a single bloody leaf anywhere. And this nasty white stuff all over the place. Let's face it — the whole garden's gone to the rack since I was last here.'

'But Monsieur,' said Meaulnes, smiling nervously, 'that was in June! I cannot stop the seasons turning.'

'So I see,' muttered Corvin contemptuously, before breaking into a broad grin and immediately clapping his hand to his mouth as his chapped lip split again.

Meaulnes asked us if we wanted to help with pruning the orchard that afternoon, and Corvin assented without hesitation. 'Don't worry,' he said to me gravely, 'I'll clear it with the old man.' The old man himself served us all fortifying carrot soup, and Meaulnes provided us with boots and gloves from his cobwebbed office. From the tool armoury he selected saws, loppers, secateurs and a long-handled pruning contraption that he balanced on one shoulder as we processed through the kitchen garden with handcart and ladders.

It was an afternoon rich in sensations that crowd back to me now as I recollect. The sky was perfectly cloudless, and the sun peeped over the saddle in the hills and scattered branchy shadows across our faces: Corvin's ruddy and sharp-featured, and Meaulnes' fleshy and pale with dark stubble and heavy-lidded eyes shaded by his cap, expressionless until spoken to, when he would frown and nod his head solemnly as though every word mattered.

I remember the smell of my hard-worked hands when I took them out of the ancient canvas gloves to rub flecks of bark from my eyes — old earth and sweat and something else unnameable — and the dark glint of sap-moistened steel, the blunt rim of a gardeners' mug nestling between my lips as I gulped Meaulnes' sweet tea, and the occasional calls of finches over the setting of ladders, the busy snip-snip and the dropping, gathering and stacking of switches.

The last rays of the hidden sun soon detached themselves from the snowy crest of Fern Top, and rooks gossiped in the beeches as the colourless chill of dusk settled over the combe. In fading light we trundled the laden barrows back to the yard, and the doctor came out onto the terrace in his woollen hat and served us hot cider-brandy punch. We drank a toast to a bumper crop and shook hands, and Meaulnes loped off into the darkness to make his lonely walk home.

That night I lay in the blessed silence of my room thinking again about the three moons and their dark planet, whose last bond was now explained. The jagged red line on Rose's face was another memorial, another record of action like the lines drawn on the photograph: it was not M'Synder or the doctor but Sam who had literally brought her back into the world, had furiously hacked her out of her sudden tomb to confront a strange new life among half-familiar faces. And after one touch of chance (not *il fato*, remember, but the chance of the moment: *il caso*) had unwrapped her scarf as she tumbled over and over and left it strung out towards the light, another had nudged the flashing steel towards her unseen, unseeing face.

Now her orphan's scar of grief seemed like a memorial to the wrong man, a man whose memorials were everywhere, while the memory of her own beloved parents lay trapped inside her just as their bodies had lain frozen inside a thousand tons of snow. Or so I speculated, shuddering and wrapping the blankets tight as two owls began calling to each other in the woods. I hoped I would see her again, but feared it too.

The next morning I was back at the shelves after my day off in the fresh air. I spent a few hours working through the music section, which I associated with Juliet, who had offered to search it, but also with her brother. The echoes of music that seemed to follow Corvin were produced not by his slender fingers but by the grace of his movements: the one quality that I envied him from our first meeting was that of *physical repose*. He was rarely calculating in his words but never in his movements — his slim body turned and drifted effortlessly without the intervention of thought, making mine, with its creaking knees and big nervous hands, feel like a reluctantly reanimated host. 'No wonder his wife left him,' you are perhaps thinking, and maybe I am selling myself short: I'm a sound enough physical specimen and those creaking joints can even cut a few dance moves when lubricated by alcohol, but this was another case of suffering by comparison — of being shown up.

At last I reached the poetry shelves and cast my eye along the rippling, intimidating spines. I was by now familiar with the library's chronological system — books were ordered roughly according to the author's first date of publication. 'Each branch of civilisation follows its own narrative,' the doctor had told me. 'The letter "A" has no claim to pre-eminence, nor have Zola and Zwingli, as far as I know, any common cause for shame.'

I found Furey on the fourth shelf down, between James Beattie and George Crabbe. I had expected one or two slim volumes — the encyclopaedia had told me he died aged just seventeen — but instead there were nearly a dozen rather stout ones: two copies of *Poems Supposed to Have Been Written by Thomas Dowley*; *The Works of Thomas Furey* in three pristine octavos; *Miscellanies in Prose and Verse by Thomas Furey*; *Furey's Poetical Works with an Essay by Walter Smeat* in two green volumes; *Furey's Dowley Poems* and several others. The boy's letter would not, of course, be hidden among his own verses — unless by some facile double bluff — but I searched anyway.

Since for two centuries Combe Hall's collection had apparently been pruned as it grew, had been compressed and recompressed until the shelves groaned with density just like the knotty espaliers of Meaulnes' orchard, it held multiple editions only if there was a good reason — a *narrative*. What was the story here? On the title page of the first edition of the *Poems* Hartley had written a hurried inscription, now fading: '*When we are gone, the words are the last bridge. If our successors keep them well, theirs shall be a boundless realm. Farewell, brilliant foolish boy that I loved.*'

Strange words caught at me as I turned the pages, whispering tangles of consonants that commanded my lips to trace them out — *enthoghteynge, upswalynge, benymmynge*: if these were the bridge, where could it lead?

As I searched and browsed the different volumes, failing to read a single poem from beginning to end but wondering what all this printing and reprinting, editing and re-editing of the same words was supposed to achieve, I realised that they were *not* the same words. For *enthoghtenyge* Smeat's Victorian edition helpfully substituted *intending*, while another edition confidently plumped for *thinking*. There were many other changes that even I could perceive — lines considered indecent (in other words, those that hit the mark) were missing, metres stumbled, rhymes rang false and the music died.

Whose words were these supposed to be? Furey had never written them (later I discovered that Smeat the distinguished philologist had contended otherwise, but, as the doctor put it to me, is it the editor's job to reverse by clumsy conjecture the stages of a poem's composition?). On the flyleaf of Smeat was written the qualification I had seen before, this time in a different hand, perhaps Stella's: '*That ye may know.*'

4

Rab the tanker-driver and Corvin greeted each other like old friends when we ducked into The Croked Hand on Saturday afternoon, and I stayed at the bar with Agnes while they caught up. She leaned across the single ale pump and studied my companion over her reading glasses with a look of amusement.

'Swinburne,' she said suddenly. 'Don't you think?' I flashed a confused smile, and she shook her head. 'Never mind. How's the good doctor this week?'

'He seems to be well,' I said. 'I haven't seen much of him, to be honest. He and Corvin spend a lot of time talking, though. I mean, they seem to get on well.'

'Do they, now?' she murmured, looking him up and down with renewed interest. At that moment he pivoted round and motioned to the back table with his glass.

'I was telling you about Sam,' he said as we sat down, 'and I might as well finish the story.' Since Wednesday we had met only briefly, though I had often heard his voice in the doctor's study or glimpsed him swaggering nonchalantly along one of the garden paths. Once I caught the slightly discomfiting wail of a violin in the hands of someone competent but out of practice.

'After the avalanche,' he began, in the more measured tone that he reserved for narrative, 'Rose went to live with Pippa's parents, and Sam and Julie got on with their lives in Derbyshire. What else can you do? Lots of people lose their best friends, after all — motorbike accident, drunken misadventure, killed in action. As for the Foresters, they died *doing something they loved* — that's the usual phrase, isn't it? At least he loved it — she preferred downhill.' This last remark, almost a joke, was murmured into his glass. It made me wince inwardly, but this was just Corvin's way — telling it, disregarding all games. Maybe he had learned it in the Navy.

'And you went to Dartmouth,' I prompted, to fill the gap.

'Yes — cut my hair and didn't see any family for a while. There was some kind of falling out with Pippa's parents — God knows why. Sam took lots of bookings for courses, I think — lost himself in work, stayed away from the crags unless he got a call-out with the MRT. I think Julie hoped he would give up climbing altogether and find something else to do, turn over a new leaf, but that winter he went up to Scotland to work with the Lochaber team and started climbing a few routes on his own. Nothing difficult, he said, just getting back in touch with the mountains, *doing something he loved*.

'The following year he began climbing hard routes solo. We don't really know how hard or how many — for the first time he kept secrets from Julie and impatiently dismissed her concerns. He went to Switzerland for a course and stayed on for several weeks without warning, presumably to climb. He starting missing call-outs, and took little interest when Rose came to the combe and refused to leave.

'What Julie didn't realise was that he was training for something. When he and Adam forced *The Temple*, the climbing fraternity had been surprised to hear that it was Adam who led through the great roof or overhang — the Pediment as it is now called, the *crux* of the route — since Sam was supposed to be the technical genius and Adam the steady hand. Adam had said it was decided by the toss of a coin the night before. The key was a short, clean wall, unclimbable in summer but sometimes glazed with a thin smear of ice emanating from a fracture in the overhang — its only line of weakness. It's what climbers call a *desperate pitch*. Now three years had passed and despite a couple of serious attempts no one had been able to repeat the climb.

'It was a fine morning in late January,' he went on, in a low voice. 'A pair of local climbers spotted Sam's body on the snow at the foot of the cliff, three hundred feet below the overhang. He had tried to self-belay but the Pediment is almost impossible to protect, and the belay had ripped out when he fell: his axes were still leashed to his wrists. Julie hadn't even known he was in Scotland.' He took another draught and gazed down at the glass. 'Of course he knew his anchors were weak, and a fall would probably be fatal.'

'Did he want to die, then?' I asked.

'I don't think so.'

'In that case, why did he do it?' Corvin seemed to acknowledge the question without responding, without suggesting that he did or did not know the answer.

'That's really as far as the story goes. Decline and fall.'

We drank quite a few rounds of Bachebrook after that. Corvin lounged back in his chair, content to watch me if the conversation dried up, or to eavesdrop on snatches of Gabriel's oratory.

'What do you do now,' I asked, 'apart from attending to your "research project" and' — he raised his eyebrows expectantly — 'drifting?'

'Well,' he replied, smiling and crossing his arms, 'if you're going to clobber me with my sister's words, I might as well say that in her letter she wrote, *"Why are shy young men so exhausting?"'* He gave a perfect impression of her low, serious voice.

'Am I?' I said, slightly put out.

'Not to me, you idiot,' he laughed. 'You don't have the hots for *me*, do you?' I blushed, remembering my absurd, misplaced covetousness (yes, even a divorcee can blush). 'Of course,' he went on, narrowing his eyes as though focusing a beam, 'you realise we'll have to tell each other everything in the end. We are the future, you and I. Two young men at liberty. Fit, educated, good with heights, and gloriously directionless.'

'Speak for yourself,' I said, consciously grasping at straws. 'I happen to be employed.' He laughed.

'And when you leave the combe? Will the bank take you back?'

'I fear it might,' I sighed, thinking again of the last volume of Gibbon stoically gathering dust in a South London suburb, and hearing the hum of the vacuum and a faint, ominous rumour of the panic.

'To answer your original question,' said Corvin brightly, 'after I abandoned ship I got a job with a "strategic consultancy" full of smooth-talking ex-servicemen. You can imagine the pitch — helping businesses to get the competition on their radar screens, or launch an amphibious assault on their target market, or steer through the minefields of regulation towards the open waters of success. Innocent fun, incomprehensibly well paid but not really my thing. I chucked it in after six months and took up drifting.'

'And what happens next?'

'We'll work on that together,' he replied enigmatically, stacking his empty glass on top of mine. 'Imagination is the key.'

On Monday (week seven, for those counting) I asked after Corvin and the doctor told me he had gone away. 'The seven-league boots are gone, you see,' he said. 'That's the only way to tell. He'll be back.'

I advanced mechanically through poetry and drama, gradually approaching the huge fiction collection. I had saved myself the treat of discovering which book commenced the narrative of narratives — which author had been crowned by Hartley or his descendants as the patriarch, the Herodotus of this cocky young literary form. I was dimly aware of several claimants (and unaware of many others). But when I climbed the gallery's small stepladder on Thursday afternoon and reached up to the top shelf I found it began with a few dull reference books: a concise Oxford dictionary, Fowler's *Usage*, Jespersen's *Grammar*, an old *Roget* and a slim volume in golden-yellow cloth with the seductive title *How to Write*. Since every book could teach this lesson by example, I thought, according to its own style, it must be a bold teacher who had no other lesson to offer.

I worked through the first few books and then slid out the thesaurus and turned it spine-downward on the roving shelf. It had smooth, regular page ends, not too thin, and behaved particularly well as I worked the now-hardened pad of my thumb over them, letting the pages curl from the right side to the left in a quick, even succession. These books were all obsolete, I reflected, in that newer and more comprehensive editions were held in the dedicated reference shelves. Indeed they seemed rather out of place on the gallery — a deliberate reminder, perhaps, that literature is not exempt from the requirement for perspiration alongside inspiration.

Suddenly my thumb felt an irregularity — there was a pause in the rhythm and then a little clump of pages flipped across together. I tilted the book and reached my thumb over to investigate, and a folded paper slid out before I could stop it and glided down into the cool air. It swooped over the railing and separated into two papers and then three, and these three demonstrated the different ways leaves have of falling — one tumbling edge over edge, another turning slowly like a record, and the third half-unfolded, spiralling corner-first as though into an invisible plughole. The first landed flat, the second slid to a halt beside the table, and the last came to rest balanced on its edge, one corner quivering.

I turned and looked down at the page from which they had fallen, my face no doubt hanging slack like the Keats miniature. The first entry was: '*Thesaurus: noun. Synonymy.*' Here was a book, I thought, as my heartbeat ground up through the gears, whose words were mere pointers to other words, endless swirling circles of references that told of nothing in themselves; and here was the page where the book pointed directly inwards, to itself. A closed circle: a sealed tomb of words. *Impossible to deduce.* I let it fall on the shelf, leapt off the ladder, bumped my head as I slithered down the stairs, tripped on the bottom step and narrowly avoided trampling the papers. I dropped to my knees and picked up the page standing on its edge: it was the start of a letter, written very close and small but in lines of perfect fluid precision like those of a legal document. In the top right corner were the words, '*Holborn, 24th day of August,*' and the letter began simply, '*SIR,*' so there was no instant answer regarding its year or recipient, but I had no doubts whatsoever: this was it. The characters of the first word were formed with exquisite looping elegance that far surpassed even my father's enviable script.

Solemnly, carefully, but with my quickened breathing filling the silence like some frantic bellows, I gathered up the other pages, got to my feet and went to the armchair. I switched on the old standing lamp (whose shade was still rather crooked after

212

the encounter with John Evelyn), sat down, laid the letter on the chair arm in the bright pool of light, and, with Hartley watching intently from the shadows and Sarah turning her sad face away, began to read.

5

Holborn, 24th day of August

SIR,

It was a blessed hand that jostled me into your path for the sake of sixpence, and a curse that swept us apart. Each knows the other Hathe What He Lacke, but the world suffers not such happy exchanges lightly. Indeed, is it not a most comely geste of Nature that all men have in abundance what she herself hath rendered useless to them, and want what they most desire? Why spoil the joke?

My particular reason for returning your friendship unopened, as it were, was that I already owed you a debt that had not been willingly offered. I have something to give in return, though it cannot make us even: you liked the good prieste Dowleie's last ballad, I think, and in time you will see all those of his works that I have writ out in a fair hand, and with much labour for there are many.

Of those men — and they be few enough — who would give so much as a penn'orth of pox for poetry, some will doubt the authenticity of Dowley. Others, I fancy, will apply their narrow wits to anything that absolves them of belief in a subchanter's son. I have wondered where my last friend would stand in this Tilt of the Toms, and would save him

214

the trouble of choosing. A game for fools!

You already know the answer: the words themselves know not the hand that writ them — that, Sir, is poetry. What matter if it were Dowley or Furey? Upon the reader, and not the writer, do the burthen and duty of ownership settle: for they are his lines now. Perhaps it was noble Dowley invented Furey, after all, as scribe and moiling errand-boy, or perhaps it was the other — these are mere prefaces. The story has passed on: it is told now by the lines themselves, that weary not of the telling so long as they are read. And you will read them and own them.

My second disclosure I make for your wife's sake as well as yours. She and I happening to meet one fair day while her husband was keeping to his chamber, I took the liberty of approach, which she received kindly, I think, out of charity. I was bold, and she unpractised at polite deflections, and we had much discourse. We met again — by Chance, I fancy — and, her husband, that is you, Sir, being alternately more attentive to my poor Scribblings and his own dressing jacket than to her, she confided in me most affectingly. I am not ashamed to confess that my admiration was soon mingled with a few potent sparkes of Lust, which took flame when I perceived the same wholesome appetites in her, and only her husband will know how well they had been satisfied of late.

He, who is most acquainted with her natural qualities of faithfulness and duty, can best imagine the unhappiness occasioned by this trial, which went the way it must. Aye, a whirlwind of fine feelings was visited upon the coarse beds of Chancery Lane, and its foul pillows watered by tears of Ecstasie and Sorrow. And if you spit jealous anger onto this

*page and think of spitting it upon your gentle wife, remember
the man you believe yourself to be and act as that man should
act. But what monster lays such a Poniard in his rival's hand,
when she perhaps stands nigh, that unhappy and unguarded
queen? He must be a heartless braggart, unless he love you
both and love Truth above all, and finds himself as it were
pressed into a corner by the converging hands of time. I arm
you thus that you might touch the blade to the bands of deceit
and remorse, that she and you be freed to love again, and
better than before if you are wise. If there be any rightful
reproaches they belong to her, but she will have none.*

*In some quarters, I own, you surpass your obedient servant
(he has tried his hand). I hope you will continue to comb the
beaches of the wide world with your pen, and that you can
perhaps give it back some little of what it has lost — God
knows, it needs mending. But the wide world don't pay enough.
Wake up, ask yourself now what it is you love, build a Temple
to it, go there and write your true name and let the world
make do with the other. Invite your friends if they are worthy
of it and ignore your enemies. As for T.F., he was born into
the wrong city, the wrong nation, the wrong time. I have done
what I could with what I had, smuggled Truth under a cloak of
lies and moiled myself out. Night falls here. I deliver myself now
into the hands of my good Prieste, as I delivered him into yours.*

*I am, Sir,
Your servant no longer, but your humble and penitent Friend,
   Thos. Furey
   dieth.*

216

I got to my feet, gave nods of respectful acknowledgment to my two silent witnesses, gathered up the three leaves neatly and knocked on the door of the study. 'Enter,' came the familiar voice: the doctor was standing behind his desk, leaning his veined hands upon it and frowning down at his work. I stepped forward *largo* and laid the letter before him without speaking. His glance rested on it for a moment and then lifted to my face.

'Thank you,' he said quietly, wearily, as though he too had suffered the hardships of the search. 'You've read it?' I gave him the same nod I had offered his thought-ancestors, walked out into the hall and thrust a long arm into my coat.

6

I entered the cottage by the dying light of my torch and struck my head squarely against the parlour lintel. Even a man touched by the sublime will utter the coarsest of oaths when his fine thoughts are mocked in this way — that crude exclamation that lurks inside him, ready to spring, ready to leave all his worthier words in the starting blocks. And I suppose that for most whom death catches at unawares, it is this angry seizing-up of the engine of language — and not a poignant theatrical direction or a cricketing metaphor — that freezes upon the lips for eternity. I hope I have more time (or not enough; the latter for preference).

I laid a few sticks of kindling on the embers of the morning's fire and the room started into eerie, flickering being as they took flame; then I buried them in coal and turned on the lamp. Dolly mewed from her basket and went back to sleep. I sat down heavily, still wearing my coat and scarf, and waited for my throbbing forehead to give up its complaining. My job was done.

When M'Synder returned from her nameless labours at the house I ducked warily into the kitchen to tell her of my success.

'Oh,' she said, turning sharply from the stove and looking up at me. The four lenses of our glasses had steamed up in the relative warmth and to observe each other around them we both held our heads crookedly, like birds. 'And is the doctor sure it's the right one?'

'It's the right one.'

'Oh. Well. Congratulations!' Her voice expressed a blend of triumph and uncertainty that accorded well with my own mood, though I lacked her foundation of serenity. 'Is he pleased with it?'

'I don't know. I'll talk to him tomorrow.'

'I do hope you wunna be hurryin' to leave us, Mr Browne. I have enjoyed our little chats. I've just got in another week's provisions, too.'

'I'll — talk to the doctor tomorrow. See what he says.'

Well, would he be pleased with the letter? Was I? Are you? The doctor had hoped it would be *a valuable document in itself*; Corvin had promised scandal; I had feared it didn't exist. Furey's disclosures were not revelatory — according to the encyclopaedia, everyone has long agreed that he wrote the Dowley poems (although there was indeed a fierce Tilt of the Toms for ten years or so), and Juliet had already hinted at Sarah Louise's uncharacteristic dalliance with the poet. The last paragraph, whose figurative temple Hartley had chosen to interpret literally, suggested Furey as the first inspiration for the mysterious creed that united the names carved into the stone tablets: a creed of truth, the doctor had called it, and yet it was born out of one of England's most notorious frauds.

But as I thus examined my response to the long-awaited, long-imagined letter after dinner, the only reaction of which I could be sure was a gentle stirring in my affections when I thought of the proud, brilliant Thomas Furey and heard his calm words whispering across the centuries, keening through all the scribbled words of Hartley that had addressed me from a hundred different books. The feeling was not unlike that faltering of my wholesome disinterest in Rose, but fainter and more resonant: it was a kind of haunting.

I did not go straight to the house in the morning: why should I? I thought. A damp wind tossed drizzle about and dragged marbled clouds slowly across the hills, and I zipped up my waterproof chin-high, nestled my hands in its cold but cosily windless pockets, set my borrowed boots into the steepening ground and let them and my thoughts wander where they would.

Corvin's disappearance without saying goodbye had given me the idea that I might do the same. If I packed my initialled suitcase and walked out of the combe, neither he nor the doctor would have any means of tracing me (a common name can be a blessing): they didn't even know the name of the bank that had employed me or the suburb that had hosted my deluded past life. Why would they want to trace me anyway? We were all square. And if I did resort again to flight, and if I turned in the winding lane as the combe disappeared from view for the last time, what words would I utter aloud over the wind in the budding birches? As a desperate man lashes out at his friends, I repeated in my mind my previous utterance, 'So long, you bastards,' but I knew it would stick in my throat. 'Farewell, my indeducible friends,' I might say instead.

All square: then what had I gained from my visit? As promised by the notice, my curiosity had been rewarded. Indeed, there was something suspicious about the steady flow of answers to my questions (only Rose had kept largely silent). Who was I to deserve such confidences? It was almost as though my sources — Juliet, Corvin, M'Synder — had been acting under instructions. If so, there could be little doubt as to the principal: who else but the all-seeing Magus with the pained smile?

I paused for breath at the viewpoint above the cottage and looked out along the combe through its veil of drizzle. Its most obvious and troublesome benefaction to Samuel Browne had been to underline his ignorance — to show him up. This chronic ache of shallowness, of missing the point, of steadily wasting the opportunity of life was surely what my old friend Keats had called '*the Burden of the Mystery*' (he was quoting another poet, but I did not know that — a case in point). And yet most people — my old self included — seemed to live their lives entirely free of this burden, crumpling suddenly if it were forced upon them by a death or the reach of some other eternal hand, tearing their hair then and wailing at the moon, but in-between-times quite satisfied in their ignorance; thus unencumbered they were happy to stay within the confines of the little maps of habit they had drawn on some corner of the huge blank sheet of the mind. Of course it was my ex-wife who had planted the burden firmly onto my own shoulders — a position surely preferable to its hanging unseen in the air above my head. She had taught me the old Socratic paradox, and the combe had driven the lesson home.

Ragged skirts of cloud were just skimming the broad, sodden ridge, and I had to stow away my useless glasses and continue in a fitting double mist of hill-fog and myopia. It is one thing to know nothing about the decline of Rome, I thought, but quite another to blunder helplessly into love or death. I have twice mentioned that I have never been bereaved. I have observed death — the sudden absences of contemporaries at school and university, and the less horrifying declines of elderly relatives and *bon-viveur* tutors. I was fond of each of my grandparents, and I miss each of them sometimes, but I did not grieve for any of them. Even my parents grieved equivocally, thanks to my mother's calm, rational will which mastered my father's more sentimental bent.

The further I advance through adulthood without suffering grief, the darker death seems to loom. Now as I plodded through the mist I wondered whether it might be possible to come to terms with grief — *to be a student of death* — in advance. Certainly the combe had provided plenty of case studies. Here I had learned that one might work day and night, wear out one's soul by the age of seventeen and resort to arsenic, or be torn almost in half on the fields of Arras though yearning to live, or drink a bottle of Armagnac and silently, happily crystallise beneath the crystalline sky, or be loving and wise a week too soon, or find oneself entombed in a giant white outfield not knowing which way is up, but knowing for minutes and long minutes that the umpire has raised his fatal hand. Then of course there was Sam himself, running barefoot into a red canvas and leaving an eddy of unanswerable questions hanging in the air behind him.

I found a new path leading around the far side of Grey Man, and the dim sky was growing dimmer by the time I joined the old grassy track that climbed into the combe from the west. As I neared the stiles at the top of the little pass and remembered Rose leading me over them, the giant figure of Meaulnes appeared ahead, loping up towards me. Droplets of water bobbed and swung from the peak of his cap and hung like improbable pearls on his fleshy earlobes. I told him I had finished my work for the doctor, and would be leaving soon. His answer came out as a sort of sombre couplet:

'That, my friend, is what they all say. Some of them leave, some of them stay.' We shook hands — it was like grasping the oversized hand of one of Rodin's seven-foot burghers — and went our separate ways.

7

There was no answer to my knock in the study's dark alcove. I was about to check the library by way of the dining room when through the open parlour door I glimpsed the silver crown of the doctor's head peeping above the back of his favourite chair. The fire was lit and an unopened bottle of wine stood in its usual place on the hearth.

'Is that my missing champion — Mr Browne?' came his dry, contented voice, though he did not stir. 'Vanquisher of prunes, keeper of promises, deliverer of the goods?' I stepped forward and stood with my rain-chilled back to the fire while he beamed up at me. He pointed to Taboni's merciless angel of truth, who glowed an eerie white in the yellow lamplight. 'She shines a little brighter today, don't you think?'

It took me a while to dry out and warm up, but the doctor fussed over me and stoked the fire and soon we were both settled with glasses of the silky, tawny wine — an old claret laid down by his father.

'Here's to young Thomas Furey,' he said solemnly, raising his glass, 'an English poet.' I murmured the name back to him, and felt again the odd haunting, the vertigo on that narrow bridge over the centuries. Tinted firelight veered and curled in the wine's dark prism.

'Hartley,' began the doctor after a long, deliberate silence, 'whom we left slumped in the stagnant wreck of his study, read the letter through twice and then hobbled slowly, dizzily over to the fire. His fire burned all year — feeling cold was a side-effect of the opium, or rather the lack of it: only the next dose could warm him. For several minutes he weighed the possibility of tossing the letter into the flames, but instead, after reading it a third time (and perhaps remembering the man he believed himself to be), he mounted the stairs to his wife's chamber and handed it to her in silence before returning to the study.

'He subsequently fell ill with some fever — all too common for him — and she nursed him for several weeks. From his bed he sent urgent enquiries after Furey and discovered he was dead and buried in an unmarked pauper's grave. The fever lingered, but when at last it began to recede Hartley found himself propelled forward as though from a run-up into a new dawn of health and vitality. He threw back dusty curtains, cleared his desk, and even climbed up to the summit of Grey Man to watch the sunrise. "*Welcome back, O Life!*" he wrote. "*Now I have strength enough to write both my names.*" An odd statement, I always thought, but the letter explains it. He and Sarah named the wrongs they had done each other (his list was long!), and forgave each other though perhaps not themselves. He begged her to tell him everything Furey had said to her in London, and she obliged, more or less.

'The next morning he ordered stacks of newspapers and journals and pored over the big questions of the day, and that autumn *Beachcomber* leapt back onto the journalistic stage. Over the next few years his articles addressed diverse subjects — the urgent American question, the abolition of slavery, the economic potential and social implications of mechanisation, and freedom of speech and religion, to name but a few — and became famous for their forceful prose. But he saved his best writing for private correspondence, holding long exchanges with many celebrated figures including the aforementioned Wilkes, Sharp the abolitionist, Arkwright the industrialist, and radical thinkers from Smith and Hume in Edinburgh to Diderot and d'Holbach in Paris. Not even your friend Gibbon escaped! These letters, lost and forgotten now, were the influential works to which I once referred. It was an exciting time for thinkers — a surge in the fitful Western progression — and Hartley was at the heart of it, always questioning, suggesting, encouraging, whether in public or private: writing both his names.

'Meanwhile in the combe he steadily accumulated his library, simply as a by-product of his insatiable thirst for knowledge — a personal slagheap of processed words. But of course he recognised its worth — if Sarah questioned his expenditure he would call it the jewel of his estate. "*The collection's true value increases as the square of its number,*" he wrote. "But who else will use it?" she asked, to which he replied, "I refuse admission to no one."'

'Was he still taking opium?' I was thinking of his gaunt appearance in the portrait.

'Yes, but much less than before. Like De Quincey he experimented with the trials of abstinence, but he decided to steer the course that would make him most productive, with the strong hand of his will on the tiller.'

'And what about the temple?'

'It was built during the middle of that decade, but the references in his diaries are few and obscure — I suppose he was thinking of Furey's advice. As Beachcomber he wrote some controversial articles about the importance of establishing an alternative to supernatural religion, whether communal or personal, but as Comberbache he kept his own temple private. "*Every statement of truth,*" he wrote in the diary, "*be it mathematics, poetry or the history of man, is a verse of my bible.*"

'Those years of health and vigour ended with the sudden appearance of tuberculosis in his early forties, after a visit to London. He was advised to travel to the Mediterranean but his own research left him unconvinced by the medical arguments, and by early seventeen eighty-two he was confined to his bed. That was the year the Dowley controversy reached its climax, and he must have read the claims and counter-claims with wry amusement — but doubtless even had he possessed the strength to write he would have stayed out of it. He died on a day of soft summer rain with his wife and young son at his side, and was buried beside the temple after a secular funeral rite directed by Sarah herself and attended by a few intimate friends.'

Heavy rain was now singing steadily against the glass behind the thick embroidered curtains. The doctor refilled our glasses and proposed a second toast, this time to Hartley, then after another long silence resumed his story.

'I suppose it is because she survived her husband by thirty-nine years that I feel a special affinity with Sarah now — she too lived three lives. She began the last by completing Samuel's boyhood education herself, acquiring more important books for the library and executing the rest of their plans for the gardens. She planted the beech in the drive in Hartley's memory, using the strongest of the saplings he had grown from seeds brought back from Greece — it's now in its third century and in fine health. With a legacy from the Bostonian uncle she established a school in the nearest town — the Liberty School — which exists to this day. She and Samuel wrote the original textbooks using the *Encyclopédie* and other works from the library. She illustrated them beautifully.'

'Tell me about Samuel,' I said. 'All I know is that the birds wouldn't sing for him.'

'Ah yes, the first of the Samuels: the dreamer. He was surely the most eccentric of the tribe. What a childhood his must have been! He was born even as the first shelves were being fashioned from the ancient boards of the banqueting table. His early memories would have been of the study piled high with those of the new volumes that his father was feverishly devouring, often reading aloud in whichever language he had to hand; of the old gardens and woods, still wildly overgrown from years of neglect; of the mysterious plans laid out on the new folio table, and then the deliveries of stone and the excavation of the great staircase up the hill. He was educated entirely at home — heaven knows, there were resources enough! — and visiting cousins were his only playmates.

'He matriculated at Jesus College with the poet Samuel Taylor Chadwick. Chadwick was brilliant and effusive and Comberbache shy and solitary, and the two had little to do with each other until the dreamer was caught by the bulldogs climbing through a college window after the curfew following a midnight ramble over the fens. He was in what he called a semi-somnambulistic state and, seeing the constable in possession of his initialled hat, gave his name as Simon Trelasco Chadwick. In the morning this led the dean straight to the real S. T. Chadwick, who despite being unjustly gated was delighted by the other's confession and the realisation that they shared the same first name and initials: thereafter they became firm friends. Whenever he wanted refuge from his whirlwind of political agitating, drunken parties and looming debts, Chadwick would seek out his nature-loving namesake for peaceful rambles in the country.

'He visited the combe on several occasions during the holidays, and supposedly discovered and experimented with the dusty remnants of Hartley's supply of laudanum — probably his first recreational use of the drug that would come to dominate his life. I think he never discovered that Hartley and Sarah had known Furey, for whom he wrote (and many times rewrote) his famous *Monody*.

'Our own Samuel is now considered a minor member of the early Romantics — his poetry has moments of lyrical clarity but is generally rather difficult, perhaps because after taking his degree he rarely left the combe for some twenty years. When his mother died — a few weeks after Keats — he finally married and reinvented himself as master of the Liberty School, where he was much loved until his death in eighteen thirty-seven — the year Victoria came to the throne.'

'And his children?'

'Only one daughter survived infancy. She married a wealthy and deeply conservative widower and let the combe. Her younger stepson, who was my great grandfather, took possession in about eighteen sixty — perhaps the only inspired thing he did in his life.'

The doctor poured out the last of the wine while I stirred the fire and added another log, which roasted silently for a while, haemorrhaging smoke. I was wondering how to broach the subject of my departure, but he seemed to read my mind and spoke first.

'Do you have any pressing need to return to London,' he asked, turning suddenly as the log burst into bright, plappering flames, 'or would you accept an invitation to stay for a few more weeks? I was going to invite you to return for our equinox gathering — or Easter as everyone insists on calling it — but it occurred to me today that you might stay on until then. There are a few specific things I'd like to talk to you about.'

'That's very kind of you,' I said awkwardly, having no idea what answer to give but feeling that something bad and inevitable had just receded.

'I'll have more time from now on,' he pursued, 'because I too reached the end of something today: my book. *Giveth and Taketh Away: a life of Thomas Linley the Elder* — finished. Linley, in case you didn't know, was an English composer of the second or third rank. He also happened to be a friend of Hartley and Sarah.'

'Why did you choose him as your subject, if he was —'

'— Unexceptional?' prompted the doctor. He drew back his mouth into the old pained smile. 'Linley had many qualities. One may be a worthy man without being a brilliant one. It was his children who were brilliant —' he paused while a squall of rain rattled faintly against the window '— but they died.'

8

'Death,' said the doctor sharply from behind his desk the next morning, like a terrible judge pronouncing sentence: 'the longest and shortest journey, the exit from the self.' Then he added lightly, 'Do you think about it much?'

He had been tidying up, and now a drifting infusoria of dust measured out the slanting girders of sunlight that leaned on their slender transoms like some radiant cargo spilling from a sunken wreck. I hesitated, and then answered, 'Before, no, but recently, yes.' Wasn't death somehow connected with the panic? *The mote which strays into a heaven of gold / And into darkness, aimless, wanders home:* my own clumsy but earnest words, an echo from adolescence. The doctor shelved the last of his books, advanced to the unlit, swept hearth and stood for a while looking down at the empty grate.

'Will you climb with me to the temple?' he asked suddenly, squinting into the sunlight. 'It exists for days like this.' Sunny days, or death days? I wondered, as we fetched our coats.

I used to find it difficult to walk slowly. When Sarah had a stress-fracture in her foot and used a crutch for a couple of weeks, I was an impatient companion and needed frequent reminders to slow down. But this was another lesson the combe had taught: if you imagine me always hurrying along the lane chafing my hands it is the fault of my account, for in truth I had become an expert dragger of feet and wanderer along hedgerows.

'I am reconciled to the prospect of my own death,' the doctor pronounced carefully, as we paced the runway side by side. 'This is important for an old man: I have built my ship. It was difficult, but a little perseverance won through. For anyone with an ounce of imagination it is an alarming proposition — this *walking backwards into death with our gaze still fixed on life*. But the truth, I believe, is that in death, at the moment of death, whether one was a good man, or a wise or a brave or a loved or a remembered man, and what one has achieved, simply does not matter — ceases to matter. These things matter so long as one is alive — they define the concept of mattering — and then they cease to matter. Therefore there is no *panic*, no anguish: that is my ship of death.'

He led me through the stone garden, past the obelisk and out into the meadow. 'So far so good,' he went on. 'But what about those left behind? Can they apply this hypothesis to the deaths of others? Did my wife cease to matter to me on the day she died? *Drive your cart and your plough over the bones of the dead* — is that the proverb we need? Death is the strangest of partings. In living partings there is a seal of fellowship in the very symmetry of the farewell: 'Bonne chance,' says one. 'And to you,' says the other. But death is the great asymmetry, the breaking of fellowship, the not knowing what to say. No, the ship of my own death gets me nowhere on the sea of grief.

'Loss: one need hardly elaborate — the word is a perfectly precise expression of the problem. Furey's death — exasperating, unnecessary, *unanswerable* — epitomises the concept. But Marcus Aurelius stands firm: "*no one can lose what is already past, nor yet what is still to come,*" he says, "*for how can he be deprived of what he does not possess?*" Marcus would have us believe that the sense of loss is just another delusion of grief — that nothing is really lost. My mind and heart have proved stubborn adversaries on this question.' I wondered whether he was thinking about Furey now, or his wife, or the red canvas in the locked room.

'It's strange,' I attempted '— I was thinking about it only yesterday. I've never really felt that sense of loss. I'm still a child in that respect.' The doctor pursed his lips thoughtfully.

'But a child is often wise,' he said. 'How do you imagine it?'

'I imagine that love — or affection, or whatever — finding its object gone, would occupy itself with a kind of fussing over the memory, fondly straightening out the faults and lingering over the characteristics most beloved, so that the love would itself erode the truth and leave you with a neat but basically unfaithful picture, something *portable* — easy to carry around in your breast pocket. And then,' I continued, hesitantly, 'the love would falter, because you can't really love a — a kind of cartoon, and you'd begin to treat it like any other picture or keepsake. That would be the final reconciliation, the moving on.' I surprised myself by articulating this thought, which had never before occurred to me. Perhaps that practice I mentioned — practising the telling of my story — was paying off.

'That is not a bad guess,' said the doctor, as we crossed the bridge and began to climb. 'Love itself as the healer. I remember my parents in that way, I think — memories faithful to them but unfaithful to the whole truth, and so more bearable because less real. Perhaps Margaret too, once I see past those final pails on the yoke. Of course, the cartoon memory, the keepsake is never quite inanimate — it has a habit of stirring, twitching in the breast pocket when you least expect.'

The doctor climbed the stair steadily, leading always with the left foot and following with the right. His deepening breaths and

232

the slow tap of his stick were like the stubborn, stoical workings of a clock, last wound God knows when, over the level murmur of winter birdsong. At the top we paused for a while to recover, gazing out at the long, smudged sketch-line of the horizon and the drifts of tiny cloud-balls settled against it. I glanced along the row of stones and for the first time an unmarked hummock at the end caught my eye.

'Here are the times of sunrise, sunset and local noon,' said the doctor behind me, angling the leather book towards the light of the open door. 'Noon today is at twenty-four minutes past twelve GMT, when the sun will reach an altitude of twenty-six-and-a-half degrees. It rose at a bearing of one-o-seven, and sets at two-five-three — we are one month or seventeen degrees of azimuth from the equinox.' He closed the book and looked up at me for a moment, as though making one last check that I was a suitable initiate, before opening the inner door.

That afternoon I accompanied the doctor all the way to the village, where he handed his finished manuscript to the shopkeeper for recorded delivery. He looked up at the church with fond attention, peered in at the low cottages and waved to a young family crossing the green.

'Shall we pay a visit to the Croked Agnes, since we're here?' he murmured as we passed the sign, and without waiting for an answer reached down for the grotesque handle. The bar was deserted, and silent except for the fire sleepily chewing on its embers. The doctor struck the bell, which gave a low, cracked chime, and then put his finger to his lips and motioned downwards with his hand. He lowered himself stiffly to sit on the crosspiece of a bar stool, while I crouched creakily beside him. Footsteps approached from the next room, entered the bar and stopped.

'Arnold Erasmus Hughes Comberbache,' snapped Agnes' voice breezily, 'get up off the floor before you do yourself an injury! And you, Mr Browne, lack even the tenuous excuse of senility.' We got to our feet and found her already pumping the ale and peering sternly over lopsided glasses like a headmistress (but do headmistresses wear red lipstick?). She nodded towards the copper bed-warmer on the wall whose polished dome had given us away. 'Chemical symbol *see-you*,' she said. 'Get it? I've got every angle covered. No Swinburne with you today?'

As dusk fell we called at the cottage for baked potatoes with M'Synder, and then went on to the dark, empty house. I lit the parlour fire (there too my practice had paid off) while the doctor, suddenly seeming worn out by the day's walking, shuffled away to find some music. The first sad bar of Allegri's *Miserere*, in which the melody itself seems to bow its head in recognition of what will follow, sounded softly in the gloom as he turned to the side-table and reached not for one of his beloved malt whiskies — *uisge beatha*, water of life — but the broad-based, slim-necked decanter at the end of the row, gleaming with the unmistakeable reddish tint of brandy: water of death. He poured two glasses and slumped into his chair.

'So,' he said. 'A student of the theory of loss only. The mind uninterrupted by the heart's objections.' It was the first time he had revisited the subject.

'There is one kind of loss that I know about from experience,' I said suddenly, my chest tightening like a drum skin for the drumming heart. The doctor waited, looking down at the sharp, flickering rim of his glass. 'My wife left me last year. Without warning. Just — wrote me a letter.' This last comment sounded ridiculous and I gave a little exhalation of laughter through my teeth. My companion looked up and studied me with interest. He asked how long we had been married, and I told him.

'I'm sorry to hear that you've been unhappy,' he said, and then nodded slowly. 'But my idea, my picture of you is clearer now. I suppose this was your mystery to hold in reserve against all my silly games. And maybe it explains why I felt I could talk to you in the first place.'

'Did you?'

'Felt I could, but didn't,' he murmured, inhaling the heavy vapour and raising the glass to his lips. 'I understand from Corvin that he has given you an outline of the circumstances of —' he paused, and his face twitched nervously '— of —' I waited helplessly. 'Of what happened a few years ago.'

'Yes.'

'Yes. It's strange, I — can't talk to him about it really. It seems so pointless because he knows, he was there. With poor Juliet it is even worse. But you — I felt myself wanting to —' He fell silent as the *Miserere*'s ghostly treble stepped down again from its famous impossible height.

'I feel that my son left me — left all of us — for some particular reason of his own: a reason I cannot imagine. Like your wife, perhaps, except that Sam didn't write any letters. Just — ran away.'

'But you don't know that he really wanted that,' I said. 'He tried to protect himself. He might not have fallen.'

'He might not have fallen,' echoed the doctor, weakly. 'Indeed. That nub of steel raked into a half-inch crack might not have slipped. Might have held. And then — would he have come back to us, his duty done?'

'I don't know,' I answered, 'but yes, I think so.' Then for a while we sat still and let the despairing voices sing themselves out. When the doctor half-glanced towards the side-table I rose to refill our glasses.

'They call it torquing,' he murmured, as I sat down. 'You know, with a "Q". You slot the pick of your ice-axe into a slanting crack in the rock so that it twists when you pull on the shaft, and that locks it in place. Such a complexity of forces,' he went on, almost in a whisper, 'the curved, flexing axe, the unseen, icy interior of the fissure, the hefting, swinging load of the climber hanging over the void.' He drained the glass and swallowed it down. 'Will it hold?' he muttered. 'Will it slip?'

One might even ask of a young marriage founded on ignorance the same questions that one asks of a man's grip on the brilliant life that he holds in a gloved fist: such a complexity of forces.

9

So my labours at the combe were finished, but my stay and the changes that it wrought in me were not. I was now the doctor's guest, and the library's demands for diligence having been satisfied I began to experience it quite differently: the light was more delicate, the cool, papery taste of the air sweeter — even the silence seemed to occupy a subtly different key. I would stroll in with a Corvin-like spring in my step, stand nonchalantly at the window for a few moments (that was part of the tradition of the place), and then plant myself before some hospitable case and seek out some particular volume that had retained a singular existence in my crowded memory, like the leaf that we can see waving back and forth among a thousand others, flashing its own particular shape and colour and exacting recognition. I would tip the book's delicious weight into my hand, open it, and browse. It would be crass to compare this newfound freedom to Geoffrey's at the foot of the Buachaille, but certainly reading, after a couple of gloriously book-free days that weekend (not one page, not a single printed word — alleluia!), had become exciting again. But where should I begin? When I told the doctor about my nagging burden of ignorance, his eyes lit up.

'Good!' he cried. 'Very good! You have crossed the first and highest hurdle. The next one is much easier — you must transform this sensation of burden, of weakness, into something more productive. Think of it as the engine of ignorance, driving you forward. What else motivates the aging student of Combe College? Ignorance is not a state from which you might one day be delivered; it should not be a reason to be dissatisfied with the present or to nurture false hopes of future wisdom; it should be a steady force, a driver of exploration and discovery.

'There is always time for an increment of learning — at least, for as long as learning *matters*. I would have liked to emphasise this to Furey, who lamented his ignorance of Latin and Greek. At sixteen he considered it too late to learn — perhaps he had some foreknowledge of brevity, of living too fast and moiling himself out. He told his mother that had he *known his classicals*, he could have done anything — as it was, he assured her, his name would live three hundred years.'

I asked which of Furey's poems I should read, and in which edition. He dismissed most of the volumes on the gallery as curiosities and brought from the study an enormous *Complete Works* dated nineteen seventy. 'Furey finally got the editor he deserved,' he said. 'This fellow had the best springs on his bicycle, and brings us the words more or less undamaged along the winding lane of years. The edition was never reprinted, however, and is now extremely rare. Recently I saw the pre-Raphaelite painting of Furey used as the cover of an English anthology from which his poems were entirely absent: perhaps his own estimate of his longevity will prove to be just about right.'

So I read the poems, slowly and with difficulty, and occasionally I seemed to hear the music that Hartley had described, and to glimpse the visions that it carried. As Furey anticipated, the dupes — the Dowleians, as they came to be called — were not really taken in by his clumsy parchment forgeries: they simply disbelieved the alternative. And who could blame them? Those whisperings of music seemed to be echoing across a gulf so wide that it must be measured not in mere centuries, but in worlds. The only miracles worthy of the name, I thought, are miracles of imagination.

I followed up the Furey with Hartley's diary and a collection of his published essays, which were full of astute predictions. Next I plunged into the translated Herodotus with periodic diversions of Gilbert White. The former inspired me to work through a Greek primer in the evenings, hunched behind the writing-plank, assiduously writing out all the exercises in my notebook despite M'Synder's teasing, while the latter sent me out into the garden in fine weather with my binoculars round my neck, stalking blurry silhouettes as they flitted from tree to tree. Izaak Walton had me peering into the stream with sinister intentions, and Stephen Graham (he of the leaf skeletons) enlarged the compass of my walks in the hills.

And then there was more poetry: after the fiendish spelling and vocabulary of the goode prieste Dowleie, the lines of Chadwick and Keats rolled off the page like smoke. I developed the habit (try not to laugh) of rocking gently from side to side as my eyes swept slowly back and forth, and this seemed to raise me further from my incapacity — I imagined myself in a little boat, bobbing over the surface of the poem where before I had floundered up to my neck. I moved on to Hardy and Lawrence and Dylan Thomas, and began to enjoy and so, presumably, to understand.

One of those productive late winter days — a day of damp stone and rolling clouds — was settling itself into a chill, whispering, moonless dusk as I walked with coat unbuttoned to the cottage for dinner. While I was washing the dishes M'Synder returned from the coal shed with the news that it was a 'proper starry night,' and I decided to go out. 'Wrap up,' she said, 'and take this.' She handed me a small dented hipflask which produced a promising sloshing sound. 'There's somethin' in it, the good Lord knows what. Prob'ly been in there for years, but none the worse for that.'

Stars, if anything, have the ability to surprise by a fine excess. Just when you think you've seen all they have to offer, you find yourself gazing up, whilst tipsily tripping guy ropes on an unlit campsite or lying back on the deck of an overnight ferry, at a spectacle that both memory and imagination have failed drastically to anticipate. So it was now as I felt my way cautiously, with arms extended to ward off the dog-rose, along the pitch-black lane beneath the darkest sky in England. The Milky Way scorned its name — what resemblance to milk in that swirling cincture of knot and filament, that dizzying interweaving of the diamond-sharp and the diffuse, blazing out between dark curls of interstellar dust?

I soon found myself standing in the middle of the lawn, encircled by a panorama in black silhouette — the gables and tall chimneys to the east and the shaggy spars of the cedar to the west connected on both sides by the gently sinuous, finely-bristled crest of the hills. Behind this comforting cardboard cut-out world, the terrible shimmering precipice of the universe yawned like death. I fumbled with the flask and tasted something metallic and fiery at its narrow threaded neck, then paced slowly over the faint, feathery radiance of new-formed frost and felt for the gap in the hedge and the archway beyond.

The memory of my dream, of stepping back into nothingness, guided my cautious feet as I negotiated the straight-edged, glimmering, answering precipices of the pools. I sat back on the revered seat and assumed Rose's crucifixion pose, letting my hips slip forward until my skull rested on the cold stone. I rolled it a little from side to side and the frozen stars seemed to come alive, flashing and flickering in their countless thousands as the invisible net of branches moved across them, winking in and out of existence like all the world's souls being born and living and dying before my eyes.

For what it's worth, I know the names of the stars — what a strange little hoard of knowledge wrapped and stacked in some otherwise desolate aisle of my brain! Hundreds of peevish little names for giant faraway things, meaningless, useless to all but boasting amateur astronomers, failing to lighten the burden of the mystery: I'll resist the temptation to reel off a list. Names and familiar shapes seemed to dissolve now in that glittering sea of light, rippling gently in a night breeze of ether as I felt on sleepy retinas the soft prickle of photons reaching their journey's end.

Suddenly I felt my shoulders stiffening with the cold, and realised my buttocks and thighs were already numb. I stood up rather dizzily, waited a moment for my head to clear, and started for the cottage whose cosy blankets would not exact such a heavy price in return for their embrace.

10

March arrived, and I chose a bright, vaporous morning to check in on the wonders unfolding silently in the grove. Shards of pale sunlight angled between the beeches and fell across the thousands of crocuses, some standing, some tipped over, like the empty goblets left scattered about after a vast nocturnal fairy debauch, stained with purple fairy-wine or golden dregs of mead.

It was quiet: even the songbirds seemed to be having a lie-in, and only the restless flapping and slapping of pigeon wings filtered down from the treetops as I wandered below. Along the garden's west wall forsythia buds had begun to open in little dewy puffs of daring yellow on wintry tangles of twigs. As I rounded the corner into the orchard I heard a familiar batter of feathers and glimpsed a flash of pink and white-on-black disappearing over the next wall, and my eye came to rest on one recently deserted branch vibrating violently in the mist.

'The arboreal spring,' said a loud, familiar voice, making me spin round. It was Corvin, standing in an alcove with his ankles casually crossed, hands in the pockets of a leather jacket. 'The evidence of things not seen.'

'You made me jump,' I said, feebly.

'Then I consider myself avenged. Look up — what do you see?'

242

I tipped my head back: a venturous bough from the nearest beech basked in faint sunlight, high above the hunched apples and pears. When I looked down he was holding something out in his slender fingers — a seed, like a stunted, shrivelled chestnut with three brittle edges. 'Evidence. It's impossible that this seed knows how to make a tree, but it does know — that's the plain truth.'

'It seems impossible, you mean.' He glanced up at the bough and shrugged, as though the distinction were unimportant.

'It's the same with Furey. The Dowleians were quite justified in their conclusions: it was indeed impossible that some teenage wag wrote the Dowley poems, poorly educated as he was, and with so little time. Nevertheless he did write them. Congratulations on finding the letter — I knew you would.'

We walked together into the kitchen garden, where rows of hardy vegetables bore testament to Meaulnes' patient labours. I told Corvin that the doctor had invited me to stay until Easter.

'Oh bravo, that man!' he said in an odd, merry voice, turning on one heel and taking the longer path round the edge of the beds. 'One more fold of the map, eh? Just when you seemed to have walked off the edge? Everyone you'd begun to get to know but thought you might not see again — Rose, Juliet, Frizzo the Clown' — here he indicated himself — 'all coming back for one last blast with Uncle Arnold and his shy apprentice. How comforting. And then what?' I hesitated, rather bewildered by this outburst. 'Well, never mind that,' he said in a softer tone. 'What have you and he found to talk about, anyway?'

'Plenty,' I said. 'There was his book, and the story of his ancestors, and then poetry, and truth, and beauty — those sorts of things.'

'Uh-huh,' he answered, returning my smile.

'And,' I added, stopping beside the glasshouse and frowning so that he stopped and frowned too, 'I've been accompanying him to the temple. One day we talked for hours about death.'

'Ah, yes,' he replied, solemnly. 'Poor Arnold quoting Marcus Aurelius again, was he?' He walked slowly on, brushing the pointed toe of his boot along glistening hands of rhubarb. '"*It is no greater hardship to be taken to pieces than to be put together.*" That was my favourite — a couple of years ago Juliet was just about ready to put it to the test by battering him over the head with his bloody Marcus Aurelius. But we each have our methods, and good luck to him.'

So another name was added to the rolls of Combe College for this brief crocus-bloom term. Corvin appropriated the study for his own obscure purposes, while the doctor and I sat reading on either side of Sarah's fireplace. One morning I arrived to find the fire lit for the first time.

'Fires in libraries make me nervous,' said the doctor, 'and you would not have noticed any warmth on the ladder. But I think we might risk a little comfort now that we are close enough both to supervise and to reap the benefit.' When we rose for coffee he unhooked the two heavy drapes of chain mail that served as fireguards and arranged them meticulously. 'Armour against the fiery darts of entropy,' he murmured, turning away reluctantly, 'and their insidious Second Law.'

On this retreat from our retreat, in the whitewashed kitchen whose cool air smelled faintly of parsnips and onions, he seemed for a few moments to recall the existence of the outside world — the profane world, my world.

'Very few people know that we exist — do you remember me telling you that?' He pressed down the wad of coffee with an ancient, tarnished spoon and slowly revolved the two halves of the percolator in his hands, engaging the thread.

'I do.' I struck a match for him and the whistling gas caught with a satisfying *woomf.*

'After all, why should they know or care? But when you go home, if you tell people about the combe, I wonder if you could do me a favour.'

'Of course.'

'Don't tell them where it is. We have no secrets, but neither do we promote our existence to the world. Of course, they might guess our whereabouts from what you tell them — I don't mind that as long as — as long as you don't make it too easy for them. And the temple — tell them about that if you must, but — just don't tell quite everything. Let it remain sacred. What do you say?'

'I'll say nothing at all, if you prefer,' I answered, thinking first of the three sketchy letters I had already dispatched and then of my rather extensive notebook.

'Oh, no, that wouldn't be fair. We have no secrets, after all. No gates, no *KEEP OUT.*'

'Just a few trees thoughtfully planted,' I suggested.

'Something like that.'

In the afternoon, as I laboured to translate a few sentences of Thucydides with the help of Uncle Samuel's school lexicon, whose sad inscription read '*presented to S.S.C. for showing excellent promise in scholarship, April 1913*', the doctor inserted into the slow duet of our breathing a deep sigh, and looked up frowning from his notebook.

'Mr Browne,' he said, after watching me for a moment, 'you are a man not only of improving classical tastes, I suppose, but also of sound financial sense.' He waved aside my doubtful expression and went on: 'As you might have noticed, we Comberbaches are neither a proliferative family nor a particularly long-lived one. To put it bluntly, I don't know how much time I have left and the future of the combe is in doubt.' I was flattered by his assumption that I was qualified to advise him, that during those three years the fabled wisdom of the markets had flashed and flickered its way into my unreceptive brain.

'Who will inherit it?' I asked. 'Rose?'

'Rose is adamant she does not want it. Or rather, she only wants the cottage, which M'Synder — who owns it now — wishes to leave to her when she herself goes to the great cottage in the sky. Decades away, of course. You might say I have been disbequeathed.'

'What about Juliet?'

'She doesn't want it either. She has her reasons, which I understand. No,' he went on, lowering his voice and glancing round towards the study door, 'it is the clown, Corvin — he is my heir, if I may put it so grandly. This is not a large house, as ancestral seats go, but neither he nor I have nearly enough to pay the tax bill. If I die, Corvin must sell the combe. Then I suppose the peerless temple will become what you once thought it to be — a folly for some latter-day lord of the manor.'

'What about the paintings?' I suggested. 'The Taboni — couldn't that be sold as a last resort?'

'The Taboni is worth something, but, I think, not enough. The dear boy would find himself ripping out the whole history of the house in order to keep the walls and the slates. That is the point, perhaps, but I'm not interested in the political debate.'

'You have recently come into another source of wealth that might be — liquidated,' I said cautiously.

'Have I?' said he, narrowing his eyes.

'Of course. Thomas Furey's last letter, in which he admits to having forged the Dowley poems and more besides, would be a sensation. I'm no expert, but I guess the American collections would want it, would give it a price. Corvin could offer it to the British Library in lieu of tax.'

'Out of the question,' he sniffed. 'It's a private letter.'

'But to whom does it rightly belong?' I asked. 'Wasn't that the first Samuel's argument for publishing his father's diary?'

'*The value of plain truth being universal,*' murmured the doctor, frowning. Then he breathed in sharply. 'No, it's out of the question.'

11

Much to M'Synder's consternation, Corvin persuaded me to join him on some cross-country runs over the hills and down into the various secluded valleys that cut into them from the east. One evening as we huffed and puffed up the muddy lane I heard again the sound of my mother's old lawnmower, and we turned to see a single round headlight bobbing after us through the dusk. We waited outside the cottage, standing in our mud-spattered shorts like two sweaty, steaming, curly-haired schoolboys, until the familiar car lurched to a halt. A slim figure got out, indistinct behind the headlight's glare, lifted a small case from the boot and stepped forward.

'Hi,' said Rose, glancing sharply at Corvin as though she hadn't expected him, but recovering quickly. 'Wow, you boys turned out in your Sunday best,' she added, looking us up and down. 'I feel honoured.' She herself was wearing a long printed skirt and prim dark jacket. Corvin bowed and took her case as the car swung into its turn and gave a coy farewell toot.

'I'll be takin' that,' said M'Synder sternly at the door, looking down at Corvin's sodden trainers and barring his way. 'What have you done to my respectable lodger?' He bowed again without speaking, the lamplight showing off a big black beauty-spot of mud on his cheek, then jogged away into the dusk leaving us only the fading tick, tock, tick of his feet pounding the track.

'I talked them into giving me early release,' said Rose later, when I was once again respectable, scrubbed, pink-cheeked, damp-haired and fragrant in my smart pullover. 'A week of private study before the holidays.'

'Oh well, our Mr Browne knows all about that,' said M'Synder, winking at me. 'He'd be teacher's pet for sure, if there *was* a teacher. Bunched over his notebook all evening, copyin' out little squiggles that nobody reads, in a language that nobody speaks.'

'Well,' I began, valiantly casting about for a riposte, 'I suppose the word *squiggle* comes from *squirm*, which comes from *worm*, which comes from the Old English *wyrm*, which is surely related to the Latin *vermis*, which is in turn related to the Greek *rhomox*. So you speak the language, for one.' M'Synder looked unconvinced.

'*Squiggle* from *rhomox*,' laughed Rose, taking her seat beside me. 'That's pushing it. You'd do better to remind her that it's the language of the New Testament — although that was Common, not Attic Greek.'

'It's all Gree— oh, never mind,' muttered M'Synder, helping herself to the salt.

The constant sight of Rose's jagged scar, for which, according to Corvin, she had always refused reconstructive surgery, troubled me even more now that I knew its precise origin — I could not rid my mind of imaginings of the avalanche, of the idea of being trapped, buried alive, hearing the faint, desperate thuds of a steel edge. The scarf she had just hung on the hook in the hall — was it the same one? Why not, let it be — the longest of those red lines drawn against the terror of oblivion.

'Doctor Comberbache will certainly make sure you keep your word, and do your studyin',' said M'Synder pointedly, serving us slices of forced rhubarb crumble with custard.

'Oh, I'll be sketching, mostly,' replied Rose. 'You know, making studies. That's what I meant.'

'Hm. Well, per'aps you should show Mr Browne the pictures in your room — he's quite the connoisseur, y'know.' Rose turned to me just as the doctor had at the door of the temple.

'Alright,' she said.

I suppose I had imagined that Rose's room would be similar to my own — plain and squarish, but instead it was long and narrow, with a bed jammed across the far end and furniture crowded along each side so that there was barely room to walk between. Laden shelves leaned precariously over the bed and a small writing desk stood at a window overlooking the lane, the ragged hedge and the stream beyond. But of course it is the pictures that I remember most — swarming over the walls, stacked under the bed, leaning against the wardrobe and pinned to its doors.

'Do you consider it a kind of communication, like writing?' I asked, looking from one to the next. I was thinking of Furey trapped in his garret, dreaming of recognition: they were the same age. Rose stood with her arms folded, watching me. She shrugged at my question.

'Communion is a better word — between my own selves, maybe,' she replied. 'It allows me to orientate myself. It allows me to — listen to my past and address my future.'

'Alas, not the reverse!' I said. 'So, a kind of diary in pictures? But you paint for other people as well, don't you?'

'It allows of that too,' she answered, simply.

Two pictures in particular caught my eye. One was a bold

watercolour hanging by the door — a pink rose against a wash of dappled green, with the petals torn away on one side. The tones of those remaining deepened from a pale base to a narrow fringe of scarlet pressing up against the massed green tint of the background, defying the tendency of watery things to merge and diffuse, maintaining an edge.

'My self-portrait,' she said, with one eyebrow raised. 'It was painted a couple of years ago, so perhaps you don't recognise me.'

'I do,' I said, smiling. The other was a vivid portrait in crayon on grey paper, hanging over the bed: a man of about thirty in half-profile, executed in two colours — chocolate brown for the shadows and cool sky blue for the highlights. A neat, handsome man with dark hair clipped short and a ruminative curl to his lips, looking out of the side of the picture and perhaps nodding slowly: ready to act, but in no hurry. I stepped closer and leaned to read some words written in crayon across the bottom corner: '*Fairer than these, though temple thou hast none, nor altar heap'd with flowers.*'

'Your father?' I said, and she nodded curtly.

'It was done from a photograph.'

On the day before the equinox the slow, resonant clip of Juliet's footsteps rang once again in the hall and the company was complete for what Frizzo the Clown had called the last blast.

'Mr Browne!' she said, pausing in mid-stride when she passed me in the dining room. Her hair was still half-caught in the collar of her cardigan, and the three slender frown lines deepened over the cool eyes. 'Still here? What have these co-conspirators done to you? Shouldn't you be earning a living, meeting friends and family, living a normal life?' My lips were parted to answer when Corvin swept in behind me.

251

'Move along, there,' he said, briskly ushering me forward into the library. 'Don't dawdle. Oh, hello sis,' he added, looking over his shoulder, 'great to see you!'

12

Rose knocked softly on my door before dawn and told me to get dressed quickly. Venus hung like a white lamp over the mouth of the combe as we hurried up the lane to the house, whose door stood open. All the doors were open — I could see straight through to the lawn, silver with dew. Juliet was waiting in the dim hall with another woman in a brimmed hat: it was Agnes. The doctor was slowly making his way down the stairs — I was half expecting some sort of ceremonial robe, but he wore simple brown cords and the Aran jumper, and now reached for his usual waxed coat. Smiles and nods were exchanged but nobody spoke.

Corvin appeared in the dining room in his wild-haired pantisocratic guise, carrying a tray of little steaming glasses — coffee with a dash of something stronger, one mouthful — and then we filed down the garden steps and across the lawn.

Venus had lost her radiance by the time our slow procession reached the top of the temple stair — she was now just a dull white speck of paint, smudged by my own faulty optics, on the greenish continuum between the blue twilight above and the deep amber glow seeping up from the eastern horizon.

We shuffled into the dark temple; the door was closed with a soft click and everyone took their seats around the circle of the sanctum.

Boy-girl-boy on one side, I noticed, girl-boy-girl on the other, just like a dinner party. A faint orange light rested on the centre of the brass calendar on the western curve, in the gap between the doctor and Juliet.

'Friends,' said the doctor at last, breaking the morning's silence. As he smiled and nodded to each of us in turn, a rayed point of light opened like a tiny golden flower on the polished silver boss that marked the equinox — opened wider, brighter, and brighter still, until the whole chamber was bathed in a warm light. All of us were turned towards it except the doctor and Juliet, whose faces were illuminated from one side only: but both were smiling.

'*In nomine nostra*,' he began, '*consideremus*.'

By the time we finished breakfast the garden was bathed in equinoctial sunshine that burned off the dew and breathed its seductive magic on a thousand buds and shoots. Chaffinches skipped about on the terrace, showing off their spring plumage and roguishly snatching breadcrumbs from under each other's noses. There was a faint warmth in the air, so that for the first time one might open a door or a window and feel no compulsion to close it. Indeed, was it not warmer outside than in? Meaulnes emerged from the kitchen garden with his shirt sleeves rolled up and collar open, and a quiet gardener's joy in his big white face. He helped us to carry a table and chairs out onto the terrace, before busying himself with assembling a mysterious contraption in the middle of the lawn.

'Who's coming for a dip?' demanded Corvin, gazing up at the sky from where he lay on the grass, with arms and legs spread in a pantisocratic star.

'I'll come,' said Rose.

'Sis?'

'Not likely,' said Juliet absently, frowning at a page of *Early Music Today*. 'Take Mr Browne.' All eyes turned to me.

'Alright,' I said. 'Where do we go?'

Rose fetched three faded towels from upstairs and tossed one each to Corvin and me, and we trooped out towards the meadow. The bathing pool was a rounded inlet of the stream where the water was deep and clear and a few weed fronds waved in refracted sunlight. I was nervously pondering questions of propriety when Corvin kicked off his shoes, pulled his shirt over his head to reveal a compact, muscular torso, dropped his trousers and underpants together and dived headlong into the pool. He emerged at the far side with a cry of delight.

'You're next, Mr Browne,' said Rose, firmly. I followed Corvin's example as quickly as I could while she looked on with a vague sardonic smile — the knotted combination of my trousers and pants got stuck on one ankle for a long, desperate moment, and then I was free and plunged in after him.

'Good for you, old chap,' he said, calmly treading water as my lungs shuddered with rapid involuntary gasps for air. 'How's that for clearing out the cobwebs?' I was still getting my bearings when I heard another neat splash, and turned to see Rose's head emerge from her own dive, her eyes shining with the shock of cold. For a few seconds we trod water in a triangle, three gasping, vivid, youthful, slick-haired heads from which three blurry white ghosts of nakedness hung suspended, kicking the void. Rose's proud eyes were fixed on Corvin; his, amused and curious, on me, and mine flitted from one to the other as I wrestled alternately with the challenges of determined disinterest and unwanted inferiority. One of the combe's several triangles, I later thought.

'Look!' said Corvin suddenly, cupping his hands together and lifting them above the surface. 'I've caught a fish.' As Rose glanced down he squeezed a powerful spray of water into her face. She surged forward and pushed him under, and then I felt his iron grasp on my ankle, pulling me down. Now we were all wrestling, hands pushing and grasping on cold, slippery, vague bodies, feet kicking, mouths gasping. I recall an arm flung up, Grecian contours falling from a slim cord of muscle to a white, faintly stubbled armpit to a glimpsed breast; the instep of a kicking foot skimming down my thigh; white fingers raked through dark hair and a burst of laughter with eyes closed tight against the spray. Then the moment was over and we were back in our triangle of heads, breathing hard.

'I've had it,' gasped Rose, and turned to the bank.

'Two minutes is about the limit if you're not used to it,' said Corvin to me.

'I know,' I said, my teeth starting to chatter. 'All systems pr-preparing to sh-shut down.' I glimpsed the long backs of Rose's legs shining in the sun as she towelled herself furiously, and then I staggered up the slippery bank myself. My skin flushed and burned as blood seethed back out from the protected core. A blackbird's song, one of the season's first, erupted from a nearby chestnut tree, and soft grass tickled my toes. Corvin was the last to get dressed.

'Alive!' he cried triumphantly towards the wooded hillside, holding his towel above his head like a trophy so that the muscles of his back slid and swelled. 'Alive and alight!'

13

Brimming with heat and health we skipped back to the house, where many lights of the great library windows had been thrown open on reluctant hinges and a fine, joyous music poured out across the lawn.

'This is Linley, Mr Browne!' cried the doctor, pointing towards the sound. 'Thomas Linley the Younger, the brilliant son!' He closed his eyes as a choir burst into song.

The music filled the house, whose doors were all thrown open (all save one). Delicious smells, laughter and the clatter of pots wafted from the kitchen, and Agnes was laying the dining table for eight.

'Will you help me to carry some drinks?' she asked, and led me to the empty parlour. She opened the cabinet, seized two glasses in each hand and then turned and studied me quizzically. Not so bad to be old, I thought, at least to have had time to think, to be one step ahead of the young. 'Does my presence here seem so strange to you?' she whispered, with a wry smile in a face that was all wrinkles and make-up. 'Yours seems strange to me, O man from London, so we are even.' A rattle of laughter spilled over from elsewhere in the house, and she smiled again. 'There is a happiness here, is there not? *A man's heart is accommodative* ...' She trailed off and frowned. 'Something is missing though, isn't it? Listen.' We faced off in silence for a few seconds, our hands full of empty glasses. 'Only outsiders can ask the question,' she said. 'What's a party with no children?'

'All hands on deck!' called the doctor's voice. '*Miraculum demonstrabitur*!' Agnes winked at me and we poured the drinks and carried them out to the terrace.

Meaulnes stood proudly beside his contraption, to which a hosepipe snaked across the lawn from the side of the house, while the seven of us lined up along the top of the steps.

'Monsieur Meaulnes is about to initiate a process whose path and consequences are unknown to science,' said the doctor, 'so hold on to your hats. Let fly, Monsieur!' The gardener stooped and turned a tap on the end of the hose, and after a few seconds the contraption began to move — a long horizontal beam tilting slowly down at one end, then swinging back the other way, then pausing for a while before creeping back slowly, then switching direction again and swinging round smartly. The effect was oddly disquieting: our eyes searched for a whimsical guiding hand where there was none, and for a while nobody spoke.

'Behold the chaotic pendulum,' said the doctor at last, crossing his arms in satisfaction, 'here created by the flow of water into a tilting tube. Designed by the late Hartley Comberbache Esquire, executed by Monsieur Meaulnes, and now to be explained to us all by Mr S. Browne, Bachelor of Science, upper second class.'

After a second visit to the temple to witness the sunset and a careful, lantern-lit descent in the deepening gloom (the steep, straight stair neatly enforces seriousness, I thought), curtains were hauled across windows and fires lit. The doctor directed a boisterous game of charades beneath Taboni's angel of truth — Corvin, Meaulnes and I calling out our guesses from the back whilst conducting a scholarly whisky tasting at the long line of decanters. Rose at first refused her turn, then proposed a book, three words, and simply pointed at Meaulnes, standing in his great woolly socks with a glass of whisky in each hand and the brooding sky of *Despair* behind him: he blushed and mumbled something in French (I caught only that ethereal name, *Yvonne de Galais*). Later we reassembled upstairs around the piano, where the opposing mirrors multiplied our small company into a dizzying corridor of merriment and motion punctuated by a thousand priceless vases. Corvin sang one of Linley's arias in a depressingly true countertenor to Juliet's accompaniment — he said this was to excuse him from playing the violin, which the doctor himself picked up instead and sawed out a rather wobbly tune, before Agnes and Juliet gave us a ragtime piano duet quite as chaotic as the ingenious pendulum.

'Make way!' cried the doctor afterwards, coming along the landing with two long swords in tarnished scabbards and a pair of white shoes. 'It's time for the hornpipe.' He drew out the blades solemnly and passed them to Corvin, who laid them in a cross in the middle of the floor and then began to limber up as though for a race. 'Place your bets, ladies and gentlemen,' said the doctor, as Juliet seated herself again at the piano. 'Sorry my dear,' he added, laying a hand on her shoulder, 'but I'm for Corvin this time.'

'Yes, Swinburne,' said Agnes.

'Le monsieur,' said Meaulnes, nodding gravely.

'Corvin,' murmured Rose.

'Well, *I'm* for dear Juliet,' pledged M'Synder, suddenly appearing on the stairs. 'And so's Mr Browne! In't that right?'

Juliet played the opening bars of the familiar sailor's hornpipe melody at a very slow tempo, like a child learning her first tune, and a thousand Corvins began to move. Straightaway I thought: forget the singing, the plotting courses, the running, the swimming, the drifting, the mysterious projects — *this* is what he was born to do. Juliet began to play a little faster and he was able to warm into the more energetic leaps and kicks, his limbs billowing to left and right while his body hung motionless in space or swayed to one side and the other like the mast of a keeling ship. The doctor and Agnes cheered and clapped. Juliet played faster. The movements became smaller and more precise, now limited to the feet only with occasional leaps from one quadrant to another, landing right on the beat. Juliet played faster still — brilliantly, impossibly fast, leaning slightly into the keyboard, frowning with concentration and effort but with lips parted in a half-smile, and the pointed toes of Corvin's dancing shoes moved faster than sight, until at last he stumbled against the hilt of one of the swords, dropped to one knee in submission to his sister, and then rose slowly to his feet while we all cheered and congratulated them both.

'I'm sorry old friend,' murmured Juliet to the piano, stroking the lid soothingly. 'Did that hurt?'

Corvin stood for a moment breathing hard and wiped his glowing face on his sleeve, then as his sister began to play a new dance he offered Rose a gallant bow and invited her to join him. She blushed and hesitated, and I felt a little twinge of yearning for her, a simple yearning of the old, pre-marriage, pre-divorce kind, of the kind that Meaulnes felt for her and that she felt for this laughing dancer. And he? For whom did he yearn as he raised his crossed arms again and shifted weight nimbly from one foot to the other? For none of us, certainly: for someone else, perhaps — I will not pretend to know.

Any hangover is rich with soulful promise whose crop, however, can be reaped only in solitude. That other part of the mind, its industrial machinery, lies idle, clogged with dehydration and lassitude, and the soul (why not call it that?) has free play: for a few precious and painful hours the hungover man is a mystic.

I spent the first of these hours lying in bed with the sheet thrown back and the cold morning air and birdsong wafting through the casement. My underpants, I noticed with a rakish smile, were on inside-out after my hasty sartorial operations on the riverbank. This recollection half-revived me and I bumbled downstairs to toast and coffee and a scalding shower, and then stepped out into the lane to share with the robin and the red squirrel my sluggish reflections on the pleasures of private study on the one hand, and the inescapable necessity to provide for oneself on the other.

'Was that spring we had,' murmured Corvin at the library window that afternoon, 'or just a dream of spring?' The morning had been cool and cloudy and now heavy spots of rain began to darken the terrace and scud down the ancient glass: nature's unhelpful restatement, it seemed, of what a thousand poets have already told us — that radiant beauty must not last. The windows were all fastened now, and M'Synder's spiced soup was back in demand.

During that week the doctor busied himself with his publisher's suggested revisions to *Giveth and Taketh Away* and Rose spent hours shut in her room, presumably working on her drawings. Juliet went to London to meet her parents, who were visiting from the 'tumbledown house' in Provence to which they had moved on retiring a few years before. Corvin said he was too busy to accompany her: 'Tell them I'll come to the T.H. in May,' he said from the library doorway as she and I stood in the dining room. 'I have some important work to finish here.'

'What work?' she asked, but the door closed with a soft click. She sighed and turned to go, then glanced back across the table to give me one last beautiful frown as a parting gift.

14

So began my thirteenth week at the sacred combe, but surely we, like Rose, are not superstitious. My interdisciplinary studies were by now going so well that I overlooked the fact that my stay was exceeding the scope of the doctor's invitation. It was a week of cold, hostile rains that hammered flat the early shoots of daffodils, tormented the muddy lane and force-fed the bloated stream with tributaries tumbling noisily off the hills.

On Friday morning I entered the library with a borrowed satchel under my arm to find Corvin seated by a merry blaze at Sarah's end of the room, wearing for the third time his Chadwickian high collar and waistcoat, with one ankle tucked up onto his knee and his hands behind his head.

'How's our visiting scholar this morning?' he asked, slowly circling the toe of his shoe. 'Would he like to play a game with me? My mind is feeling simultaneously agile and indolent today.'

'I was planning to work on my Gibbon,' I said warily, pushing back my wet hair and taking off my rain-spattered glasses to wipe them.

'Oh, but Gibbon is a patient fellow,' he returned dismissively, 'and I'm not. Brew us some strong coffee and I'll set up the game.' I returned from the kitchen to find two chairs arranged symmetrically before the fire, and between them a table bearing a large backgammon board. 'My gift to Arnold from the Gulf,' said Corvin as he laid out the counters. 'I bought it in the market in Basra. As it happens, he dislikes the element of chance and prefers chess and draughts. I like the element of chance: I find it instructive. But we often buy gifts for ourselves inadvertently, don't we? Take a seat.' We played — I needed reminding of the rules, but in the first game, to my surprise, I gammoned him. He flashed an inscrutable smile and reset the board. Later he won a few games but I kept throwing doubles and won the match comfortably.

'So — you win the right to choose,' he said, clearing the board and folding it shut. 'Will you listen or tell?'

'I'll listen,' I replied, trying to keep up. 'But even I've realised what day it is today — why should I believe a word you say?'

'Because I'll begin my story at noon,' he replied, slipping a small pocket watch from his waistcoat and eyeing it significantly, 'so if I tell a single lie, the joke's on me.'

The wind was rising, wrinkling puddles along the terrace and flinging the rain this way and that. I could once again hear the restless tap-tapping of the wind-dial behind the locked door, but if Corvin heard it he made no comment. At noon he began to tell his story — the story of his life — 'heavily abridged,' he said, 'like all stories.'

He spoke for perhaps an hour at a time, dividing his past into chapters between which I was to study or rest or eat my lunch — 'while I make up the next bit,' he added mischievously to himself, as though I was not supposed to hear. He reached the present year, even the present day, as dusk was falling, and seemed quite ready to continue the narrative when the doctor knocked at the door (odd to knock at one's own door, I thought) and shuffled in from the study.

'*O critics, cultured critics!*' he said, grimacing and waving his

263

manuscript. 'I've finished the accursed revisions. Come dine with me and do your worst — burlesque me, boil me down, do whatever you like with me!' I tried to comment constructively on the passages that he read out across the table, while Corvin seemed preoccupied and kept largely silent as the wind boomed and moaned around the combe.

'Now you have the past,' he resumed as if there had been no interruption, as we returned to our seats in the library after dinner. 'But in recent weeks I've also been thinking about the future. You've been trying not to, I suspect, but don't worry — I have ideas enough for both of us.'

'Such as?' I asked, remembering his strange words in The Croked Hand as he stacked his empty glass on top of mine.

'Well, I'm going to write a book. There — I've said it. I've been thinking about it for quite some time now — even while I was in the Gulf. But you've helped to show me how it might be done.' Is that all? I thought. One more mumbling book to add to these thousands? Is that really the *noblest and best path* he can imagine? But I envied his — yes, his decisiveness.

'What kind of book?'

'A book about this place — about the combe and its history. It deserves one, surely. Of course I'll change the names — that gives me more freedom to invent.'

'Why would you need to invent anything? Why not just tell the truth?'

'I don't know, old chap,' he replied in low voice, leaning towards me. 'Maybe I've had enough of this bloody creed of truth — I have a craving to make something up, but I want to do it *by the book*, as it were. The key was to come up with a suitable narrative voice, and I think I have.'

'Go on,' I prompted, frowning.

'An outsider. An earnest young fellow with a slightly mincing gait, wandering eyes and a tendency to wear ill-fitting clothes — of course, he won't describe himself that way: a narrator must be slightly egotistical to be convincing. He'll tell the story of the combe as revealed to him during his visit.'

'And what then?'

'If people buy my book, I'll write another one.'

'And if they don't?'

'I'll write another one anyway.'

'And if they don't buy that one?'

'Oh, then I'll study medicine,' he replied, waving his hand impatiently, 'or computer programming, or banking. What was your job title?'

'I was a quantita—' I never could get that word out, and tried again: 'a quantitata— a quantittertatter— a *quantitative* analyst. *Quant*, for short.' He shrugged.

'That'll do, if all else fails.'

'And what were your ideas for me?' At this he raised his eyebrows, pursed his lips and looked heartily amused. But before he could answer we were interrupted by a tearing, splintering crash that shook the very fabric of the house — suddenly not so sure of itself after all. For a moment Corvin's face remained frozen in that expression of mirth, now painfully inappropriate, before we both leapt to our feet.

'Hello!' came a thin, wavering voice from the study. 'Man overboard, hello!' We rushed in to a scene of alien disorder: cold air swept into the room from the great window, the doctor lay twisted on the floor by the side table surrounded by broken glass and porcelain, and spots of rain were landing one by one on the leather of the hallowed desk.

It was that mighty low branch of Hartley's beech tree, big as a big tree in its own right and heavy with sap and glowing shoots — it had pitched up and down, up and down all evening as the gusts swirled and howled around the house, and had buckled at last and fallen. As it struck the gravel it had keeled sideways like a ship run aground, and one quivering spar had lunged through the study window just as the doctor set his teacup on the mantelpiece. He had cowered back from the flying glass and stonework and lost his balance, wrenching his one good knee and banging his head as he fell heavily against the side table.

Now we all sat in the parlour: Corvin and I hot and breathless from our efforts to move the furniture away from the window and cover the worst of the breach with an old tent canvas, and the doctor pale-faced, wrapped in a blanket with a neat dressing on his forehead and a bag of frozen peas on his knee.

'Well,' he said, wincing as he shifted in his chair, his mouth now fixed in the pained smile as though the wind had changed on him (I suppose it had).

'Well,' echoed Corvin with a sigh, 'it could have been worse.'

15

Telling M'Synder and Rose about the accident had been my job, and of course my reassurances could not prevent them hurrying back with me to the house. M'Synder went straight in to see the casualty but Rose stood for a while in the drive, staring at the fallen branch and the tree's gaping wound, the scattered debris and the wrecked window whose stonework hung precariously like a Piranesi vault. She said nothing, but for a moment those iridescent green eyes were wide with alarm and disorientation, as though she saw something I had missed. An inscription, perhaps: '*et in arcadia ego.*'

'It could have been worse,' I parroted meekly, glancing up at the tree still thrashing and moaning over the house. She eyed me sharply as if to say 'what would you know?' and hurried inside. We found M'Synder standing over the doctor, asking solicitous questions but at the same time slowly surveying the neat bandage, the blanket, the leg raised on a cushion, and the mug of cocoa. She looked up at Corvin with reluctant approbation, and then turned to the dying fire and peered into the scuttle.

'I'll fill 'er up,' she said, seizing it resolutely and stumping out of the room.

Meaulnes made a welcome appearance the next morning, and he and I cleared several fallen branches out of the lane so that when the patient's stubbornness at last relented, a four-wheel-drive ambulance was able to churn its way up the combe before noon and carry him away for treatment.

'Suspect mild concussion and a cruciate ligament injury,' he murmured to the paramedics as they carried his stretcher through the hall, 'compounded by osteoarthritis. Oh, my dear Mr Browne, please taketh and giveth away the manuscript to the post office — it's already overdue.' He was still muttering as they loaded him into the ambulance: 'A prod from old Hartley, you think? No, it was just that Second Law doing its work — I've been entropised. Prognosis: patient to be back on his feet in a week, but unlikely to cope with stairs, *especially if staircase is long or steep or lacks handrail*. Consider stairlift or bungalow. Next patient, please.'

Rose accompanied him to the hospital, while the rest of us continued clearing up and M'Synder made arrangements for a stonemason and glazier to fix the window. The weather turned bright, the sharp April sunlight picking out bristling shoots of vivid green along the banks of the lane and in the trees arching and swaying over it. Rose returned and reported that all was as the doctor had predicted, and he would be home in two days to rest.

'We'll have to make up a bed on the ground floor,' she said. 'In the parlour, I suppose.' I rather enjoyed her new persona as mistress of the house, fierce and sensible, snapping directions to me and Meaulnes and even M'Synder, but she seemed to draw the line at cheery, self-assured Corvin, in whose company she shrank once again into artful adolescence.

The doctor's eyes, when he returned early the following week, had lost their sparkle. He sat rather glumly in his wheelchair and stared at the bed we had carried downstairs and positioned across the parlour window.

'You've all been very kind,' he murmured awkwardly. 'Now, I wonder if I might have a little peace, and a little Bach. *Composed for connoisseurs,*' he added with a bitter smile, '*for the refreshment of their spirits* — that's what I need.'

Corvin seemed uncomfortable with the doctor's new predicament. He was a man of many talents, dressing wounds among them, but he was not a patient nurse.

'Since Arnold wants a few days' peace and quiet,' he said breezily the next day, 'and since I'm not a very peaceful or quiet housemate, how would you like to come up to Ben Nevis with me this weekend? I could take you up that North-East Buttress.' Rose looked up from her sketchbook frowning, but said nothing. 'I am reliably informed that the storms washed away most of the snow, and now the fine weather has dried the rock nicely — the ridge routes are in summer condition, more or less. Trust me: you'll love it.'

'What was that nasty step called?' I said doubtfully, adjusting my glasses and trying to look delicate. 'The Man-eater?' Corvin was having none of my vacillation.

'The Mantrap!' he cried, leaping to his feet, then glancing guiltily at the door and lowering his voice. 'Guess who's going up that first, ladder-monkey!'

He led me up to the vast attic, where one whole room was filled with climbing equipment — coils of rope, straps and strange clusters of ironmongery hanging from nails on the rafters like giant multicoloured bats above dark Jacobean chests full of the same. He looked me up and down and smiled.

'Let's get you kitted up.'

So I boarded a train for the first time in three months: left the sacred combe far behind but carried perhaps its rarest curiosity — Corvin — on the seat beside me as we darted through the lamb-speckled wonders of Cumbria and the southern uplands of Scotland. It was a long journey, and we talked. I told him everything, I think, just as he had predicted — or at least everything that you have yourself read in this account (as to what remains untold, about my marriage or anything else, you and he are free to speculate).

'Don't mind me,' he said at one point, slipping a notebook from his pocket and writing a few lines. 'I always carry one of these on the train.' I talked more, and he wrote a few more lines.

Upon reaching Fort William at dusk we clambered over a low hill that obscured the comforting lights and sounds of the town, and then stumbled and cursed our way across a lumpy, scratchy moor to the banks of a river which produced a blank, eerie noise in the darkness. Further up the valley a vague shadow loomed against the sky. Corvin searched about judiciously and, having found a flat, mossy platform sat down on a boulder beside it.

'Welcome to our humble abode,' he said, cheerfully. 'Make yourself at home.'

'Won't the sound of the river keep us awake?' I asked.

'Oh, the ear is accommodative,' he replied, opening his rucksack and pulling out a small sleeping bag. 'In half an hour you'll hear nothing.'

He was right, and after sleeping soundly I opened my eyes to a blue April sky thronged with benevolent clouds.

'Still or sparkling?' asked Corvin, carrying our two water bottles from the riverbank. A reckless, rootless feeling came over me as we tied our boots and packed away the sleeping bags — it was like that moment of looking back at the patch of flattened grass as you leave a campsite with the tent on your back, but this heather had suffered not even the imprint of a tent, nothing attached to the ground — we simply stood up and walked away. The human instinct to settle was for a moment troubled by an even older one — the one that had got humanity to wherever he settled in the first place — then it passed and we were just two lads out for a walk.

As we trooped up the path the mountain drew nearer — the dark alter ego of that friendly, rounded Ben Nevis of family holidays and the *Three Peaks Challenge*, its monstrous grey buttresses looming forward from the distant, corniced edge of the plateau hanging sharp against the sky. Snow lay thick in the famous gullies and was scattered liberally across the higher slopes. An air of menace hung about the last of the buttresses, a jutting silhouette at the head of the valley, soaring a thousand feet straight to the summit.

'Which one are we going up?' I asked, trying to identify the least threatening of the many ridges and spurs. Corvin smiled and looked straight ahead towards the last.

'Just think of it as a series of ladders,' he said, 'one on top of the other. And here you have no books to worry about — you can hold on with both hands.'

When we stopped for a sip of water deep under the shadow of the first cliffs, I gazed up and tried to recall the photograph in the locked room, which showed the mountain under much heavier snow.

'Where's *The Temple*?' I murmured. Corvin nodded towards the steepest cliff of them all, crossed by overhanging faults like a suit of armour with plates stacked one upon the other. One overhang was deeper and darker than all the others. 'The Pediment,' I mouthed silently, craning my neck. Corvin followed my gaze with narrowed eyes, the wind flicking at his long corkscrews of hair.

'Do you feel it?' he whispered. 'The pull, up towards the sky? The lure of the unattainable?' I did feel something — a premonition of vertigo, a kind of panic in my stomach that reminded me of something else. I took a slow breath.

'Sometimes you have to admit defeat without a fight,' I said, serenely. Which fights, I wondered, were left to me?

'And sometimes not,' replied Corvin. '*Consideremus.*' We stood in reverent silence for a moment, then he turned and bounded on up the path. We passed the lonely climbers' hut with its wind turbine thrumming away uselessly, and later crossed beneath the looming bulk of our own buttress — behind which, to my relief, there was an easier way up.

'At the lower grades, mountaineering is wonderfully pragmatic,' said my guide, pointing out the way. 'It's all about finding the line of least resistance.'

'And at the higher grades?' His lips twisted into a grim smile as he glanced back along the cliffs.

'You've seen what *that's* about.'

He led me across a steep, slabby hillside back towards the buttress, which we joined on a broad platform above the lowest cliffs. Already the valley was far below and the climbers' hut a tiny squarish speck, but the mountain seemed to loom above us higher and steeper than ever. There were no more easy ways up.

'This is where we rope up,' he said, shrugging off his rucksack and laying his slim fingers on the wall of rock that barred our way. 'We'll use running belays. Put on your harness and helmet and screw your courage to the sticking place.'

We barely spoke a word to each other on the journey south. Corvin dashed off a few more notes and gazed out of the train window while

I read my book — Borges — and relived the strange new euphoria of pleasure and fear I had experienced on the shattered side of a mountain.

After a couple of hours in one particularly busy carriage, Corvin bumped my knee gently with his own. 'I like trains,' he declared in a level murmur without turning his head, as though we were birdwatchers in the presence of a rare flock. 'But sometimes I lose the knack of them, and feel a silent rant against humanity rise up within me.' He paused for a moment, perhaps checking that no one else had heard him, then continued in his low monotone: '"Look at yourselves!" the rant says, "Reading your tawdry papers and thumbing your gadgets! Overwhelmed by cleverness and anxiety, good intentions and a terminal loss of imagination, fooled by sly convention, crippled by the woes of specialised competence and the joys of generalised ignorance, like circus animals when the crowds have lost interest. Come away, you silly oxen! The combe awaits you! There is no guard to bribe, no gate to keep the riff-raff out! Come away! Do not go gentle into that *London Lite!*"' He again fell silent for a few seconds. 'Then I recover myself, open my senses, observe the ever-renewing gallery of expressions on preoccupied faces, notice a familiar book in an unlikely hand, catch a coded fragment of lovers' talk or the friendly words exchanged by strangers, maybe meet someone's idly wandering gaze and look away. Yes, I like trains.' He opened his notebook and said no more.

We had to run for the branch-line's last service of the night, and then made our way perhaps ten miles in darkness, across fields, over stiles and fences and through black woods to the mouth of the combe. Corvin knew the way, of course, and I followed, panting and sweating as I tried to keep up.

16

At breakfast I asked M'Synder how the doctor was feeling, but she only smiled reassuringly and said, 'I think I'll let you go and see for yourself.' In the lane I met Corvin pounding down from the house in his running shorts and a dress shirt with cuffs flapping open.

'Doctor alright?' I asked as he shot past.

'Never better!' he called over his shoulder, and was gone.

On reaching the house I knocked at the open parlour door, and then peered cautiously round it to find the bed gone and the chairs back in their usual places.

'Is that you, Mr Browne?' called his voice from behind me, in a kind of mirrored *déjà-entendu* of his once calling me from the parlour. 'I'm in the study. Please do come in.' He was seated at his desk working as though nothing had happened. The dismembered hulk in the drive and the large, blank boards screwed across one side of the window were the only reminders of the storm.

'Sorry I was such a miserable Casaubon last week,' he said, brightly. 'I'm feeling much better now.'

'You can climb the stairs already?' I asked.

'Ah, no, I'm afraid I was right about stairs — neither of my corroded old knees seems to want to take that particular responsibility. I asked them nicely, but we came to something of a stand-off on the bottom step.'

'But the bed's gone,' I observed.

'Yes. I issued new instructions. I've settled myself into a different room.' I looked around — there was no bed here.

'The library?' I guessed. He gave a short, dry laugh.

'Oh dear, no — that would be rather antisocial, or perhaps hyper-social, and besides, I couldn't possibly sleep under Hartley's gaze.' I knew what he meant — if my attention had wandered from the Spartan congresses, or the fire had been too warm and my eyelids had begun to hang heavy, it was always the luminous urgency of the portrait that re-engaged my mind's machinery. 'No,' he went on, pointing over his shoulder, 'the morning room is to be my bedroom now — you know, the one that's been locked up.' The mourning room. He looked at me steadily. 'I don't think Sam would want to be *confined* in there anymore.' He went on looking, and gave a soft smile that did not seem pained at all. 'I've tidied the place up a bit — let him out.' I relaxed my practised silence and returned the smile.

'I'm glad,' I said, and he nodded, the wrinkles of his smiling eyes spreading across that face that was speckled brown like a sound autumn leaf.

'What is more,' he went on, slowly, '*I have found something.*' His gaze dropped to a weird object encircled by his two hands on the desk — it was a magnifying glass in the shape of a giant, bulbous eye with brass lids. This he now began to slide with his fingertips by infinitesimal degrees across a piece of paper, so that swollen whorls of ink rose and fell inside the glass. We both leaned closer.

'Furey's letter,' I said.

'Indeed,' he murmured, continuing his painstaking scrutiny. 'There is some faint scoring on the last page, and the text of Uncle Prune's thesaurus has leached a mottled sheen of ink onto the paper, making visible the depressions. I hope to take it to a friend in Oxford for closer examination. As you know, torn fragments of paper were found beside Furey's body.'

'What is it, then?' I asked. 'A last poem?' He glanced up and smiled again. 'Is it Dowley, or Furey?'

'The good priest himself. Short but incontrovertibly genuine, unlike the other supposed "last poems" doing the rounds. Might boost the market value, eh? Would you like me to quote you a line?'

April is the miracle month in England, and I suppose there is a kind of cruelty in miracles. No other month comes close — October's work has the same bewildering swiftness, but dying is easy. The combe surprised me by its fine excesses wherever I turned. On a windless day the birds could taste as I did that mysterious promise of summer in the air, and oh, how they sang! Birdsong danced in through every window and onward through the ragged gaps in my soul, skipped and chattered and laughed along its derelict corridors, quickened it, bothered it, distracted and jumbled and drowned out its tentative repairs and left a smile of surrender on my face. An old blackbird (the oldest are the true masters) took possession of the cottage roof and poured mindless ecstasy into my waking, while wrens cheered me along the lane with piercing volleys of sound above the gentle, persistent prattling of the dunnocks with whom they shared the hedges.

One such windless afternoon found me sitting in Corvin's alcove in the now blossom-heavy orchard with a long, lazy kiss of sunlight on my eyelids, a sheaf of letter paper lying idle in one hand, a pen in the other, mesmerised by the drumming of a woodpecker in the nearby grove: a deep, shuddering, unworldly resonance, a drumming through the thin bark of the present, perhaps, into the tree rings of my own past, brief but coming again and again so that I could think of nothing else — could only wait for the next deliciously unenlightening burst, until the world shifted a little, the next delicious burst didn't come and I opened my eyes.

'It's a pity you'll never the see the gardens in their full glory, in high summer.' So remarked Corvin later that same afternoon, as we walked together across the lawn. Now that the doctor and M'Synder seemed both to have accepted me as a settled inhabitant of the combe and made no mention of my departure, it was this young pretender, having held me here since his return, directed my steps, steered my very thoughts as once he had steered a mindless hulk of steel, who again exerted his will.

'Yes, it's a pity,' I said casually, concealing a pang of resigned sorrow. Was it decided, after all? Did I not have a say?

'You'll just have to imagine it,' he went on, waving his hand across the budding vista: 'A foaming wave of delphinia in alien shades of blue; the intoxicating smell of a heap of wet grass roasting in the sun; Arnold in sandals, short trousers and a panama.'

'Now that last item I can't imagine,' I said, laughing.

'What about the ruddy-faced clown,' he suggested quickly, 'seated in the quiet, breezy shade of the treehouse with a laptop computer and a bottle of beer that he's just retrieved from the cooling waters of the stream?'

'Alone?'

'Of course — alone, aloof, having a prospect of the distance only.' A swift shadow fell across the garden as clouds rolled over the summit of Grey Man, and for a moment Corvin seemed to lose his enviable repose, to shift awkwardly, self-consciously as he squinted at the sky. I was almost reminded of myself. 'Only his doubts attend,' he muttered.

Rose went back to school at the end of this, my fifteenth week. Thanks to the blackbird I did not sleep through her departure this time, but joined her for a last coffee in M'Synder's parlour while she waited for the car.

'Good luck with your exams,' I said.

'Thank you, Mr Browne.' She folded a white shirt-collar down over her pinstripe jacket and smoothed it with quick fingers.

'Won't you call me Sam, just once?' She looked back at me with her steady child's gaze, gently pulled outwards at one corner by the scar.

'Alright. Sam. I've drawn a picture for you — a memento.' I certainly blushed, but didn't seem to care anymore: I wouldn't see her again.

'You shouldn't have, really —'

'It didn't quite come off, I'm afraid,' she said, turning to M'Synder's letter-rack, drawing out a small paper and laying it before me on the table. It was a meticulous ink drawing of the view from the little landing window — there was the stream in its thistly meadow, the lane from which Corvin had once raised a gloved hand, the lamp hanging over the steep-sided porch, the bent hawthorn from which the robin had first performed his quiet serenade —

'What bird is that?' I asked, in a level voice.

'It's a jay,' she replied, cheerfully. Oh, why spoil it with a jay? I thought. Why? 'A big, colourful thing,' she went on. 'It landed there in the hawthorn while I was drawing and stayed for ages, bobbing its head and looking up at me. It *wanted* to be in the picture, I think.'

'Well, thank you very much,' I said, looking up into those sharp green eyes for one, two heartbeats before the soft clatter of a car summoned her to the door. 'It will mean a lot to me.'

17

One morning I crossed the bridge to find an intrepid van parked in the drive. The portly stonemason stood nearby talking to Meaulnes while the doctor looked on from his wheelchair. They were evidently concluding their discussions about the repairs, and now as I watched the mason lifted a heavy parcel from the van and handed it to the giant gardener, who hefted it up under one arm and loped away to his yard.

'What are you working on?' asked the doctor shortly afterwards, as he crutched himself steadily towards me down the long green carpet of the library. The soft thud and creak reminded me of voiceless, one-legged Harry in The Croked Hand. The borrowed man's credit was still good, by the way — his would not be the first to run out, after all.

'Gibbon.' I was nearing the end of the eleventh volume.

'Balls to Gibbon!' he snapped, making me jump. This was, I thought, an unfortunate phrase to aim at the poor historian, who had medical troubles in that region. 'I have a name to breathe some life back into you,' he continued, standing over me with the crutches as though he might prod me with one. '*Shakespeare*. A most reliable guide to history. And have another for no extra charge: Dostoevsky!' I told him I had read *Crime and Punishment* at school. 'Then this week you will read *Hamlet* and *The Brothers Karamazov*,' he shot back. 'Both are compulsory texts at Combe College.'

Parallelograms of afternoon sunlight draped themselves over us while a gentle breeze wafted from a single open pane. The doctor lowered himself carefully into a chair and laid down the crutches, and we had the last of those talks he had promised on my first morning at the combe.

'Perhaps you think this conflict between reason and superstition a touch outdated?' he suggested as we again discussed the inherited creed. '"Hartley and his Enlightenment pals raised the standard," you might say, "and the other side died a slow death: reason won." Well, it is true that superstition and religious dogma (I choose my words carefully) have been relegated to the level of eccentricities — to which, incidentally, all men are surely entitled. Why, I know a well-intentioned retired GP who is obsessed with one composer to the exclusion of all others, even parades him around inside his own name! Ridiculous! But to return to the point, what use have the victors made of their conquest? You agree, I hope, that a daily grind of materialism sprinkled with sentimentality is not enough.'

'Yes, I agree.'

'For me — for us — truth is the sole, simple absolute. All the other so-called virtues and vices are mere cartoons of human behaviour — change your point of observation, look at them side-on, and they change shape or disappear. And I don't mean some mystical conception of truth, of course — just the plain truth. Like —' he seemed to cast about for an example, then fixed his eye on me. 'Did you ever cheat on your wife?' I bristled, but the answer was easy.

'No.' His rejoinder was swift.

'Did you ever have the opportunity to do so?' He held my gaze as I flickered a cursory torch-beam back into memory and glimpsed again those cosy Friday nights at home.

'Not really.'

'Truth begets truth, you see? Doesn't it feel good?' It didn't.

I plunged into *Karamazov* as instructed, and was still riding it like a magnificent, foaming wave when Juliet arrived unexpectedly, on Friday. My eyes were drawn away for a moment from the spell of the narrative and followed her as she came to stand at the library window, half-turned away from me and towards the white, bright, cloudy afternoon sky, cradling the favourite coffee mug, one knee drawn forward to rest on the sill, the heel lifted. *I wish I could have drawn her then.* Sometimes my whole life seems to be a diary of such wishes. Where do they come from, and what are they for?

'I was just telling Arnold and Corvin about my coming to a new understanding with a teacher-friend at the school,' she said, blowing gently into the mug. 'I'm afraid they were rather shocked. But Arnold was the one preaching about paths not yet passed by — do you remember?' I nodded. 'Well, I liked the look of this path, so I've taken it. The rest remains to be seen.' I hesitated for a few seconds, letting the adjustment settle before replying.

'I'm really glad to hear it,' I said, remembering that horrible moment in the garden when a raw January wind was blowing hair across her face. 'I hope he'll make you happy.'

'He's a divorcee, of course,' she said, 'but I suppose we all make mistakes.'

On Saturday the air was warm. Corvin and Meaulnes were busy in the glasshouse all morning, while the doctor, Juliet and I sat at a round table on the corner of the terrace reading and talking. The doctor rambled away happily about the past — he explained, for instance, that his father had been a pioneer of crampons on Scottish mountains before the war, when the British climbing establishment considered them instruments of Satan. 'He used to call them his pins and needles,' he told us fondly, 'because that's what you got from the tight leather binding. When he was cut dead by the president of the SMC at its annual dinner he called after him cheerfully, "And I thought you only cut steps!" Ah, he was proud of that. Now everyone wears them, of course.'

Later he hobbled inside to rest. Corvin appeared with a tray of gardening tools and sat cross-legged in the sun sharpening them, humming to the rhythm of the whetstone while Meaulnes watered the ranks of budding tulips along the side of the lawn.

'What is that tune?' I asked suddenly. 'I keep hearing it.' Corvin's slender brows dropped into a playful frown.

'That? I think I picked it up from Meaulnes. Old chap,' he called, twisting round, 'what's that tune you're always warbling at?' The gardener bunched his lips and gave a rendition for us on the spot, in a delicate, trilling tone of which even the old blackbird might have been proud.

'That one?' he said. 'It came from mon père. He used to sing, you remember, but I cannot. *L'amour est mort* — these were the words, I think.' Corvin's frown deepened.

'*My love is dead,*' said Juliet to her open book, and we all turned to her. '*Gone to his death bed, all under the sallow tree.*' She looked up and gave a sad little smile, then got up without another word and wandered away across the lawn.

'What *is* that?' I had heard it, or read it, before.

'It's the refrain from Furey's famous roundelay,' murmured Corvin, thoughtfully. 'Arnold once told me that Sarah Louise had set it to music, and sung it at Hartley's funeral, but the tune was lost. You don't think — where did your father get that song, old chap?'

Meaulnes shrugged. 'Not from France, I think. Maybe from the old caretaker of Madame Stella? Who knows?' He returned to his watering, whistling softly.

'What is a roundelay anyway?' I asked.

'Just a song with a repeated refrain,' said Corvin. 'I rather fancy it represents the interplay between life and literature' — then his hazel-brown eyes lit up — 'but is life the verse, and literature the repeating refrain, or is it the other way round?' I thought for a moment.

'I suppose that depends on whether you believe more in the possibilities of life or those of literature in making sense of it.'

'Exactly! Men of action and men of words. Isn't it grand? A motif for a book, surely, or part of a book.' He looked around for Juliet, and then saw her sitting motionless on a bench in the cedar's dark shadow. '*L'amour est mort*, indeed,' he murmured. 'Love is dead — a characteristically elegant mistranslation by a Frenchman. But love, it seems, is not dead after all.'

Juliet left the combe the next day, promising to return at the midsummer that I would never see.

18

I was blessed by *il caso* with one week in the combe for each year of Furey's life, and now I had reached the last. The weather stayed fine, but I felt another shift of mood and tone as Corvin and I walked in the gardens — we sighed and smiled knowingly like friends at the end of a long holiday, revisiting the settings of a tantalising near-happiness across which the shadow of impending departure had already fallen. He brought me to the beech grove early on the Friday morning to see the reflected stars of dew glittering red and green on the soft, indigo sea of bluebells that had now welled up from this endlessly fertile tract of sacred ground.

'Here's a question for you,' he said as we crossed the bridge. 'Is it a worse crime to use a dead man's words without acknowledging his authorship, or to attribute to him words that he never wrote or said?' We followed a faint path downstream.

'I'm not sure,' I replied. 'I suppose you should avoid both.'

'There the creed agrees with you, of course. Whereas the world of literature has declared the first sin deadlier than the second, which it simply calls historical fiction. I incline to the opposite view. But for a novelist the passage between these two pitfalls gets rather narrow and tortuous in places.'

Some way off in a clearing behind the kitchen garden, we could see Meaulnes standing with a hammer in one hand and a chisel in the other, contemplating a great sawn section of the fallen bough that stood on end, as tall as him. He began circling it slowly, his big dark head on one side.

'You just have to make a choice,' I suggested, as we passed a weeping willow that blocked the view. 'Limit yourself either to absolute truth or absolute fiction.' I knew this was wrong — after all, didn't I judge any collection of words according to whether I *believed* them? Corvin stopped and turned, letting the damp willow fronds brush over his face.

'You'll have to remind me,' he answered mockingly: 'what exactly is absolute fiction, and where can I find some?'

The telltale dimpling of frogspawn interrupted monochrome reflections of branch and sky in the long pools of the water garden that afternoon. It was during one of those chilly grey interludes with which spring loves to tease us that the doctor's heir, standing effortlessly on one leg opposite the fatal stone seat and sketching the scene rather badly in his notebook, again took up his thread.

'At the very least,' he said, scrawling an imagined seated figure onto his drawing, 'I have to make sure my narrator is a submissive sort of chap. He will observe whilst interfering as little as possible.'

'The husk of my physics education makes me sceptical,' I replied. 'An observer always interferes.'

'Quite so — there must be assumptions, approximations. Even then, numerous problems remain. For example, I might sit this lanky fellow beneath the star-tree on a particular night and have him contemplate infinity. In truth, the seat was empty all night — not even an insomniac bird landed on it, only a hard frost that had no choice in the matter — and we don't mind that. But what if there was a full moon that night, and I have done away with it to protect the celestial display? Now I have not only sketched a fiction onto a truth, but poked my pen into the very workings of the solar system! It's outrageous!'

'But your whole book is just a picture,' I objected, impatiently. 'Ink on paper: everything in it has been created, the solar system included.'

'You flatter me,' he muttered, flipping the notebook shut. 'I do what I can with what I have.'

And what *did* he have? He waited until evening to answer that question — we were walking the perimeter of the meadow, whose trees and grasses glowed like a bed of old embers in the half-light of a half-sun slipping behind the pass at the end of the combe.

'Symbols!' he hissed suddenly. 'Those are my chief weapons! My book will be crammed with them, even if I'm not sure what they all represent.' He flashed an impish smile. 'That way I'll make my readers write most of the book for me.'

'Wouldn't that make it — well, pretentious, by definition?' I said, taking the bait. 'Surely you must know what you want to symbolise first.'

'Not at all — it's natural for the symbol to come first. It appeals to me precisely because it seems to represent something, then it gradually leads me back to the source. One came to me in a vivid dream last year, and I've only just worked out what it stands for.'

'Go on,' I prompted, impatiently.

'It stands for everything that I will try and fail to write about: the unwritten, inaccessible truth. It's an acknowledgment, an apology to my reader. *Even after a tetralogy* (and I won't be writing one of those), *almost everything is still left to say.*'

The sun was gone now, and beyond the meadow the faint line

of the garden wall led the eye to a knot of trees, a peeping chimney, the yellow glimmer of a lighted window.

'And what's the symbol?'

'Ah — you'll see. Suitably horticultural. I'll put it somewhere prominent.'

19

My story has been a gentle one — like most stories, if you count the ones that just happen without being told. Perhaps you hoped that Rose and I would fall in love and drive poor Meaulnes to some desperate act of jealous violence; or that Juliet would be persuaded to replace one Samuel with another; or perhaps you deduced a fundamental reason for the failure of my marriage that pointed to Corvin as my salvation. But no. For my part I have indeed come to love each of them — I have felt in these few weeks affections sharper and stranger than those born of years of friendship in the profane world — but none of them need a Samuel Browne. There is only one vacant seat in the sacred combe and that will never be filled, so my puerile fantasies (and yours) remain just that.

Now I climb the temple stair for the last time. It is Saturday evening, and a dove calls sleepily from her roost as I leave the trees behind and climb the last few curving steps into the celestial realm. There is the ninth stone at the end of the row, set neat and clean in the nibbled turf:

Samuel Taylor Comberbache 1967 – 2000

There are no flowers, no discordant trinkets from the Heraclitian world. I turn and look out; from this lonely promontory I cannot look down into the combe, but only out and away, over the treetops to the long, long line of the horizon until I'm ready to rotate my gaze and the rayed handle and the direction of my thoughts — to open the black door.

I think of Thomas Furey: I am touched again by that yawning vertigo on the bridge of time as I scan the sweeping whip-line of the world, a world whose furthest and finest possibilities are always unimagined, but a world in which we can at least be sure that at the same moment on Good Friday in the year seventeen seventy, opium addict Hartley Comberbache looked up sharply from the abyss of his own destruction and remembered that life was good, and teenage apprentice Thomas Furey sat down in his native city to write the famous will that would set him on the road to London, and an even younger Mozart, glowing with friendship for a sweet English boy named Linley, walked out of the Sistine Chapel and wrote from memory the score of Allegri's closely guarded *Miserere*, whose theme would be borrowed centuries later by a young widow for a piano sonata she would play once only, because it brought tears to the eyes of an old man she had come to love.

The sweep of the world, did I say? Oh, but our eyes can see further than that: now we have lenses and mirrors and the *Hubble Deep Field*. Look upon these works! Look upon them! The names of the stars are not useless — in the face of such terror why not resort to our best defence, the defence of language — why not give a name to each and every one? *Stephan's Quintet* is better than a blank panic, just as new verse is better than wailed refrain.

But as the sun sinks in a silent rage I think too of the truth unnamed and unwritten, unwritten by Furey, or Gibbon, or the doctor's father: Geoffrey's epilogue might have described his tearful return to the mountains but it said nothing of his experiences at the camp — of the starving Russians on the other side of the fence, to whom he once threw a loaf of bread, the effect of which in the Russians' yard was so horrifying that he never did it again though they died before his eyes — or the best friend who didn't believe it for one instant when an anonymous letter told him that his wife was living with another man. Truth unwritten, truth written and lost, truth forgotten, truth half-remembered, truth that never wrote so much as a postcard.

I think of cool mahogany under my fingertips; a few petals tumbled on frozen loam; a wraith of coal smoke as I kneel on a faded rug; a rattle of rugby boots on the pavilion steps. I feel the gentle lifting and unfolding of compressed memories from an archive at once inauspicious and expectant, like a piano's keyboard or like a library whose books are all blank unless you slide out the right one and watch the pages fill up with words. There is more unwritten truth inside me than the bony-fingered sideshow of my present self can comprehend — a greater store of life on which to build an undecided future: I was wrong to feel shown up, and I laugh now at the galloping hooves. Why panic about an innocent delusion, innocently encouraged? I have followed my curiosity and healed myself by accident. By accident I have joined the thriving culture of separation — could, if required, speak of my 'ex' casually and without bitterness. That chapter of my life has folded itself up and disappeared as though the combe were a conjuror's hand, and only my undecided future remains. But it is not here. I can't stay any longer — what good is a combe except for a writer? And, to be frank, what good is a writer at all? I suppose doubts attended even my wife, but it was not her business to communicate them: if decisive Corvin is to unpack the old Russian doll of a man writing a book about a man writing a book about a man writing a book, will he really find something startling and precious hiding in the core? Or will we be left, you and I, with just a very little man writing a very little book? Yes, in the combe I have discovered a new cause to serve — or rather a cause has been assigned to me — but like all causes it rests upon an assumption.

I mistook the identity of the principal, of course — it was not the kindly, shuffling doctor but Corvin who granted confidences, unlocked doors, set out the board and counters and laid down those rules that he himself was free to disregard. I deliver myself now into the hands of this clown, this ruddy-faced pantisocratist, as I delivered him into yours. And yet at the same time he delivers himself into mine.

Night falls. The clouds in the west are like stretched silk: stretched, perhaps, between the wings of my soul where now a soft, sad music of voices rises, that perfect resonance at last, summoned out of my own self — a fuzz of tears behind the eyes, nothing more or less than a shuddering presentiment of brevity, appalling and final like an arrow that finds the heart through the back. Time sears and saps like the icy water of a bathing pool from which there is no climbing out. I think of Thomas Furey and turn at last to the black door of this Temple of Light from whose ruthless prow no benevolent saints or angels look down, to offer up my miserere prayer to a different kind of god.

20

'Will you reveal your deception?' I asked as we paced the smooth, tessellating slabs of the runway on the first day of May. 'Will you take off your mask at the end of the book?'

'There will surely be no need to be explicit,' replied Corvin, toying with his notebook, swinging it between his finger and thumb. 'Even with all that chatty stuff about the narrator being unsure of his approach and Salvator Rosa glowering down on his labours, my readers will understand the difference between truth and fiction. But perhaps as I wrestle with the final chapters I'll catch a glimpse of the book I should have written but didn't — if so I might throw down my cards just to cheer myself up, and, of course, to honour the creed.'

We had passed the gates to the rose and stone gardens, and now approached the end of the promenade, where a sun-bleached table stood on a terrace beneath a blossoming cherry tree.

'Then your readers will assume that you've simply invented me — that I'm merely a narrative convenience, a Dowley to your Furey —'

'That's precisely what you are,' he said firmly, smiling as he sat down.

'But I'm as real as this damned table,' I protested, laughing and slapping my hand down on the warm, weathered grain of beech. 'As real as anything in this valley — as real as you!' He was still smiling, but thoughtfully now. It was almost my last sight of him: the breeze stirred and white petals began to fall, tumbling edge over edge or turning like records, mottling away lines and colours and the weathered grain and the span of these bony fingers like the last words on a page. Somewhere in the grove, a jay screamed.

'Quite so,' whispered the honest clown, taking up his pen.

Dedicated to the memory of Thomas Chatterton.

ACKNOWLEDGEMENTS

The title is John Fowles' translation of the phrase *la bonne vaux* from Restif de la Bretonne's *Monsieur Nicolas*, as discussed in the former's novel *Daniel Martin*. The character Geoffrey Hughes is inspired in part by the mountaineer and writer W. H. Murray, combined with some experiences of the author's grandfather and a dose of fiction. Rose's secular Grace is from Albert Camus' *l'Etranger*. Various other writers are quoted in the text with or without acknowledgement, as permitted by Corvin's interpretation of the creed. The climbing route *The Temple* is very loosely based on the Ben Nevis route *Centurion* (VIII,8), with significant topographical alterations. Samuel Taylor Coleridge enlisted with the 15th Light Dragoons in 1793 under the name Silas Tomkyn Comberbache.